Gold Star Christmas

Edwin C Brannan II

ISBN: 1499121849
ISBN-13: 978-1499121841
Library of Congress Control Number: 2014906965
CreateSpace Independent Publishing Platform
North Charleston, South Carolina

Dedication

This book is dedicated to the friends, service members, and family who have selflessly supported me, and to our nation's fallen heroes and their Gold Star families who have made the ultimate sacrifice in the defense of this great country.

God bless the USA.

Contents

Acknowledgements

~

This book, like all of our accomplishments over the last fourteen years, has been a joint effort. I would be a fool to believe that I could have accomplished anything without the support of my loving wife, Jenny. To our children, Christopher and Clara, thank you for your patience, love, and support. Thank you to our crazy family for memories and an interesting life that gave me the imagination to create and tell a good story.

To the little girls who stirred emotions in me I never knew I had and who inspired me to write this story, I pray you find peace. Your father was a dear friend and is missed by all with whom he served. To their mother, you are a dear friend and patriot. Thank you for your support during this endeavor.

Thank you to all who serve or have served and those who support them. A special shout-out to the men and women of the US Army, Navy, and Marine Corps!

Last, but certainly not least, a very special thanks to my editors! For anyone who has had the unfortunate experience of proofing any of my writing, you know how painful it must have been to proof and edit this manuscript.

1

A Bad Dream

~

"Wake up, Eddie!" she whispered, standing in the dimly lit hallway just outside the tiny bedroom of their ratty, flea-infested trailer. The bedroom had a seventies-style décor with built-in closets, dressers, and cheap, drafty picture windows. It was barely large enough to fit the queen-size hand-me-down bed. Jenny had learned early in their relationship not to wake him suddenly from a deep sleep. She normally avoided waking him at all.

Unfortunately, what she had just seen on the news needed attention. His eyes were swollen and slightly bloodshot. His breath still reeked of alcohol, and his mood was as irritable as usual in the morning.

He grunted. "What?"

"A plane just crashed into the World Trade Center in New York City," she said. The words did not quite register in his booze-soaked brain, so he rolled over and closed his eyes. *Typical*, she thought to herself, and walked the short distance back to the living room.

As she continued to watch this nightmare unfold on the local news, it became clear this was not an accident. A second plane struck the adjacent tower eighteen minutes later. Overcome with emotions, she started to shake with fear and began to cry. She could hear him finally starting to stumble around the obstacle course they called a bedroom.

She knew if he saw her reacting like this, it would develop into an argument, so she tried to compose herself before he made his way into the room.

"What the hell is wrong with you?" he said. She explained what she had been watching as he flopped onto the battered couch. His whole demeanor changed instantly. She had seen this look before. He was staring at the television, but he was not seeing anything. It was as if he were seeing something a thousand miles away. When he got that look, there was no need to speak to him, because he wasn't going to respond. It was a trance of some sort. He was in a different world or in a different time, remembering something, but he never spoke to anyone about it.

She knew he was a combat veteran, but he never talked about his experiences. His family and friends told her he was not the same when he returned home. After several awkward minutes of silence, he stood up quickly, grabbed the keys to their old red Ford minivan, and headed for the door.

"Where are you going?" she asked. He didn't even turn around as he left. She began to tremble and weep again, feeling alone and afraid, and wondering what was going through his mind. She knew the kids would be awake soon, and more news was coming in continuously, so she stayed glued to the television while she could, praying that people were not hurt and that he was not going to do anything stupid.

✳✳

As Ed exited the shack on wheels they were living in, his mind was racing. Memories of the first World Trade Center bombing flooded his thoughts, and a terrible feeling overwhelmed him. He knew this was not over. Climbing into the van, he prayed he was still in bed just having another nightmare, but the sun, the smells of the trailer park, and the visual cues of broken-down vehicles and junk told him this was no dream. He had no idea where he was going or what he was going to do. He had quit another job two weeks ago and had been applying and testing for state jobs, but he knew staying at home with Jenny would just drive him crazy.

Every radio station was broadcasting something about the events. There was no escaping it. He decided to take the country roads to his mom's house in a nearby town fifteen miles away. He knew she would be at work, and he could be alone there.

The drive was normally quite relaxing for him. It was fall, and the leaves were already turning beautiful colors. The weather was near perfect, and the countryside on the road he took was his idea of paradise. Rolling hills, meadows, pastures, and streams intermixed with freshly chisel-plowed fields and scattered old farmhouses.

But this morning, nothing was comforting about the drive. He saw no beauty. He saw nothing but the road in front of him and began to remember.

The radio was broadcasting something about the fires billowing from the towers, and his mind went immediately to burnt flesh. He could smell it. In an instant, he was back. This was not the first time he had experienced a flashback of Somalia, but it was the first time he was sober. It scared the hell out of him. Horrible images of mangled and mutilated bodies being offloaded from helicopters danced around uncontrollably in his mind.

Nausea overwhelmed him as his vision started to tunnel. He quickly swerved to the side of the gravel road, ripped open the door, and began to dry heave. With each violent wave, his body tensed, and he started to drip with sweat. After what seemed like hours, he was able to compose himself and continue in a haze. He was still reeling from the flashback, with his mind fading back and forth from past to present, begging for his thoughts to focus. He finally reached his mom's house without crashing, and staggered to the door. He prayed she had left the door unlocked so he could have some peace.

Her house was an average-sized three-bedroom, two-bathroom, ranch-style home with a finished basement in a quaint little subdivision. It was always meticulously clean. The woman obsessed over every detail—nothing too lavish, but it was high class compared to the rat's nest they were residing in, and he enjoyed the solitude it allowed him during the day. Today he knew he would need it. He did not want to turn the television on, but he had to know what was happening. After five minutes, he wished he had just gone to the couch and fallen asleep.

A third plane had struck the Pentagon, and a fourth had crashed in a field in Pennsylvania. As he suspected, these were not a couple of random accidents. America was under *attack*. The nausea overwhelmed him again, and his skin glistened with a cool sweat. He recalled an old oath made just prior to receiving his end-of-active-service paperwork from the US Army. He remembered promising himself if ever his country went to battle and he was able, he would return to duty and fight again. It was a debt he never imagined would have to be paid. Now, with two babies and a girlfriend, and still fighting a war in his head, how would he be able to meet that obligation without losing what was left of his mind, his family, and his God?

The following hours were a whirlwind of emotion. He remained glued to the television, but called to comfort Jenny. He knew how fragile she was and couldn't believe he had left her and the kids at home alone while something so devastating was happening to their country. The two towers had fallen, and death tolls were mounting. Estimates were in the thousands, and no one seemed to know if it was over. He needed to summon the courage to return home and ensure his family was safe, but he didn't want her to see him in his current state.

He feared he was more shaken than she was. He also needed to explain to her that he would be leaving, and she must make a choice—a choice he was not sure she could make. He knew that she had contemplated ending their relationship. He was sure the only reason she was still with him was for the kids, but that was how they came to be together in the first place.

Two years ago she had ended a long-term relationship with another man on bad terms. Jenny and Eddie hooked up playing euchre one night. Eddie was tall and dark haired, with piercing brown eyes, and he made her feel like a princess that evening. He was twenty-five, a partner in a couple of bars, and by all outward appearances seemed to be a great catch—nice, funny, and fun to be around.

She soon found he definitely had his demons. The businesses were failing. He was drinking too much, and there was something wrong. He was angry. He was not physical with her, but he could get violent with others, and he had a temper.

Two different people lived inside him: one when he was sober, and one who would come out when he had too much to drink. The sober person was the sweetest, kindest, most loving man she had ever met, but the drunk was the exact opposite. They dated for about two months before she got pregnant, and all hell broke loose when she told him. She often wondered if she should have ever told him.

Without hesitation, he had asked, "Are you getting an abortion?" They were both Catholic, so she couldn't believe he had just asked her that.

"No," she replied. He went on a tirade, saying that having a child was not an option for him, and she was trying to trap him. He was acting insane. He was scaring her. She told him she would call him later and left.

※※

Jenny was sitting at the table with the kids when he came back into the trailer. She looked up at him, her shoulder-length blond hair frazzled and her beautiful crystal-blue eyes glistening. He could tell she had been crying. Her nose was amber from the tissues she had been using, and her bottom lip gently poked out, still quivering like a child in agony. The sight of her made him feel even worse. Her beauty and innocence were what had always attracted him to her. He walked to her side and gently rubbed her shoulder.

The kids could tell something was wrong, but they were glad to see their daddy. Christopher grinned widely, and the much smaller version of his father raised his arms for his daddy to pick him up from his high chair. As Ed reached for him, he fought back tears. He grabbed his son in his arms and hugged him, wondering if this would be the last night he would spend with his family.

It was obvious to Jenny he was upset and something was on his mind other than what had been going on out on the East Coast. His demeanor was odd. He was direct and to the point, and rarely showed any affection toward her or the kids. She could tell he had something to say and wondered what it was, but she wasn't sure she wanted to know. He looked defeated before he even said a word, as if he knew the answer before he asked.

Her curiosity finally got the best of her, and she asked, "What is going on, Eddie?"

His head slowly moved from his son to her, and their eyes met. She felt as if he were staring through her when he spoke.

"Jenny, our country has been attacked. I promised myself a long time ago if we ever went to war, and I was able, I would go back. I know I haven't been the man of your dreams, nor have I been the father you wanted for the kids. I have no right to ask you for anything, but I do love you and the kids, and I want to be a part of your lives. The only way that is going to happen is if you decide to come with me."

She sat speechless for a few moments and then asked, "Go with you where?"

"Tomorrow morning I'm going to the recruiting office and reenlisting in the military. You don't need to give me an answer now or even anytime soon. This is something you should take some time to think about, but I've already made my decision."

She couldn't believe he had just sprung this on her after what had happened this morning. He really was crazy. She couldn't imagine how someone who was dealing with the issues he was dealing with would even consider putting himself in a situation like that again.

He sat his son down, walked over to his daughter, and picked her up, cradling her in his arms and rocking her gently. She was a beautiful little girl. With brown hair, brown eyes, and a beautiful smile, she looked like a little Berenstain Bear. The emotions going through his mind were overwhelming, but vengeance was coursing through his veins. He could feel it with every beat of his heart. He knew who was responsible for the attacks without any evidence.

He knew how wrong it was to feel this way, but he wanted nothing more than to seek an eye for an eye. How could he feel this way holding such a beautiful child? How could he feel such hate when he was capable of pure compassion? This had been and would always be his internal struggle. His grandmother saw it in him as a little boy. She saw him struggle with the choice of good or evil. Maybe everyone struggled. He didn't know, but what he did know was that someone would have to atone for the attack on his country.

Jenny was still in disbelief, but this was often the case in their relationship. She figured this was just another one of his rants that would pass in a couple of hours, so she went about her daily tasks of taking care of the kids and keeping the house in order. Ed thought this would be a great time to sneak back to his mom's house.

As he headed toward the bedroom, Jenny thought to herself, *Well, I guess that was pretty short-lived. The hangover must be kicking in.* Then soon after he left the room, he came back carrying a briefcase she had never seen before.

"What is that?" she asked.

"Some old things I never thought I'd need." She didn't know what that meant but was surprised he was able to keep anything hidden from her in such a small place, which she kept as clean as possible. She should have learned by now not to underestimate him; he truly lived a life of duplicity at times. She didn't think he was intentionally deceptive; it was just his nature. When she initially got pregnant with Christopher and he lost it and made some threats, she decided to go stay with some relatives in the country. She thought there was no way he knew where she was, until a couple of months ago. She threatened to leave with the kids and said he would never know where they were.

"Like when you were with your cousin at his farm?" he asked. The way he said it and the smile on his face had scared her, but she had just laughed at him.

"Keep it up, you psycho, and you will end up a very lonely man!"

※※

Before he got to the door, he stopped and reached for her hand. He pulled her gently to him, put her head on his chest, and held her.

"I do love you," he whispered. "I know you love me, and I know I am not what you asked for. It's OK if you can't come with me, but this is something I have to do, Jenny. You may not understand this now, but if you come with me, I know someday you will. I love you." He kissed her and the kids and left abruptly, a man on a mission.

❈❈❈

Having no idea if he had just lost his family or not, he jumped back in the minivan and headed to his mom's house. This time, he took the less scenic route. It was a fast, uneventful ride, and a mind blur. The countryside, cars, and road zoomed by as thoughts raced through his mind of how he was going to explain this to his mom, dad, and brothers. His mom and dad had divorced when he was eight. He and his brothers went with their mom as most kids did, but Eddie was attached to his dad's hip from a young age.

It didn't take long for his darker side to kick in and push his mom into allowing him to go live with his dad. They stayed in his grandma and grandpa's basement for years until they could afford a little apartment a half block down the street. Then he spent most of his time with his grandma, going to drink coffee with her friends and his great-aunts. She showered him with affection and treated him as if he were her youngest son. They went everywhere together—church, shopping, coffee—and they loved each other's company. His grandpa was house-ridden and a bit of a pain in the butt, so for her, having Eddie around was a breath of fresh air. They were close. If she hadn't been in his life, he would not have turned out as good as he had, and he was not that good.

When he reached his mom's house, he went back in, turned on the television, and got the updates on all the events. Initial reports were off, but it was still very much a tragic day, and his decision hadn't changed.

He opened the briefcase for the first time since putting all the documents in it at the end of his service. He had considered burning all of it once or twice to see if it would make everything go away, but like a good soldier, he followed orders and kept it tucked away. Unfortunately, he was never a good soldier. He never liked what he did in the army. When he joined, he had wanted to go infantry in the Rangers and then on to Special Forces. He had had the opportunity to serve with both units in a support role. That had always embarrassed him and was the primary reason he never talked about his service or mentioned any of his mental health issues.

He knew he was dealing with post-traumatic stress disorder (PTSD), but had no idea how a support person could have it. Men who called themselves leaders taught him that anyone who had those feelings was weak, and he figured that if PTSD was real, it was reserved for real warriors, not someone like him. Those so-called leaders were wrong, and he was too. He knew that myth had unfortunately been the cause of more veteran deaths than combat.

As he pulled each document and award from the old case, he reminisced about his time in the army. The good, the bad, and the ugly times all came flooding in, causing a roller coaster of emotion and mixed feelings about whether or not this choice would be the correct course of action or just another reactionary drama in his life. A man guided by his emotions is either a fool or a saint, and he was no saint. When he came to the certificate of commendation from Third Ranger Battalion and read it aloud, a sense of pride filled his heart. He remembered those days. He had just lost his grandfather weeks before the operation, turned nineteen six days before it, and became a man during it. Out of all the decorations and accolades he received while on active duty, this was the one thing he was truly proud of.

His unit supported the task force, so he was not assigned to the Rangers. That did not affect his loyalty to the men who were out on that mission, ran that mile, and lost their lives. He and three of his closest comrades spent thirty-six hours on radios coordinating medical evacuations and patching internal Combat Support Hospital communications for seventy-six wounded and eighteen fallen men. There was not a day in the last eight years that he had not thought about that event and if they could have changed something to bring more of them home. That was the drive behind his decision.

He had no idea how long he had been sitting there when he was rattled by the garage door opener coming to life. *This should be interesting,* he thought. *At least it won't be as bad as telling Jenny.*

❈❂❈

His mom came in with a concerned look on her face. She had never been good at dealing with him. Their relationship had improved over the years and had gotten much better since the births of his own children, but he was always a pain in her butt. She knew the events of the day would be difficult for him and her youngest son. They were both veterans and had friends serving, but she knew Ed had a lot more going on than he let on.

Ed was like most of her friends who came back from her era's war, Vietnam. They were changed, and they did not talk about it to anyone. If they did talk about it, it was in whispers together in a corner; and when an outsider came around, there was nothing but silence until the outsider left. It made people uncomfortable and caused more speculation about how messed up they were. But what were they supposed to do, announce to their family and friends, "Hey, I'm having a hard time dealing with the fact I had to take another person's life so he couldn't take mine"?

Maybe that was the right answer, but it's the last thing you wanted to tell people you love. Ed was dealing with a different situation. He just did not feel like he had brought enough of them home, and he was not out there with them. Guilt is a powerful thing. No one educated him on how operations work. It takes bullets, beans, and Band-Aids to win wars. In other words, every element, from the infantry cook to the medic and everyone in between, has to do his part to win the war. The biggest component, though, that no one ever hears about is the one back home: the warriors' support networks. Their family and friends.

When his mom entered the kitchen, he quickly threw all the paperwork into the case and shut it. She, like Jenny, had never seen the case before and wondered what it was. She had only seen her son in uniform one time, when he was in Georgia graduating from Advanced Individual Training at Fort Gordon. She, Ed's brothers, and his stepfather, Steve, were living a couple of hours away; so they all went to see him graduate. He was the honor graduate of the class. It was a proud day for her to see him standing there in uniform being honored that way. He enjoyed having them there as well, but that wasn't something anyone would have known.

※※

Ed asked her to sit down. When she did, he asked, "Do you know what happened today?"

"Yes, it's horrible. How are you feeling?"

"I'm going back in, Mom." She looked as confused as Jenny had. Her facial expression said everything he needed to know, and as usual, his only emotional response was anger.

"You know, I don't know why I bother trying to tell you anything or attempt to explain why, because everything I do is wrong," he raged. "Here's a news flash for you, Mom. I didn't come here for your approval. I came here to let you know what I was doing and that I would be leaving soon. I don't know if Jenny and the kids are going to come with me. Please try to be a better grandmother than you were a mother!" As she sat there stunned, in tears, as he usually left her, he stood and stormed off in anger.

Ed's mom was used to his uncalled-for outbursts toward her and had learned years ago, as Jenny had, that it was best to let him vent and to not escalate the situation by arguing with him.

Steaming from the interaction and cussing under his breath, he slammed the door and stomped his way to his vehicle, looking like a mental patient off his medication. *Why bother with this crap?* he thought.

Since he was in town, he thought he would swing over to his brothers' apartment and see if they were home. Maybe they would understand. He figured his youngest brother would. He was an Airborne Infantry Ranger with First Ranger Battalion just a couple of years ago and was now working road construction after being honorably discharged. They were always close, even though they had not lived in the same home since they were young. When Pat went into the army, he took Ed's advice and took the path Ed had wanted. Pat was a natural. Ed was disappointed when Pat decided to get out, but it was his life, and Ed wanted what was best for him. He was doing very well.

When he got over to his brothers' apartment, Andy was there. Andy was the middle brother. He and Ed loved each other but never had a great relationship, and their interactions could get tense if Pat was not there to keep things calm. Ed explained to Andy what he was planning to do. Andy told him how silly he thought it was.

Ed just laughed. "Coming from you, that doesn't surprise me. Tell Pat to get hold of me when he gets home." With that, he decided the next stop would be his dad's house.

The drive would give him time to do some more thinking, and it was a peaceful route. He and his dad had a rocky relationship after his grandma passed away. They remained close, but were always better friends than they were father and son. Maybe they were more like brothers. He loved his dad, and more than anyone, his dad understood him. His dad never served in the military, not because he did not want to. His dad was medically deferred from the draft during Vietnam, but many of his friends went. That had been rough on his dad. He felt guilty, and he made up for it with undying loyalty to all his friends who went.

Ed spent a lot of time with his dad growing up. He went hunting and fishing with him, and more often than he should have, he went to his dad's friends' parties. He remembered a story of his dad's about a friend of his in the veterans hospital. His friend was in the mental health ward for some reason, and Ed's dad took him cigarettes and played cards. His dad would sneak him off and take rides. He recalled his dad telling him during one ride the man told his dad that when he killed himself, he was going to kill Ed's dad too, so he would have a friend in hell. Despite the threat Ed's dad kept going to that hospital to visit him until he was released, and he and that man remained friends. Loyalty ran deep within his blood. You could also call it stubbornness.

Ed's dad and stepmom lived off the highway just outside Beardstown. As he approached the turnoff to the county road, he decided he would make a pit stop to visit a couple of other people he went to see from time to time for advice. They didn't have much to say; if they had, he would have needed to be in the mental health facility where his dad's friend was kept for a brief stay. The Catholic part was in the back corner of the city cemetery. Their family plot was in the far corner, a spot he was quite familiar with. He spent a lot of time out there with his grandma when she was alive. They spent countless hours grooming family members' plots and talking to the deceased as if they were there. He never thought it was odd and did not think this stop was either. He found it peaceful.

Ed thought the one thing this little town did right was to maintain its cemetery. As he pulled through the gravesites, he thought of the fallen that day and prayed for them and their families, begging they had met a quick and painless end and that their families would not suffer at length. He asked God for the strength to carry out his plan, knowing his intent was not pure. As he slowly approached his grandparents' head-stone, tears filled his eyes again, this time not of sorrow, but of thanks. He loved the two of them with all his heart. He sat for several minutes in silence, speaking to them in his mind, wondering if they could hear his thoughts and wondering, if his grandmother had lived, if he would have ever left this town in the first place.

After a short prayer and telling them he loved and missed them, he continued to his dad's house. He could see the roof of the house from the gravesite. He hoped his dad would not try to convince him to stay. He didn't want any more arguments, and the last person he wanted to upset or disappoint was his father.

The short distance to his dad's house didn't leave a lot of time for thought, which was comforting. He had spent too much time inside his head today already, and he needed to be clear and concise in his message to his dad. And he wanted to be out of there before his stepmom got home. He loved her, but he did not want to deal with that emotional train wreck today.

The gravel, pothole-filled drive to the house was a nuisance. By all outward appearances, this was a beautiful country home. It was about three thousand square feet, with four bedrooms, two and a half baths, a full basement, and a two-car garage, plus two buildings sitting on six acres. Unfortunately, as soon as you walked in, you realized that beauty is skin deep. The place was a wreck, but it was their home.

His dad was having coffee, sitting at his normal perch on the barstool next to the kitchen island. A few years ago, he would have been half in the bag with a beer in his hand, but diabetes had slowed him down a bit.

When Ed came in, as always, his dad grabbed him and hugged him, just as his grandma used to, and told him he loved him.

"How are you doing?" his dad asked. Ed told him what was going on and what he was planning. "Son, I know you well enough to know that it doesn't matter what anyone says. I'm sure your mind is already made up, but you have to understand something. It isn't just you anymore. You have two kids and a woman who depend on you."

"I understand that, Dad, but you have to understand where I am coming from."

"Eddie, I don't know what you or any of you guys did overseas. I never went, and I never will, but I am smart enough to know you don't owe this country, me, or anyone else any more than what you have already given!"

"That's just not how I see it. The last thing I want is to go get messed up in some piece-of-crap country, but I can't stay here and let these kids go fight when I have been telling them to go in the military. Hell, if I can go and just keep one of them from ever knowing what I know, maybe I can finally close my eyes at night without thinking about that place. Maybe there is nothing noble about my intent; maybe it's just revenge or selfishness. It doesn't matter what I'm doing here. It is a better opportunity for the kids and me. I should have never gotten out. I listened to everybody else but me. I loved what I was doing. Nobody could handle that. 'Why aren't you in college? You're wasting your life. You're better than that.' Whatever."

His dad stopped him. "Listen to me. I support what you want to do, but you need to think about this. You need to give your family time to think about it. You know what you are getting into, but Jenny doesn't. You have two kids with her and haven't even asked the girl to marry you, but you're asking her to leave home with you. Just please be careful. I love you. Now calm down and go home."

"Dad, I'm sorry. I will, but I think you already know what's going to happen. I will let you know what's going on. I love you too." With that, they hugged, and he headed out of the house and pulled out of the driveway, back toward his family.

⁂

It was getting late when he pulled in, and she figured he was drunk. She prepared herself for anything. When he came in looking worn-out and sober as a judge, she was shocked.

"What's wrong?" she asked.

"Nothing is wrong, Jenny. I am tired, and I plan on going to the recruiting office in the morning. I would like to spend the evening with you and the kids and then get some sleep so I have a clear head when I go in there."

"You're really going to do this?"

"Listen, I get it. Everyone thinks I am incapable of keeping a job. That I am some screw-up who is broken or messed up in the head. Well, you know what, that may be the case. I don't know anymore. I know I don't like what I see in the mirror. I haven't since I took that uniform off. It was the one thing I took pride in doing. I was not a good soldier in garrison. I definitely had discipline problems, but forward I was good. You know where they're going. They're going where I'm needed. Therefore, like I said, I want to enjoy time with you and the kids, get some rest, and prepare for tomorrow. Jenny, I don't even know if they will take me back in, so don't get all worked up yet. They'll probably think I'm as big a screw-up as everyone else does."

"Eddie, no one has said that. Are you OK? I've never heard you talk like this. I support you, but this scares me. I don't know anything about the military, and what happened today is horrible. The last thing I want to do is lose you."

As she spoke the last words, she began to weep. He went to her and held her closely. They sat there in each other's arms for hours, watching their children sleep, both lost in thought, wondering how all of this would work out and praying they would never lose each other.

2

Honor, Courage, and Commitment

~

He woke early on the twelfth. It was a restless night. The only thing comforting was the woman next to him and the little boy jammed in between them who insisted on having one hand on his dad and the other on his mom's lips. It was a bizarre ritual he developed early in his life, partly due to his dad not wanting him to cry, and because he was their first child. Clara, on the other hand, had no need or desire to be near anyone when she slept. Like her father, she wanted to be alone, with no one touching her.

As he gingerly and quietly exited the bed, trying not to wake the two of them, he heard her voice. "Where are you going?"

"I'm going to the bathroom to get ready. Let's have some coffee, and we'll talk before I head to the recruiting office." With that, he headed to the bathroom.

As he looked in the mirror, fear resonated within him. What he saw was not the young man who had left the service six years ago. The "food blister," a not-so-kind military term for an overweight individual, he saw staring at him was in no shape to be running from the police, let alone running into a firefight. The skeptic in him began to take over. His inner voice told him, *You are a fool! You have failed at everything you have ever done. What makes you think you will accomplish anything this time? You are going to go waste your time when you should be out getting a real job to support your family. You are a piece of crap.*

This inner dialogue was quite common with him. He was harder on himself than anyone else could ever be. Anyone who truly knew him knew this and could overlook his faults because they knew he was kicking his own butt worse than they ever would.

As he finished grooming and proceeded to the tiny bedroom obstacle course, he maneuvered his way to the closet and started to find some clothes, only to realize she had already selected something for him to wear and laid it on the bed for him. She was as much a mother to him as she was a lover and friend. He knew she took care of him, but he rarely said thank you and had a difficult time expressing any affection.

Since he had grown up with such a loving and nurturing grandmother who told him multiple times a day she loved him and who squeezed the life out of him when she hugged him, you would think it would be easy to show the same affection. Maybe at some point it was, but now it seemed to him that anyone he cared for left or died, and he would not put himself in that position ever again. He distanced himself from close relatives, friends, and past relationships—anytime he felt in danger of growing too attached. He recognized this as a character flaw but had no desire for any added pain; unfortunately, the lack of love is what caused the greatest pain in his life.

As he dressed, he watched his boy sleep and wondered what it would be like to be innocent again, to start over. He wondered if he and Jenny could provide him and Clara with what their parents were unable to give them: a stable home. He feared that with his mental state and the choices ahead, that was going to be impossible, but he wanted nothing more than the best for his children and Jenny. He just didn't know if he was supposed to be a part of that equation.

Jenny was in the outdated kitchen she had decorated in a cowboy theme, complete with an overhead wagon wheel her mother had given them and a cowboy wallpaper border. It was a cute décor. She was good at interior design and made the best of the ratty conditions they were residing in. This was the third home she had painted and made her own since meeting Ed.

She never could have imagined the roller-coaster ride she was jumping on when she decided to go out with him. There were days when she was the happiest woman on earth, and other days when she wondered what she was thinking. Today she was wondering, *What did I get myself into?* She had made coffee and breakfast for him. She was cleaning up and doing busy work to keep her mind off how the coming conversation would go as he entered the living room.

To her surprise and delight, he looked good and was in a pleasant mood.

"Good morning, love!"

"Good morning, plumkin." She thought that nickname was cute, but scowled at him for the remark. He had started calling her that when she was pregnant with Christopher during Halloween. His sense of humor was one of the things she enjoyed about him, except that she was often the target of his jokes.

As they sat for breakfast, he said, "I know you haven't had a lot of time to think about it, and I don't want to push you, but are you considering coming with me if they take me back in?"

"I love you, and we will be with you, Eddie," she said.

He wasn't sure if he heard her correctly or not, but he wanted to believe his ears.

"I love you too," he said with a smile. "Thank you. I have a lot to do today. I will head over there and talk to the recruiters. I hate those guys, so this should be an interesting day."

"Try not to be an ass! If you want to do this, you can't go in there and act like you are the one running things. You are not the boss anymore."

It irritated him a little, but he knew she was right. After losing the businesses, he had had a rough time. Going from management to worker was difficult, and he had not transitioned well. He knew if he didn't figure it out and went back in with the wrong attitude, there were far harsher penalties for insubordinate behavior in the military than being fired.

That morning's drive was much different from the day before. He took the direct route to the recruiting station. He knew exactly where it was. The location had not changed since he entered it for the first time when he had just turned seventeen in 1991. He paid no attention to the cars, countryside, weather, or scenery. His focus was only on what would be said and how he would answer any questions. Before he left the house in the minivan, which they called the Red Rooster, he ensured all his documents were in proper order and arranged by date. He felt prepared, other than he knew he would be questioned on his physical appearance.

He prayed to not lose his temper with them and hoped there would be a fellow combat veteran in there who would understand his dilemma. As he approached the station, the butterflies in his stomach had him about to throw up. He sat in the parking lot, staring at the door for several moments, before summoning the courage to open the van door.

As he walked to the door, his knees felt weak, and he wanted to turn and run like a coward. He was second-guessing everything he was about to do. Nothing seemed right with this decision. He didn't want to go back into the same job or military occupational skill he had prior to leaving and knew that would cause some problems. His reasons for going back in were simple. In Somalia, he felt that he didn't do enough to save those men, and he wasn't going to let that happen this time. If he enlisted, he was going to be a medic, or he would have a reason to stay home.

He entered the army recruiting office and was greeted by the sergeant at the desk.

"Good morning, what can I do for you, partner?"

What an arrogant little butthead, Ed thought. *Now I remember why I don't like you guys.*

He snapped back to reality and said, "Good morning, Sergeant. I am Ed Brannan, and I am interested in reenlisting."

"Are you now?" the sergeant said with a sly grin.

You little ass, Ed thought. *I see from the ribbons you are wearing on your chest you have done nothing in your career but sit behind a desk and*

lie to young men, so don't start jacking with me, or I will smack that smile
off your fake face and call it a good day!

Remembering Jenny's advice from that morning, Ed said, "Yes,
Sergeant."

"Well, let me see your two-fourteen, and let us see what we can do."
Ed had a momentary sigh of relief and thought it might not be as bad as
he had expected.

As the recruiter went through his paperwork, he asked all the
pertinent questions. Ed answered appropriately and maintained his
bearing. His thoughts were on the task and on his family's future, not
on the smugness of the man in front of him questioning his desire to
reenter.

"Well, I think we can get you back into your prior job, communications," the sergeant said. "And there should not be an issue with your
reenlistment code three, because it was an early out for college, as long
as you can get some references. You have had a DUI. That is not a real
problem either, since it was several years ago, so we can get waivers for
all that stuff. You need to retake the Armed Services Vocational Aptitude
Battery test, go to the Military Entrance and Processing Station, and
you should be good to go."

Ed expected his DUI to be an issue. He also knew he would need
to take another ASVAB test to ensure he met the minimum education
standards for entrance. Additionally, everyone enlisting or reenlisting
into the military must go through MEPS to enter the service.

"I am interested in medical," Ed said. "I don't want to go back into
communications."

The cocky little recruiter looked him dead in the eyes, laughed, and
said, "Well, that ain't happening!"

Ed was infuriated. He turned as red as a fire engine and could contain his rage no longer. He stood.

"Listen to me, you little arrogant piece of crap," he said. "I was over
chewing sand when you were playing with Legos, and I am not about
to sit around and listen to a punk like you tell me what I am or am not
going to do. I worked with marines in Mogadishu and know they have

navy corpsmen serving with them. I noticed the navy recruiter is in today, so maybe I will just go speak with him."

This did not go over well with the sergeant or his lead recruiter in the back, so they both recommended he do just that. With that, Ed exited the army office and headed next door.

When he opened the door to the navy office, he was surprised to see a senior chief sitting at the desk. The only other encounter he had with a senior chief was in Mogadishu, and it was not a pleasant one. Few encounters with persons of authority had been pleasant for him. He remembered being on watch as a young private first class, when a little old crusty guy who reeked of cigarettes came up to him and demanded he wake him and the captain up at 0430.

The little old crusty guy wore an anchor with "USN" and a star on top for rank, and Private First Class Brannan had no idea what that meant, so he thought, *Who the hell does this guy think he is? I'm not waking his little old butt up. It looks like he could use some sleep anyway.* It turns out the last person in the world Ed wanted to piss off was a navy chief, especially a navy Fleet Marine Force corpsman senior chief. Ed had a knack for finding the exact people you should never mess with and pissing right in their cereal.

Zero four thirty came and went. Ed had forgotten about it until the little fella was breathing his stinky morning breath heavily and angrily on his collar. It scared the heck out of him, so he jumped up. The senior came unhinged with a tirade of curse words only a chief with a long history of combat assignments with the marines could so eloquently throw together. With each word and thump on the chest, Ed moved backward, stunned a man of this size was so intimidating. If Ed had not been so scared and had not been the target of this man's aggression, he would have found it inspiring.

The commotion aroused the entire command element, and Ed's sergeant major came creeping in. He was an older man as well. Ed thought he was older. He was probably only forty-five, but that was *old* to Ed. He was hunched over from years of service and carrying combat loads. He was a draftee from Vietnam who made the army a career, a quite distinguished one. Ed respected the heck out of him. They spent many hours out on the smoke deck. Ed didn't smoke, but he would listen to him talk about everything and anything.

When Ed saw him coming, he was relieved until he saw a look he had seen before, but never toward him. He knew he had messed up. The senior chief continued as the sergeant major joined in. Ed locked his body, and in unison they delivered one of the harshest tongue-lashings he had ever received.

At one point the senior said, "You tall, lanky prick, I'll bite your damn knees off so I can bring you down to my level and kick your empty head in!" He was a military poet only those who have served could appreciate, and Ed would laugh about it later, but at that moment, he wanted to be somewhere else.

❆❂❆

As Ed entered the recruiting office, he said, "Good morning, Senior Chief, I'm Ed Brannan." The senior chief peered over his glasses, stood, and reached out his hand.

"Good morning, I'm Senior Chief Troxell, United States Navy. How can I help you?" Ed explained his situation, told him of the encounter next door, and discussed his desire to become a corpsman as the senior chief browsed through his paperwork. As the army recruiter had already said, the senior chief thought the reenlistment code and DUI needed a waiver. He also added that he would need a waiver for the two children and did not recommend getting married until he enlisted. He told Ed he would need to retake the ASVAB, go to MEPS, and he looked fat, so he needed to tape him before they went any further.

The tape test for body fat measurement is not reliable, but it was the standard for the armed forces. Males must be at least 22 percent body fat or lower. The percentage is calculated by subtracting the neck from the waist measurement and comparing that number to the age group, which gives you the body fat percentage. Ed was approximately 24 percent. That was 2 percent too much, and for the senior chief, that was a waste or waist of time, so he asked Ed to come back in a couple of weeks when he was in standard.

"Fair enough, Senior Chief," Ed said. "I'll see you next week."

The recruiter smiled and said, "All right, I will see you next week."

※❀※

As a recruiter, Senior Chief Troxell had heard it all. He was pretty sure this food blister was not coming back in, but he was a man who followed regulations, so he documented the visit, filed the copies of Brannan's paperwork, and put a note in his computer: "Twenty-four percent body fat, he says he will see me in a week, yeah, right."

※❀※

Undeterred by the fat comment, Ed left the navy recruiting office feeling excited. The feeling that he was making a bad choice was gone from his stomach. He walked slowly by the army office and stared in the door, making sure to make eye contact with the two recruiters in their chairs inside. He gave them a one-finger salute, hoping they would come outside for some civilian battle training. Fortunately for him and them, they just returned the gesture and went about their business. He decided to laugh at them and head home to get his fat butt ready for the navy. He and the army had now officially ended their relationship for good.

As many people know, getting out of shape is easy. Unfortunately, getting back into shape is not as easy. The proceeding days were not fun for him or Jenny. Diet and exercise are painful for someone who has existed on beer and pizza for the last five years. Pure determination is a driving force for a man like Ed, and with support and a little prodding from Jenny when he didn't want to get up to exercise, he dropped the 2 percent fast. He checked himself daily and rechecked himself the day before he returned to the recruiting office. He was sure he was in standard and ready to go. Jenny didn't know the first thing about what he was talking about. She just cooked what he asked and woke him up when he said to.

A week had passed since he first walked through the door, and as before, he came in and addressed the senior chief sitting at his desk.

"Good morning, Senior Chief."

"Good morning," the recruiter said. "Nice to see you again. How can I help you?"

"I'm in standard and ready to enlist."

The senior chief stood, looked him over, and said, "It looks like you've lost some weight; let's see if you are good to go." He took his height, weight, and measurements, and checked the chart. He was 22 percent. The recruiter looked surprised and told Ed to look at his computer. He turned his screen so he could see the note he wrote.

"I obviously underestimated how bad you want back in the fight. I will not do that again. We have a lot of work to do. Are you ready?"

"Senior Chief, I have never been more ready for anything in my life!"

As they were sitting there discussing what they needed to complete, in walked a familiar face. His youngest brother came strolling in, cocky as ever. Pat was next door, talking to the army recruiters, when he noticed the Rooster sitting in the parking lot. He remembered Andy and his parents saying Ed was talking about going back in.

"What's going on?" Pat said.

"I'm joining the navy as a corpsman."

"I guess I'll see you on the other side of the pond then. I'm going back to Ranger Battalion." With that, he laughed and went back next door.

The senior chief asked who that was. Ed said that was his younger brother and gave the senior chief his history. They completed all the required forms and scheduled the ASVAB test. He gave Ed the reference paperwork and said he needed three strong references from credible people. He added that his past service would be a benefit, but he should talk to some teachers and former employers. He also said he needed to continue to diet and exercise, and he would be willing to exercise with him. Ed agreed and said he wanted to be assigned with the marines, so he knew he had to get in much better shape.

The rest of the week was a frenzy of activity. Ed was working out twice a day, on his own and with Senior, and getting his references while the senior chief was scheduling his test. Fortunately, there was an exam that Thursday in a nearby town, and Senior secured him a seat. He explained that Ed needed to meet a minimum score to qualify for corpsman prior to entering the testing facility. He had taken the exam two times before and always scored higher than the requirement, so he was not worried about meeting the minimum score. The only things painful about the ASVAB test were the length and the number of sections. You were given a preliminary score immediately to determine if you met eligibility, so you didn't waste the recruiter's time and they didn't waste yours. As inefficient as the military could be, most things worked out.

Ed's scores were well above the requirements for corpsman, and he completed all his other requests earlier in the week, so the senior chief scheduled his first MEPS visit.

❋❂❋

As Ed was going through the motions, trying to secure reentry into military service, Jenny was busy keeping the house, kids, and him maintained. She was also the sole source of income for the family. She was babysitting and doing accounting work on the side. Ed was so far behind on his bills from the businesses, he had long ago quit trying to pay them and focused only on the essentials. With no income and too much pride to ask for help, he was depending on Jenny until he got back into the military, so he focused on getting in as fast as possible.

Jenny's thoughts were on the kids and getting their things in order. She was also concerned that there had been no mention of marriage. Ed had failed to mention that he needed to get in before they got married. She knew he had enough going on, and she didn't want to add any more stress to his situation, but she was wondering what she was signing up for. Little did she know that this was just the beginning of her new life.

※※

The Military Entrance Processing Station was the same as Ed had remembered. Fast-paced, rude medical personnel were mixed with recruiting and administrative staffers and a whole lot of hurry up and wait. The night prior, the senior chief had dropped him off at the Holiday Inn in St. Louis, Missouri. He had a room to himself, which was a luxury at MEPS. The morning started at 0300 with a nasty hotel breakfast that was worse than any chow hall could ever serve. The meal was followed by a shuttle ride to the federal building and a fun-filled day of poking, prodding, physical exams, and administrative nausea. He made it through the process and to the final desk to select a job/Naval Enlisted Classification (NEC). Ed wanted corpsman, and the only other job he would consider was Seabee, the navy's construction battalion.

When he told the petty officer he wanted to be a corpsman, the young man's eyes lit up, and he nearly jumped out of his seat with excitement.

"When do you want to leave?" he asked.

Ed was amazed, but overjoyed, and announced, "Today."

"How about two weeks?"

Still in shock, Ed said, "That sounds perfect." The petty officer finished punching in all the details and explained he had to get the waivers approved by the detachment officer in charge, and he would want to speak with Ed. He left and returned shortly and asked him to come with him to the commander's office. The office, which was tucked away in a separate part of the building, was not that impressive. It was definitely not what Ed was expecting for the commander of such a large detachment, but he did not dare say anything.

The commander was a pleasant man. Ed could tell he was an administrative type, but if he was the only thing that stood between him and his goal, he would eat some humble pie and kiss the man's ring, if that was what it took. Fortunately, the commander was already signing the paperwork. He just wanted to meet Ed as a formality and ask him about his decision to join the navy and his service in Somalia. Ed was never comfortable discussing Somalia. He never felt he did anything special there, but he obliged the commander's request. He explained the details to the commander.

The commander stood. "Thank you, and welcome to the United States Navy."

Ed thought that was awesome. It left him with a sense of pride he had not felt in many years.

"Thank you for the opportunity, sir." When he exited the commander's office, he went to the room to swear in. He recited the oath and was given copies of his contract. The senior chief met him at the entrance in his government vehicle to take him back home. They discussed plans for physical training, Delayed Entry Program training, and other pertinent information he needed to have prior to his final MEPS visit before departure to Great Lakes.

✖✖

Two weeks was not a lot of time to get everything in order and to say his good-byes. It was definitely a confusing time for Jenny. The man who was being so loving and spending so much time with them began to distance himself again. More and more, he focused on physical training and what he was taking with him, as opposed to her and the kids. It frustrated her more each day.

When she finally summoned enough courage to confront him about it, a huge blowout occurred. She immediately wished she had just kept her mouth shut. He went on a typical tirade. The old Ed was back. She knew what would come next. He would grab his things and go stay somewhere else until he left town, so he would not have to be an adult and deal with any emotions. He was incapable of any response but anger. *Good riddance*, she thought as he slammed the door.

She did not shed a tear. She was as mad as he was this time. Over the last couple of weeks, she had done everything to help him and to support the entire family, and this was the thanks she got. So typical. *Good*, she thought, *that makes it a lot easier. I'll figure it out on my own.*

She did not expect the door to open and to see him come back in with his head hanging like a whipped puppy, but she thought it was amusing and felt like she had finally won a battle. He apologized and said she was right. She thought about asking him to say that again, but knew better than to push it too far. Even a small victory was nice after the last two years.

⚹⚹

The last weeks were not uneventful, but they went smoothly. Ed made his rounds to his family and friends to say his good-byes and to let everyone know he didn't know when he would be back home. He finally explained to Jenny that he had to wait to enlist and finish boot camp to marry her because of the additional waiver issues if he had another dependent. She had no idea what he was talking about, but didn't think he was making up a story to avoid taking her. He asked her to work on selling the trailer and getting things ready to move once he had orders. He explained that when he completed training, they would receive orders to a permanent duty station, and they would get base housing there.

They discussed the medical benefits and other opportunities of military life, and he told her about the disadvantages. He was as honest as possible about the low pay and the amount of time he would be gone. He did intentionally leave some things out—not to deceive her, but because he did not want to scare her away.

On October thirteenth, the anniversary of the day the navy was established, he got into the senior chief's car with his carry-on bag and paperwork after kissing his family good-bye, and started his journey. As they pulled away from the recruiting office, he saw Jenny crying, and he fought back the tears forming in his own eyes. He knew he would not see them for two months. He had never been away from Jenny and the kids for more than a night or two.

His first enlistment had been easy. It was just him, and he was glad to be getting away from that one-horse town. His grandma had died a year earlier, his relationship with his dad had disintegrated quickly, and he had been bouncing from his grandpa's house, friends' couches, and sometimes the backseat of his car. This time he was leaving his own home and family behind, and it hurt.

The two-hour drive was a time for him to ask some last-minute questions about boot camp, navy life, and what to expect when he arrived in Great Lakes. He had developed a friendship with this recruiter that he hadn't had with his army recruiter, most likely due to the man's honesty, integrity, and work ethic. He told him of his first encounter with a navy senior chief. They both enjoyed the tale and had a good laugh. Senior passed on some wisdom to the young recruit on the way to MEPS.

"The navy is simple: work hard, study, and take care of your sailors, peers, and leaders. If you do that, you will promote fast and do well."

When they reached the fine government-contracted accommodations, the senior chief shook his hand, wished him luck, and told him to stay in touch and to call if he needed anything.

The routine was the same as it had been the other times he had been there. This time, he wasn't as fortunate and ended up with a roommate for the night. He was a young kid from Missouri, a real pain in the butt. He was going into the army and knew everything about it. Ed didn't bother telling him he was an army veteran and everything he was saying was complete bull. He figured he would find that out on his own soon enough.

Fortunately, the little pain in the neck did the one thing you are told not to do and went out to the bars with some other knuckleheads, so he had peace and quiet for most of the evening. At 0300, the little dork did not want to wake up, and Ed considered letting him sleep it off, but knew that was not the right thing to do, so he kicked him out of the bed. As he hit the floor looking like a child who fell out of his bunk bed, his eyes were like piss holes in the snow, and he reeked of stale cigarettes and cheap beer. *Damn, now I know how Jenny feels*, Ed thought. He figured he had done enough, so he headed downstairs for coffee and the shuttle to the station.

The final time at MEPS before entrance was a shorter version of medical, admin, and swearing in. Members were put in groups to ship out. Those heading to Great Lakes were herded over to the navy staging area. A civilian called Ed over to the side.

"Here are your orders," he said. "Do you have your vehicle?"

Ed looked at him oddly. "I can take my vehicle to boot camp?"

The man laughed. "Son, you are not going to boot camp. You are reporting to Transient Personnel Unit at the Naval Training Center. You are an Other Service Veteran. An OSVET. You will complete transition training and be awaiting orders to your 'A' School, Hospital Corps School at NTC."

Ed was still confused, so he said, "I was under the impression I was going to boot camp. Am I going to a different type of training?"

"TPU is just a transient command where you will get checked in and issued uniforms and your orders for your follow-on training. If you do not have transportation, we will put you on the plane with these guys going to boot camp, and you will take the bus with them, but do not get off the bus at Recruit Training. Tell the bus driver you need to go to TPU at NTC. He will know where to take you."

Ed said, "Yes, sir," while thinking to himself, *I have no idea what this guy just said to me! Oh well, I will figure it out when I get there. This should be interesting.* The civilian told him if he was going on the flight with them, he was the group leader.

Group leader. Ed reminisced. He remembered a story his dad had told at the Veterans of Foreign Wars a few years ago. He and his dad had been uptown having a few beers and decided to go over to the VFW to have one. When they got there, they ran into a bunch of Ed's friends, many of whom were his dad's age. One remembered his dad from MEPS. They were drafted together. Dad was medically deferred for hypertension, but Randy went to Vietnam as an infantryman with the 101st Airborne Division. He was a great man. He was one of the many men in that club who helped Ed through his struggles with PTSD.

Ed's dad was oblivious to all of this, but it was not his fault. His dad decided he would tell everyone that the only reason Randy made it back from Vietnam was because he was Randy's group leader going to MEPS, and if he had not been such an excellent first commander, Randy may not have lived. They all thought it was hilarious, including Randy. Ed was embarrassed as hell his dad told such a bullshit story to a bunch of combat veterans. Ed didn't think the VFW was the place for a silly story like that, and he didn't think an outsider had the right to tell such a story, but those warriors allowed it for two reasons. One, they respected the man telling the story and knew he was tough as nails. Two, they loved his son.

※◈※

Prior to leaving, the staff gave a final warning about the urinalysis that was given in the morning and gave everyone an opportunity to turn in any contraband. Ed found this amusing for some reason and smiled. It pissed the civilian off, and he thought he would intimidate Ed with some harsh words and a stern voice. It had the opposite effect on Ed. Ed said if they were so stupid that they would show up high or with that crap in their system, why not just let them go make big rocks into little rocks in Leavenworth prison. The civilian did not think it was as cute as Ed did and told him to keep his comments to himself and move out. Ed shut up and moved on.

On the way to the airport, he listened to all the myths and stories coming from the conversations around him. It was rather amusing. He remembered all of this from before. Then, like now, he just sat back listening, thinking how utterly ignorant some people were. At the airport, he found a quiet corner and read a book until their flight boarded. He ensured that all the members of his group boarded the plane for Chicago.

Upon landing, they went to the Uniformed Services Organization and waited for the bus to the Recruit Training Center. The volunteers at the USO filled the recruits full of snacks and drinks while they waited for the transport. As they waited, more stories were flying around. It was getting annoying, until finally a recruit division commander (RDC) came in, rallied the wannabe sailors together, and herded them to the waiting buses. Ed filtered his way through the masses at the back of the crowd and found a spot at the front of the bus. Normally, it was a spot no one would want to be in, but he knew he would not be getting off with this group.

The RDC got on last and announced there would be no talking. *Thank you, God*, Ed thought. The silent forty-five-minute ride was relaxing. As they pulled through the gates of Great Lakes, Ed could feel the buttholes pucker and bus seats pinch all around him. It was hard for Ed to contain his laughter. The buses pulled in line in front of a group of RDCs in formation. Like a group of starving lions ready to feed as soon as the doors opened, they pounced, yelling and screaming, "Get off these buses!" and "Move, move, move!" It was comical from the other side. Ed sat there as the shenanigans ensued. One of the RDCs saw him sitting there watching and came at him immediately.

"What the heck is your problem, Recruit?" she said.

"I'm an OSVET going to NTC, Petty Officer." She looked at him and then to the driver.

"When we have the rest of them clear, take him over to TPU," she said to the driver. The driver just nodded, and she moved out smartly. *That was a lot easier than I thought it would be*, Ed thought.

As directed, when the chaos had moved on, the driver shut the door and proceeded to the Transient Personnel Unit, which was just across the street. It was close to 2200 hours now, so Ed was curious if he would have a bunk to sleep in or if he would be on a cot. Oddly enough, the overnight staff was well prepared. They checked him in, issued him linen and a room, and gave him instructions where and when to report for classes in the morning. He took the linen, his key, and bag, and headed to the barracks and found his room. It was a pleasant surprise to find he had his own room. There was a pay phone to contact Jenny and the kids to let them know what had transpired, and to tell them they would be leaving two months earlier than expected because he wouldn't be going through boot camp.

※◎※

Jenny had just put Clara in her room and was lying there with Christopher in their bed, daydreaming, when she heard the phone ring. She jumped up and made her way to the living room. She did not expect to hear from Ed, but calls this late were normally bad news. When she answered and heard his voice, she thought the worst. Her mind drifted, and she was not paying attention to what he was saying. She imagined he had gone down there, gotten pissed off at someone, screwed everything up, and needed a ride home.

When she finally realized he was in Great Lakes and checked in, she felt horrible she had doubted him. He was still telling her what went on and sounded enthusiastic about them reuniting sooner. She was not as happy. It meant she had to work harder to get things in order, but at least they could expect a paycheck at the end of the month. Their conversation was brief. She could tell he was exhausted.

"I love you, plumkin," he said. "I will call you soon."

"I love you too," she chirped. "Be careful and don't get in trouble."
She hung the phone up and thought, *Wow, he did it. We're in the navy.*

She made her way back to her baby boy. He was restless, and as soon as she lay down, his hand found her lips. It was useless to push it away. He would just move it right back in place until he fell into a slumber. It was sweet and irritating all in one. She lay there wondering what the life of a navy wife would be like. She had never shied away from adventure. When she had graduated from high school, she moved to Atlanta and lived there for several years. Much like Ed, she wanted to get away from their small town and see what was out there.

Unfortunately, things didn't work out as she had hoped, and she came back home to work at a local factory. She was apprehensive and intimidated by the unknown, but she was looking forward to something new and praying to be stationed somewhere near the ocean. She loved the beach and wanted to live next to the ocean.

As a child, she had always wanted a family. She had not expected things to work out the way they had, but she hoped they could make things work for the kids. She did not want them growing up the way she and Ed had. Not because they had horrible lives, because they hadn't. She just wanted a better life for all of them. The way they were living was not working out, and this could be a blessing. She could only hope this was the right path.

※※

Ed woke early and prepared for the day. He was eager to get started. When he got downstairs to the dayroom, it was a flurry of activity. You could recognize all the new check-ins; they were the only ones not in uniform. As usual in the military, there is a certain dynamic within every unit. The new people congregated in one area, and each group formed up in different areas. Ed kept to himself and just observed what was going on. When it was time to move toward the muster area, everyone made their way to formation. Each group assembled into platoons by check-in day. In the dayroom, the new group not in uniform was to the far left. All the personnel in this unit were either other service veterans or navy veterans, so they all had prior active-duty experience and knew drill and ceremony.

When the petty officer in charge of the formation came out and gave the command, "Fall in," they all took their places in rank and file. He covered the plan of the day, gave instructions, and ordered, "Carry out the plan of the day." With this, everyone fell out of formation and went to his designated training area.

Ed's classroom was in the main transient personnel building, an old World War II-era brick building with large ship anchors in front. Ed found out quickly that navy terminology and the customs and courtesies were slightly altered from the army. Buildings were treated as if they were ships. The entrances were quarterdecks, hallways were passageways, doors were hatches, latrines were heads, and so on. It was confusing for him.

He was also baffled by the rank. He knew the rank structure. He had learned it from his experience in Somalia, but he started hearing BM2, SK3, HM1, and other ranks that were confusing the heck out of him. He decided *petty officer, chief, sir,* and *ma'am* would have to do for now. He waited until fifteen minutes prior to the assigned class and proceeded into the room, found a chair, and took a seat. As he waited, more sailors from his group piled in.

At 0900, a petty officer first class boatswain's mate (BM1) came in and passed out welcome packages with all the information inside, including a *Bluejackets Manual.* He explained that the personnel department would be getting their orders ready for their follow-on training, and the group would be responsible for getting their own uniforms and taking their swim test, medical, dental, and physical fitness tests.

"All the information is in the package," he said. "You are all NAVETs or OSVETs, and I am sure you can figure it out. If not, ask a shipmate who has been here for a while to help you out. Your folder has your assigned duty section. You will muster each morning at oh-eight hundred and each afternoon at thirteen hundred hours. You will check the watch bill on the quarterdeck and ensure you maintain your watch. Are there any questions?"

Ed was the only one who raised his hand.

"What?" the BM1 asked.

"BM1, is that our training?"

"Yes. Are there any OSVET Reservists in the room?" One person raised his hand. The BM1 explained that unfortunately for him, he would be going back over to Recruit Training Command and going through boot camp. Ed thought that was funny and let out a chuckle, which the BM1 did not find amusing.

"What is funny?" the BM1 asked. "Are you a Reservist too?"

"No, Petty Officer. I think it is funny that we all go to the same training, but for some reason, Reservists have to go through boot camp, and we do not." The BM1 shook his head and asked the Reservist to come with him. He told the others to carry out the plan of the day.

What the hell did I get myself into? Ed thought.

The first thing Ed wanted to do was get his uniforms and quit looking like a newbie. It was one of the first things on the checklist, so he headed for the Navy Exchange clothing sales. The army had two uniforms. Ed looked at the list and thought the navy had around seventy-two. That was definitely an exaggeration, but looking at the endless list of uniforms and racks of different styles of uniforms, it seemed like seventy-two to Ed.

The most interesting and best-known uniform in the navy is the enlisted service dress blue uniform, better known as the crackerjack. Ed found out the hard way that the buttons that looked like a butt flap on long johns were actually the front of the trousers when he mistakenly put them on backward the first time. The women at the Exchange clothing sales department were amused at his ignorance. After spending six hours wandering aimlessly through the rows, grabbing anything and everything, and then returning them and getting the right ones, he ended up getting all of his issue and figuring out how to properly wear the new uniforms.

The rest of the week, Ed knocked out the checklist as fast as he could and went to every muster. He met two navy vets and read the *Bluejackets Manual* cover to cover, so he had a better understanding of the navy. It was not boot camp, and he was not as prepared as a sailor would be coming out of Great Lakes, but he was smart enough to get by. The first morning he rendered honors to morning colors, he felt a pride he had not felt in many years and felt a warm tear flow gently down his cheek as he stood there at attention, saluting the nation's flag.

❊❊

Next came Hospital Corps School. Ed's immediate impression was that he had made a horrible choice. When he checked in, he walked into the graduation hall for check-in muster. A Hospital Corpsman

Recruit (HR) Student Awaiting Training or Transfer (SAT/T) was conducting the muster, and it was a cluster bomb. She was a rude and unprofessional little pain in the rump, and Ed took issue with her attitude. She took it upon herself to interject into a conversation he was having with a navy vet who was in the same class as him. Ed asked the young recruit if she understood rank structure and if she knew she was interrupting two people senior to her. She explained to him that she was in charge, and he needed to shut up. Well, that did not work out well for her. Ed dressed her down as if she were one of his old privates in the army.

An instructor overheard their interaction and came to her aid. Ed was told to fall in and conform or he would have a difficult time during his training. Ed asked the petty officer if he could speak to the chief of the day. She said he was not going to speak to anyone, and he needed to get out of her face. Fortunately, a chief who had been watching everything came over and defused the situation. He corrected Ed and pulled the petty officer to the side. Ed didn't hear the entire conversation, but he could tell it did not go the way she had intended.

Later that day, a lieutenant in the nurse corps who was wearing master parachutist wings, a Silver Star, and a Purple Heart approached Ed. Ed wondered how in the heck he had those, since he knew the Master Blaster Jump Wings were not authorized on a navy uniform. He found out he was a former Second Battalion Ranger medic and Special Forces Eighteen Delta who went to nursing school and transitioned to the navy. They spoke a few times during Ed's time in corps school, and Ed was glad to see a friendly face.

He began class that week and completed the first week of training with a regular class. The first week was basic life support.

Following the first week was the Christmas holiday break, and since this was his first leave period, Ed took two weeks of leave. Jenny came to pick him up for the holidays.

Jenny was busy getting the house and kids ready for the coming move. She had managed to sell the trailer and moved in with her dad until they married and could move to their permanent duty station.

They did have a steady income coming in, and although it was not a lot of money, it was one less burden she had to manage.

The wedding was not much of a ceremony, and it was short notice. They did it on January first, just two days before Ed returned to Great Lakes. The rings they purchased from the local Walmart did not fit properly. They asked their priest to marry them in the church rectory and had two friends and their children with them. Jenny's friend later told her she was concerned because Ed did not even look at Jenny during the vows. Regardless, they got a babysitter, celebrated by going out to one of their favorite watering holes, and announced to their family and friends that they had finally tied the knot.

Ed returned to corps school on the third. Thankfully, during that time frame, the navy was experimenting with a thing called the Accelerated Pace Program. Ed was in and out of corps school in four weeks. He wasn't sure he had learned much, and apparently the program wasn't a great success, because the navy canceled it after a couple of years. He did learn the basics and graduated with a high grade point average. His family was able to attend the ceremony, and he was proud to have them see him stand to be recognized as one of two honor graduates in the class.

※※

Jenny, the kids, and Ed's mom and aunt all came up for the graduation. Jenny was so proud of him. She had never seen him like this. He was smiling, and he looked handsome in his uniform. She had no idea he had so many decorations, but she didn't know much about his service. She could see the other people checking his awards out, and it made her even more curious, but she knew not to ask. Their time together was going to be brief since he had received orders for training in Camp Lejeune, North Carolina, at Field Medical Service School for eight weeks, with follow-on training in Pensacola, Florida, for twelve weeks. He would fly out that afternoon. They would arrange to meet in North Carolina and in Florida when he reached Camp Lejeune.

Ed gave everyone hugs and kisses, said he loved them all, and grabbed his gear. He was disappointed to leave them, but he was ecstatic at how well things were going and could not wait to get to the marines.

Jenny felt abandoned again.

3

Semper Fi

~

Jenny and the kids traveled back home as Ed flew to his next destination. The military was familiar to Ed, but the navy was not. He arrived in Jacksonville, North Carolina, late that evening. The airport reminded him of the small local airfield in Springfield, Illinois. He didn't know what to expect, but assumed he was going somewhere much larger than Jacksonville turned out to be.

Jacksonville was a typical military town. Any community that surrounds a military base features the same local businesses. Scattered throughout were a mix of bars, nightclubs, and exotic dance clubs, with barber shops on every corner—and of course, tattoo shops, lots of them. Ed was one of few service members who just did not like tattoos. He always laughed when asked if he had any and said, "Scars tell a better story!"

Camp Lejeune was twenty minutes from the airport. Ed loved cab drivers. He found early on that if you want to know the pulse of a town and know how to have a good conversation, jump in the front seat, introduce yourself, and just start talking. That was exactly what he did. The elderly man driving was not used to a friendly and polite person jumping in his cab, so he was delighted to tell Ed whatever he asked about the area and more. As he was telling Ed about his time in the marine corps, Ed's mind drifted to a rest and relaxation trip he took to

Cairo, Egypt, while deployed in Mogadishu. It was early 1994, during Ramadan. The weather was beautiful, and the accommodations were phenomenal. The R and R arrangements had been made through the air force. *They knew how to live!* Ed thought.

They arrived at the Cairo Airport and reported to the air force terminal for the safety and country brief. Following the briefs they loaded into vans and were transported by escort to the hotel. It was a desert, but the landmarks you would expect to stand out did so immediately. The Giza Pyramids were massive. Approaching them was like driving from a valley up to the mountains. For a country boy who never thought he would leave Illinois, seeing one of the wonders of the world was amazing. What struck Ed as odd was that the city was so close to these great feats of engineering genius. It was almost sad, but tourism was a source of income for the country, so it made sense. The vans pulled into the Moving Pick Lounge, a beautiful five-star facility with full-service everything. The grounds had a breathtaking view of the pyramids, plus a gorgeous pool, spa, restaurant, smoke lounge, and most important for Ed, a huge, brass, fully stocked bar.

They arrived late that night and decided to have chow at the restaurant and call it an early night so they could sightsee in the morning. Ed agreed, but that really was not his intention. His plan was to eat with the group, walk back to his room, and then walk directly back to the bar. That is exactly what happened. He was nineteen and didn't know the drinking age for Egypt. He did know Muslims did not consume alcohol, so he was hesitant, but thought, *What the hell.* He approached, smiled, and asked for a beer. The bartender was an extremely tall, very nice Egyptian man who spoke fluent English.

"What brand would you like, sir?" he asked.

Ed thought for a moment. "Sir, I'll have a local beer if y'all have one."

The bartender gave him a wry grin and said, "Yes, sir, we do." He grabbed a twenty-four-ounce bottle of the local brew, poured it into a nice glass, set it out a napkin on the highly polished brass bar, and said, "Thank you, sir. My name is Muhammad, and I will be your server this evening. Please let me know if I can get you anything else."

"Thank you, Muhammad. My name is Ed. I'm from Illinois. You ever been there?"

Muhammad laughed and said, "No, sir. I have been to America, though. I was on the Egyptian basketball team, and we traveled there to play. It was a beautiful country, and I enjoyed my time there. I hope to go back someday."

Ed smiled. "Thank you. I miss home. You have a beautiful home too. This is the first time I have been here. Where do you recommend I go while I am here, and how do I get there?"

Ed sat with Mohammad all night, listening, telling stories, and drinking the local beer. It tasted horrible, but it was beer, and it was cold, so he was happy. At one point, he had a group of the staff playing basketball with a bunch of wadded-up bar napkins and a trash can. Mohammad was good. He stuffed Ed's shots several times, but Ed chalked it up to him drinking twenty-three of those skunk beers.

He received some great information from the man and his new friends. They gave him contact information for one of their cousins who drove a cab. His name was Mohammad too. Ed found out that was a common name. The night went faster than he had expected. When he was tapped on the shoulder by his group's senior officer, he nearly crapped his pants. She asked him if he had been up all night.

When he looked at his watch and realized it was 0700, he said, "Yes, ma'am. I'm going to breakfast, and then I'll go to bed and meet up with the group later." She was not pleased with him, but this was R and R, so she gave him a break.

The group had breakfast, and Ed headed to his room as they headed off to the see the sights. Walking by the pool, still in a drunken stupor, Ed leaped. The cool water mixed with the chilly desert-morning wind was enough to sober him up a touch and give him a brilliant idea.

"Why would I go to sleep when I am in Cairo, Egypt!" He headed to his room, showered, brushed his teeth, and attempted to get the horrible beer taste out of his mouth. He got dressed and retrieved the soaked cab number from his pants pocket. He called the front desk and asked the receptionist to contact the driver and call when he arrived.

Shortly after he hung up, the phone rang, and the pleasant voice announced that his driver was waiting for him in the lobby. Ed was about to violate a bunch of the rules from his safety brief, but he never bothered to follow the rules. He did what he wanted to do. He strolled by the pool, avoiding the urge to leap in this time, and went to the lobby to meet his driver.

Mohammad was a short man in dingy clothes that smelled of cheap cologne and stale clove cigarettes. He had brown stained teeth and spoke English, but was not as proficient as the bartender. It did not faze Ed. He remembered the places he was told to visit and wanted to go to the pyramids first.

He introduced himself to Mohammad. "Hi, I'm Ed. Are you Mohammad?"

"Yes, sir," said the man.

"Cool. I got your number from my friends last night. He said you are his family, and you would take care of me."

He smiled and said, "Yes, sir. My pleasure. I will take you all around Cairo for your whole stay and charge you cheap. We have deal?"

Ed smiled and grabbed Mohammad's hand. "We have a deal, my friend."

The following days were amazing. Mohammad was a man of his word, and he did take care of Ed for cheap. Ed was sure Mohammad didn't leave the hotel. At one point he let Ed drive the cab—not a safe or smart idea, but they both got a good laugh out of it. He saw Cairo in a way he was sure no other outsider had seen it. He was invited to the Ramadan evening meal in the bazaar by Mohammad and enjoyed the meal with the driver's family and the locals. Ed learned a couple of valuable life lessons in Cairo. Do not drink the local beer. Be polite. Always go to the bar, and always get a cab and meet the driver. He also learned the air force lives a lot better than any other branch of service.

❋❖❋

Ed drifted back into his current conversation as they were pulling into Camp Lejeune's main gate. The driver asked for his orders and his identification to show the guard. They were allowed through and directed to the Naval Hospital Quarterdeck, where Ed paid the man, thanked him, and went to check in.

The Naval Hospital Camp Lejeune was near the main gate along the New River. It was a nice facility that serviced the medical needs of the area's active and retired, and their dependents. It was not a big hospital, but it did an amazing job taking care of the marines, sailors, and their families. The petty officer on duty saw Ed walking in.

Ed went to the desk with his orders and said, "HN Brannan reporting, Petty Officer."

"Good evening, welcome to Camp Swampy," the petty officer said with a grin. "You can relax. You aren't in training anymore, and it looks like you have been around. Where are you from?" That was a common question in the service for service members and their family. It was a great way to start a conversation.

"I was in the army, and I'm from Illinois," Ed said.

"Where did you get that accent?" the petty officer asked.

Ed laughed. "Not everyone in Illinois is from Chicago, and my mom lived in Virginia and Georgia when I was a kid. I probably picked it up bouncing around."

He checked in, got his orders for the following day, and got a ride to the barracks. He was surprised to find he would be in a room with three other sailors and sleeping on the floor. It was temporary, but unacceptable. Unfortunately, there was nothing he could do about it, so he had to just suck it up, shut up, and drive on. He was there for four days before he reported to Field Medical Service School. Many others were not as fortunate.

Field Medical Service School was on Montford Point, off Highway 17, next to the New River. The base had been utilized during World War II to train African American marines in support roles and was later called Camp Johnson, named after historic Marine Sergeant Major

"Hash Mark" Johnson. He got the nickname "Hash Mark" for all the service stripes he had on his uniform from years of dedicated service.

The school was scattered across the northeast side of the base. The buildings were in horrible condition and were World War II era. The barracks were open bay-style block buildings with heads in the center and dayrooms at the forward hatches. Each barracks housed two platoons, one on each side, and they each had two heads and two laundry rooms, with two platoon sergeant rooms. The rear hatch opened up to a smoke deck, picnic tables, and mops.

Ed decided the check-in process was lame. He expected to get some physical training and yelling. The staff did plenty of yelling, but he was surprised they did not do more physical training (PT). Most of Ed's classmates were intimidated by the in-your-face attitudes and by the stories they had heard, but not Ed. This was something he had experienced before, with the added bonus of PT. Up to this point in his naval career, he wasn't impressed with his choice. The morning he met the Field Medical Service School (FMSS) instructors, that all changed instantly. Ed knew that second that he had found his new home. The marines were a special breed of people, but they were his kind of animal.

The sailor on duty gave instructions to be prepared to receive the new instructors at 0500 the following day. Ed found this odd, considering they were being awakened every morning at 0400, so he set his alarm for 0330 again. It was a good idea. He was showered, shaved, and dressed when all hell broke loose. Lights went on, trash cans went flying, doors were opened and slammed, and the instructors were yelling at the top of their lungs.

Ed should have been freaking out, but he was happy. This was what he had been waiting for. They instructed everyone to get in line. Ed locked his locker and rack and stood at attention next to his bunk. A marine staff sergeant came flying up to him. He was about five foot eight and tiny, wearing a marine utility uniform with a duty belt. His eyes came about to Ed's name tapes, and he was on his tiptoes staring up at Ed and yelling. His breath smelled like dog poop and coffee. Ed was about to throw up on him. He was a masterful curse-word poet, like most military instructors, and Ed couldn't help himself. He smiled. The staff sergeant went berserk.

What followed reminded Ed of the scene from a movie. He said, "What the hell are you smiling at?" Ed corrected himself.

Ed knew he had lost his military bearing and proper courtesy. It was unprofessional, not to mention belittling, to smile at someone yelling at you, so he said, "Staff Sergeant, I screwed up. I am just motivated to finally be back with some warriors."

The staff sergeant liked the answer, but he wasn't going to let Ed off that easy. He made Ed do some push-ups and other exercises before he proceeded. He then told Ed to go shower, shave, and get dressed.

"Staff Sergeant, I am already prepared for the day," Ed said. Off he went again, and Ed did another round of PT. He tried again, and Ed did another round. This time the staff sergeant didn't waste any more time on a futile battle of wills. Ultimately, had he chosen to proceed, Ed would have lost, but he went on to people who needed more attention.

※※

Field Med was outstanding physical, field, and medical training, truly some of the best training Ed had ever had in his military experience. The staff was professional and demanded the students act the same. The marine corps was definitely Ed's new home. He learned so much in such a small amount of time. Ed was ready to get to the fleet and get in the action.

Since Ed had joined and started training, the United States had invaded Afghanistan and pushed the Taliban out of the major areas. Ed's friend Tyson did the jump into Kandahar Airfield with the Third Ranger Battalion. Ed couldn't believe he had already missed that action. He needed to get through training and into the fight before it was over.

Jenny and the kids were doing well. They planned to drive out with Ed's mom to attend graduation. It was awesome how engaged Jenny was with his new career and how curious she was about what he was doing. He loved her and missed her and the kids so much. It would be difficult to leave them. He wrote to them often. He had even started writing poems and drawing pictures for the kids. He was not a great poet. He often wondered if Jenny really liked the poems or if she told him to keep sending them because they made her laugh.

※※

Sitting in the kitchen of her dad's double-wide trailer, with the two kids in high chairs, Jenny was reading another one of Eddie's letters to the kids. She was amazed how often he called and wrote. She was more overwhelmed that he was sending her poetry and drawing pictures for the kids. She had no idea he was artistic. She thought the poems were sweet and the drawings were cute. Both were done quite well. She knew he hadn't liked the training he was doing before he got with the marines and could tell by his attitude and voice he was excited by his new duties. She couldn't wait to see him again.

They were driving with Karen, Eddie's mom, to meet him in two weeks. The drive to North Carolina would be fifteen hours. The kids had never traveled in a car that distance, and Jenny was stressed about having them in their car seats that long, but she wanted to see him.

She had everything prepared for them to move when he received orders, and she prayed they found out soon where they would be permanently stationed. The anticipation was grueling, and she talked with her family and friends about it often. She knew it was driving them crazy, but she had no one else to talk with. The kids were great listeners, but they didn't talk back. She knew that wouldn't last forever.

She was concerned about money. Eddie was not making much, and creditors were still calling constantly. They qualified for and received federal support from Women, Infants, and Children (WIC) and food stamps, as many junior enlisted families do. That fact amazed her. She never guessed that the country's military would be forced to receive welfare to provide for their families. Eddie had no idea she had applied for and received the assistance. She knew he would never allow her to accept aid from anyone. He would never apply for unemployment when he was out of work.

※※

During his training Ed became close with three of his platoon members. They were all around the same age and had joined to fight. They were all over six foot tall and loved to party too. Each weekend, they loaded up in Travis's car and found a cheap hotel room, loaded the bathtub full of beer, and got torn up. Ed's buddies had cell phones and let him use them to call Jenny and the kids whenever he wanted, so he bought the beer. They all agreed it was a good trade.

Ed always thought it was simple to meet new friends in the military. Everyone was in the same situation. When he had checked in, he didn't know anyone, but he knew he had something in common with those around him. They were in the military, and that was all they needed to strike up a conversation. Civilians believed there was a huge rivalry between services. There is between services; however, like a family, the branches of service can talk about one another all day long, but as soon as an outsider says something out of line, everyone teams up and lays it on him.

The last two weeks flew by for Ed and Jenny. Ed completed training, turned in his gear, and prepared for graduation. Jenny prepped the kids, packed, met Karen, and hit the road. Ed and his buddies had stayed at a local Motel 6 for several weekends and recommended it to his mom. The motel was a short distance from Camp Johnson and on the main route in, so he thought it was a great place for them to stay. He didn't put a lot of thought into the fact that the place was old and outdated. The price was good, and he thought the staff was friendly. When Jenny and his mom arrived, their opinion was not as high as Ed's was, but they made it work.

Jenny used Karen's cell phone to call Ed's friend Travis when they got in. She told them they had arrived and were at the hotel. Ed told her the details about graduation: when, where, and how to get to Camp

49

Johnson. They talked for a while, and he talked to the kids as they listened. He talked to his mom and then went back to the barracks to crash for the night.

The next morning, everyone staged his gear, did a final cleanup, and completed inspection. The platoons marched to the main classroom and staged for entrance. All the families were in the classroom, waiting for their loved ones to enter. The classroom was the old base theater. The building was a wooden structure with whitewashed wood siding and a large front entrance. It was probably beautiful in the thirties when it was constructed, but it was in need of refurbishing.

The senior military instructor filed the students into the classroom. They all remained standing until he marched to the front of the stage, about-faced, and gave the command, "Take seats." In perfect unison, the entire class sat. Coordinated chaos. Sitting on stage were four large chairs, a podium, and all fifty state flags. In the far left corner was the American flag with the navy and marine corps flags flanking it.

At 0800, the senior military instructor announced, "Attention on deck." Again in unison, the entire class stood at attention as the commanding officer, command master chief, training officer, and chaplain marched to the stage. As the official party took their seats, the assistant training officer, a senior chief, took his place at the podium and began the ceremony.

The ceremony was short, but moving and conducted flawlessly. As the official party exited, the senior military instructor returned to the front of the stage and announced, "Class dismissed." With the announcement, the sailors and families roared to life.

It took them a while to find each other, but when their eyes met, it didn't take long for Ed to get Jenny in his arms. He held her tightly for several moments and then kissed her forehead and whispered, "I love you," in her ear. She noticed he was thinner and more firm than when she had seen him in Chicago. She liked the marines too! They had turned her fluffy hubby into a firm man. He then found the babies and gave them their hugs and kisses. Clara didn't want to go to him, and he didn't show it, but it hurt him deeply. He knew it wasn't her fault. She hadn't seen him in some time, and he didn't look the same.

Christopher knew him and was excited to see him. He wanted to play. Ed's friends did not have any family at the ceremony, and they had made their way over to meet his family. They introduced themselves to Karen, then Ed introduced them to Jenny and the kids. Jenny was amazed at how big two of them were. Madden was a huge African American man. Ed was six foot three, but Madden was almost a head taller than he was and had arms the size of Ed's legs. He was a gentle giant, though. The kids immediately saw that and wanted to play with him.

Fortunately, with this graduation, they had more time together. Ed did not have to fly to Pensacola, Florida, until the next morning. They made plans to go to Chili's for lunch and some drinks and then just hang out at the hotel. Two of Ed's buddies didn't have to check into their units until the following day, and they were going to stay at the hotel too. Travis was checking into Pensacola on permanent orders, so he was going to eat with them and start driving.

Ed's family got a kick out of the stories they were hearing from these clowns over lunch. Jenny was getting her first taste of her new life and enjoying it. Ed's mom picked up the tab for all of them, and they were appreciative. They finished up, said their good-byes to Travis, and headed to the hotel. On the way to the hotel, they had to make a stop to get beer and ice for the bathtub cooler so they could show Ed's family how to do this right and what they had been up to for the last eight weeks. In the morning, they all woke early, got packed, said good-bye to their friends, and took Ed to the airport.

Ed didn't want to draw out the good-bye. He didn't like them. He asked his mom to just drop him off at the terminal. He and Jenny got out and grabbed his bags. They talked about Pensacola and if she would come down to see him. Then he gave her a kiss, said he loved her, and kissed the kids good-bye. He told his mom he loved her, said thank you, and promised he would call her soon. He picked up his gear and walked away with that nagging pain growing in his stomach.

Ed was looking forward to his training in Pensacola. In corps school, he chose aviation medicine based on his senior chief's recommendation. He told Ed it was similar to army flight medic. In Somalia, Ed's main responsibility was communicating with the medical evacuation (MEDEVAC) helicopters. He loved flying and hoped to get orders back to Camp Lejeune with a marine helicopter squadron. In the airport, he picked up a newspaper and read about what was going on in Afghanistan and around the world on the flight.

※◈※

Traveling home, Jenny was feeling alone again. She hoped this was not going to be the routine. She was happy Ed was doing well and loved the way he looked. She couldn't stop thinking about him. She also thought it would be nice to be stationed in Jacksonville, North Carolina. It was a small town and next to the beach. She liked it there. More than anything, she just wanted them all to be together again. She noticed Clara's reaction to Ed and feared the kids would grow up knowing their dad only from letters, phone calls, and pictures. It scared her, but she remained optimistic. She knew they were better off now than they were months ago, and she shouldn't be complaining or worrying.

Pensacola was a wonderful duty station on Florida's Gulf Coast Panhandle, with clear blue water and white sand beaches. Home of the navy's Blue Angels and naval aviation, it was by far the nicest place Ed had ever been to train. The only comparable paradise he had visited was Mombasa, Kenya. He went there on R and R while deployed to Somalia. They stayed at the Nyali Beach Club resort for three days in early September 1993.

He had only been in country a month when he was chosen to go on R and R. They sent him because his grandpa had died, and they couldn't allow him to go home because he wasn't immediate family. Ed was upset; he loved that old man, but he understood the policy, and he didn't want to leave the mission. Mombasa was wild, a coastal city with a huge shipping port. The only other commerce was tourism and prostitution. Ed spent most of his time at the hotel bar, drinking whiskey and Coke.

He was drinking one afternoon by himself when an older Australian man sat beside him and said, "Hey, mate, there is a much more efficient and cheap way to drink that. You Yanks are not the brightest fellas." Ed had no idea what the person had just said, nor did he realize he had just been insulted, or he probably would have hit him.

Ed looked at him strangely and asked, "What?"

"Order two whiskeys and split the Coke between them. They charge more for the Coke than the whiskey, Yank."

Ed caught on. "Well, thanks for the advice, sir, but my name's not Yank. It's Ed, and if you call me Yank again, I am going to yank your head off!"

The Aussie got a good chuckle out of the comment. He pulled up a chair and said, "Well, Ed, my name is Wally. Pleasure to meet you." They enjoyed the rest of the day and must have enjoyed quite a few drinks. When Ed woke up, they were in some mud hut somewhere in between Mombasa and Nairobi. He had no idea how they got there, and he felt like someone had kicked him in the testicles until he had passed out. Wally saw him moving around and started laughing hysterically at him.

"Ed, my young friend, I don't know about the rest of you Americans, but you are not much of a drinker."

Ed laughed. "Wally, you are an alcoholic. I'm not sure anyone could keep up with you. What day is it?" They both got a kick out of that. They made their way back to Mombasa in time for Ed to catch hell for leaving without telling anyone and to make his flight back to Mogadishu.

※※

Checking into Naval Aerospace Medicine Institute for Aviation Medicine Technician (AVT) School, Ed soon realized he had been bamboozled. AVT was not anything like army flight medic. In fact, it was nothing more than a physical examination technician. He was not happy. He immediately requested to speak to the leading chief petty officer (LCPO) about terminating his orders and being assigned to Camp Lejeune. The LCPO agreed to meet with Ed.

Ed explained to the chief what he was told at corps school and that he was not interested in this type of position. The chief was unfazed by his plea and told him he had one of two options: suck it up or fail out. Once again, Ed was irritated with how the navy operated. He knew if he failed out, it would damage his record, and he would be assigned wherever the navy chose to send him, so he decided to make the best of it. He also decided he would put no effort into this course. He would PT and party while he enjoyed Pensacola.

✳✺✳

When Ed called Jenny and told her what was going on, she was amazed by the news. She didn't think it was fair and didn't understand how they could do that to someone. She could tell he was upset and hoped he wouldn't get in trouble. She just wanted him to finish and get orders. She was tired of being alone and wanted her husband back. The kids were great company, but she needed adult conversation too. She was also jealous that he was always going out with friends and enjoying himself while she was home taking care of the kids. She didn't think he understood their money situation, and she did not dare tell him they were receiving assistance.

She did her best to comfort him when he called, and they decided she would drive down and stay for a week when he graduated. Then he would drive home with them, and they would move to their new home. That sounded great to both of them.

The rest of the twelve weeks dragged on for both of them. For Ed, the training was monotonous administrative crap, but he loved the PT. Jenny's life was just a daily routine of cleaning, feeding, paying bills, playing with and taking care of the kids, and diapers. Having two children eighteen months apart was a chore with two parents in the home. It was a nightmare for one parent. She was counting the seconds by the time she packed the car and loaded the kids for their trip.

⁂

Ed finally got his orders when Jenny was on the road. They received orders to Marine Aircraft Group (MAG) Twenty-Six, Second Marine Aircraft Wing (MAW), Marine Corps Air Station (MCAS) New River, part of the Camp Lejeune area. He was excited about the orders, but he was still pissed about his new job. He knew Jenny would be pleased with their permanent duty station.

When Jenny arrived, Ed secured them a room at the navy lodge on the beach across from the Navy Aviation Museum. It was a gorgeous lodge with beautiful palm trees, balconies overlooking the gulf, and a great restaurant and bar within the facility. They had a wonderful week taking the kids to see the sights, to visit the beach, and to watch the Blue Angels practice. They watched Ed's graduation, got his orders, packed, and loaded up for the long drive home.

They had two weeks of leave to get their household goods packed up, say their good-byes, and make the trek to Camp Swampy. When they made it back to town, Ed realized how busy Jenny had been over the last several months. Everything was ready to go. She had boxed and labeled everything, scheduled the truck, and had all their things arranged for fast and efficient pack out. She would have made a good sailor.

They spent a lot of time at the lake with Ed's mom at her camper. They all loved it out there. It was located at a neat little private campers club called Pine Point on a five-hundred-acre manmade lake with forty campers and one hundred social members and their families. It was always a good time. Ed and his brothers grew up there. His stepdad joined Pine Point right after they had started the club. Steve and Ed's mom had always kept a camper there.

Ed's mom threw a big going-away party for them. A lot of their family and friends came from the surrounding area to see them off and wish them luck. Ed's brother, Pat, pulled him to the side and let him know he had reenlisted and was leaving soon. He also told Ed that he was going to be an uncle. Pat's girlfriend was pregnant. Ed was grinning from ear to ear with the news.

Two days after the party, they all stood outside Ed's mom's house, packed and ready to roll out together this time. It was going to be a long drive, but they were all sad to leave. Ed's parents did not want to see them go, especially the grandkids. Jenny's parents felt the same way, but everyone knew it was for the best. Hugs, tears, kisses, and more tears were shared before they climbed into the moving truck and hit the road.

They drove for four hours before stopping to get gas and letting the kids stretch. They got some food and made plans to drive another four or five hours and then stop for the night. They were both already exhausted from driving and the stress of moving, but the excitement was driving them forward to their destination.

When they reached West Virginia, they found a small hotel off the interstate and got a room for the evening. They settled in for the night and let the kids watch some videos to settle them down from the drive. Pizza was everyone's favorite meal, so they placed their order for delivery and waited patiently for supper. When it arrived, they ate and went to bed. In the morning, they pressed on and arrived in Camp Lejeune at 1600. Familiar with only one hotel, they decided to stay at the Motel 6. It was not Jenny's first choice, but she was in no mood to argue with Ed, and she was just too excited to be at her new home.

4

Bougainville Drive

~

Eager to start the day and hopeful to find suitable housing for his family, Ed got up early, did his normal routine, and headed for the base housing office on Tarawa Terrace. He was unable to secure a house prior to leaving Pensacola and hoped to get the keys to one today.

He had called the office three weeks ago and knew he might have to wait up to a month for housing. He wasn't keeping his family away for another month because the navy could not get orders completed in a timely manner, and he was not about to tell Jenny the information, so now he was in a jam. He was not leaving that office without a house. He believed if you wanted something bad enough, you asked and worked hard, and you would get it. He thought things were that simple, and that's why it was frustrating for him when people made life difficult.

It was a muggy and humid morning in late August. When Ed opened the motel door, it felt as if he had opened a sauna door.

Sweat formed instantly on his brow as he turned and winked at Jenny, blew her a kiss, and said, "I love you, plumkin. I'll be back shortly with the keys to our new palace." He laughed hysterically as he shut the door and marched smartly to the Rooster. The drive to Tarawa Terrace II was quick—left onto Marine Boulevard, right on Western Avenue, all the way down to the entrance to the housing area.

Tarawa Terrace II butted up right next to Camp Johnson, with a small trailer court and Boy Scout Camp separating the two. Military housing was the same all over the world. Like all government contracts, the cheapest bidder got the job. Cheap was good, but it was also cheap and often poorly constructed. The lawns, playgrounds, and streets were meticulously groomed, and the exterior of the homes were manicured to look presentable. The military was all about presentation and appearance. Unfortunately, they were like a nice-looking onion at the grocery store that spoiled from the inside; once you started peeling the outside layers, you realized what you really had.

Ed made his way through the maze of houses. It was a bustling neighborhood already full of activity, with marines, sailors, and spouses commuting to work, kids walking to school, others waiting for buses, and families playing at the park. Ed thought about how much better this would be for his family than where they had been less than a year ago, and he knew his decision had led them in the right direction. He begged to be granted one wish: to leave with keys to a home today. He could not bear going back to his family with news of yet another failure.

At the housing office, he parked and sat for a moment in the van. He summoned the courage and prayed again, "Please give us a house." He had not been to church in many years and was not sure whom he was asking or if anyone was listening, but he thought, *What can it hurt?* He put on that charming smile and strolled up to the office. He entered as fear grew deep in his gut, and he wanted to throw up, but he managed to move forward and approach the elderly man sitting at the desk.

"Good morning, sir," he said. "I am Hospital Corpsman Brannan. I just arrived from Illinois with my family. We received orders three weeks ago when I was in training, and I was unable to arrange for housing at that time. I was told to report here when we arrived." The man introduced himself and asked Ed to have a seat.

He punched the keyboard, scrolled through his computer, and made small talk for a while. Then he said, "HN Brannan, you are in luck this morning." Ed looked puzzled.

He was not used to things going smoothly, so he asked, "Will we have a house soon, sir?"

The man smiled and said, "I am a retired marine, Doc. Corpsmen took care of me for years. Marines take care of their docs too! How about today?" Ed's smile grew larger, and he would have hugged the man, but he knew how inappropriate that would be.

Ed thanked him several times before the man stopped him and said, "I read you, Doc. No need to thank me for doing my job. Now go get your family and take care of this paperwork. Return it to this office within two days." Ed thanked him again anyway, shook his hand, and floated out of that office on cloud nine. He could not wait to get back to the hotel to tell Jenny and get their belongings to their new home. He hadn't even bothered to look at the address.

The drive back to the hotel was maddening. It seemed to take forever. When he reached the hotel, he leaped from the Rooster and ran to the room, leaving the van door wide open. He beat on the door like a wild animal. Jenny was inside getting the kids ready when she heard the banging. She nearly came out of her skin, and both kids were so frightened, they began to cry. She grabbed them and ran into the bathroom.

Ed started yelling, "Jenny, Jenny, we got a house!" at the top of his lungs. People in the adjoining rooms and staff from the hotel were opening doors and peering at him as if he were insane. He realized how silly he looked. His face flushed red, and he yelled, "Sorry, I'm just excited. We got a house! You all have a good day."

※※

Jenny finally came to the door with the kids wailing in her arms. Ed grabbed them all and squeezed them tightly. He released his bear hug and said, "We have a home." He reached inside his front pocket and pulled out a set of keys, dangling them in front of Jenny and the kids, rattling them and dancing around like a baboon. The kids loved it and started to giggle.

He is a moron, Jenny thought. *Did he go drinking?*

It didn't take Jenny long to pack their things and get ready to leave. She didn't want to spend one more second in that hotel. She thought it was the dirtiest place she had ever been. She knew Ed liked the place, but he was ready to get *home*. They got their things packed up and headed to Tarawa Terrace II on the same route Ed followed earlier. Ed took the lead in the moving van as Jenny followed in the Rooster.

❊❊

Ed finally looked at the address and thought to himself, *I wonder if that retired marine thought it was funny putting a sailor on that street?*

The address was 2625 Bougainville Drive, Tarawa Terrace II, Jacksonville, North Carolina, 28543—the new Brannan home for the next three years.

What better first base home for a young navy family than on a street named after a battle in which the navy fleet left the marines and corpsmen on Bougainville Island? Ed thought. *They came back for them, of course, but how ironic our first home while stationed with the marines has to be on this street. I hope this is not some bad sign.* Ed didn't believe in that sort of thing, but Jenny did, so he didn't dare say anything to her. He figured why spoil the moment with some bull crap like that. She wouldn't worry about it if he didn't mention it.

Ed remembered driving on the street when he went to the housing office earlier, so he was confident he knew where to go. As they entered the gate and took the first left, he scanned the house numbers. It was a short distance before the entrance to their parking area, and he saw their new home. It was the house on the left corner, part of a five-plex, single-story, apartment-style structure with cream-colored vinyl siding and a brown-shingled roof. A humongous oak tree stood in the large front yard, flanked by manicured bushes with pine straw along the front of the complex, with breaks for the entrances. The grass was beautiful; it looked like a perfect spot. It was definitely far better than the dump of a trailer they were living in and better than sharing a home with Jenny's dad, or so they hoped.

It was midmorning when they arrived, and fortunately there were no vehicles in the parking lot. Ed maneuvered the truck around and backed it up close to the front door. Jenny backed the van into their assigned parking space and got the kids out of the car. They were all so excited to see their new home, it was hard to contain themselves. Christopher was running around the yard, wild from being cooped up in a car and hotel for days. Clara wanted down and was trying to wiggle free from her mommy's clutches. Ed and Jenny were grinning widely. They were happy to be together and to be at the steps of their new home. Ed inserted the key and, with a turn, opened the door.

The intense smell of pine oil cleaning solution was the first thing that hit them. The smell was so overpowering, it brought tears to their eyes. Ed knew the military saying, "If it smells clean, it is clean." Apparently, the housing managers applied this principle as well. The apartment was seven hundred and fifty square feet. It had three bedrooms and one bath, plus a full kitchen and a small screened-in back porch. Their initial tour took three minutes tops. The home looked clean, had a fresh coat of paint, and all the appliances worked. The décor was standard vinyl tile and white walls, with cheap cabinets and appliances.

Ed knew what to expect; it was free! Maybe it wasn't exactly free; he would be giving up his Basic Allowance for Housing, an allowance paid to service members who choose to stay off base instead of living in the barracks or in base housing. The allowance was normally enough to find a comparable home or apartment in the area, but rarely could junior enlisted afford that luxury. Those who chose the option often found themselves in deep debt early in life and often stayed that way or ended up in bankruptcy by the end of their careers.

They spent the rest of the day unloading the truck and van. They set the kids up in the far left room with some toys and a television. They played and kept themselves entertained while their parents worked diligently to get everything unloaded. They did not want to keep the truck any longer than they had to. The less money they spent, the more they could keep from the do-it-yourself (DITY) move. DITY moves were an option service members could choose instead of having professional movers transfer their household goods. It was time consuming and a lot of work, but if done properly, it saved the government money, and the service member made some cash. When they finished, they loaded the kids in the van, and Jenny followed Ed to return the truck to the nearest dealer.

They returned home and began unpacking. Ed was not much help when it came to household chores. He got in Jenny's way. She preferred he go do something else, but he thought he knew how to do things more efficiently than she did. It was a battle of wills that often led to a verbal battle. They had not had a confrontation in some time, but they had not spent a lot of time together over the last year. Jenny had become accustomed to her own routine, and Ed was used to his. Two storms were on a collision course and were about to meet in the Brannan household, the first of many tropical depressions that erupted.

It was late, and they had just finished eating pizza again. They had managed to get a lot done that day, and Ed wanted to get some sleep so he could report to his new command in the morning. Jenny wanted to continue working. Ed had not been alone with his wife in their own room for many months, and he just wanted to put the kids to bed and for them to go to the bedroom as well. His intent was romantic, but his follow-through was anything but, and as usual, it led to a series of misunderstandings that caused the first day in their new home to end in a disaster.

When Jenny continued to work on the house and ignored his request, he said, "Are you freaking kidding me? Is this the way I'm going to be treated after busting my ass for the last year to get us here?"

"You're an asshole," Jenny erupted. "Do you think you're the only one who has been working to get here over the last year? I guess I haven't done anything but sit around."

"Yeah, that is exactly what you have been doing!" Jenny was shocked by his complete disregard for the struggles and efforts she put forth daily to provide for him and the kids.

"You know something, you have always been a selfish son of a bitch," she said. "You have no idea what I do every day, because before you finally got a real job, you were too damn drunk to know what was going on around you." Ed was furious when he heard her say this. She had never spoken to him like that, and deep down he knew she was right, but he was not going to be insulted by her.

"You're right. I have never done a damn thing for you, have I? You were living a grand ole life before you met me. I mean, hell, living with your mom at thirty had to be your life goal. I know that was always one of mine." He was brutal when he got mad and could spit out the most evil and hurtful words with ease without thought. He destroyed her with his comments, and she shuddered as she began to weep, falling to the floor in a clump and curling into a fetal position.

He knew instantly he had taken it too far again. He hated hurting her like this and wanted to grab her and apologize, but that damn pride of his refused to allow him to be human and do so. He left her lying there, went to the bedroom, and slammed the door.

※※

Jenny was lying there crying, thinking, *Why did I come here? I'm all alone with this psycho. He doesn't love me. There is no way someone can talk to someone he loves like that.* She summoned the strength to get up and compose herself as she continued to think. She wondered if they were going to make it, and if they did, would the kids be affected by all of the constant fighting? She prayed he would change and they could be a happy family like the one she always dreamed of.

※※

Ed woke early the next morning. He showered, dressed, and stealthily exited the house without waking Jenny. He knew how wrong he was the night before, but he had no desire to apologize and hoped it would all blow over by the time he returned from work this afternoon. He thought to himself that he needed to quit getting so mad and acting like that. It reminded him of his dad's disposition when he was young, and although he loved his dad dearly, the last thing he wanted was to have his temper. He jumped in the van and drove to Marine Corps Air Station (MCAS), New River's Medical Clinic.

❊❊

Jenny heard the front door open and close. She had cried herself to sleep on the floor next to the kids in the small bedroom when Ed had shut himself in the night before. She couldn't believe he just left without saying anything to her. Actually, she could believe it; she expected it from him. She knew he would return that afternoon and act as if nothing had happened.

"What a *jerk!*" She crawled off the floor and went to her kitchen. She was an amazing person. She had learned to adapt to cruel behavior early in life. For whatever reason, she seemed to attract it. She was the target of her mother's rage when she was young. As she grew older, she believed it was because her mother didn't like her dad and took it out on her, but it did nothing to soften the pain it caused her. "Tough as nails" is how her dad described her. Appropriate description coming from a master carpenter!

As she sipped her coffee and thought of what had transpired, something dawned on her. She realized what had upset him. *The fool was just trying to get me in the sack.* She smiled as a tear ran down her cheek. She didn't understand him. Maybe she never would.

She spent the rest of the day unpacking and maintaining her normal routine of diaper duty and feeding and entertaining the children. She was a working machine; *efficient* was an understatement. *Screw you, Eddie Brannan,* she thought, giggling under her breath. *I'm a lot better at this than you!* When she had completed the tasks, she realized they didn't have enough furniture to fill a tiny home like this one, and they barely had enough money to buy diapers. Where were they going to get the money to buy what they needed to make this place presentable? She thought if he knew what financial shape they were really in, maybe he would show her a little more appreciation.

Little did she know that other than not knowing about the federal assistance, Ed was quite aware of the dire straits they were in concerning finances. He was broke, and he knew it. He may have failed at his business attempt, but it was not from being ignorant of finance. He also knew how hard she worked. He just refused to acknowledge she was putting forth as much or more effort than he was. He was stubborn as a mule—another fine trait he inherited from his dear ole daddy, God love that man.

❊❊

Ed sat in front of the clinic in the Rooster, thinking to himself, *Here we go! Let's do this, Brannan.* He looked over his uniform and hair, made sure he was in order, and exited the van. He walked smartly to the entrance and entered the clinic. It was a hot morning. The heat and nerves had him sweating instantly. The tan brick clinic sat back in a crop of pine trees. It was a newer building than most of the structures on base, but it had the same steam pipes going to it as the rest of the air station. *Lowest bidder!* Ed thought. *The government is a model of efficiency.* Coming from a man who had lost everything he owned, he should have remembered the old saying, "People who live in glass houses shouldn't throw stones."

He entered the clinic and proceeded to the front desk, where a younger HN was working. He asked where he could check in. The HN directed him to the administrative offices through the glass hatch to the starboard side of the desk. *Just say freaking "right" and "door,"* Ed thought. *I'm not impressed.* He went through the doors and followed the signs to administration. He entered and spoke to the Hospital Corpsman Second Class (HM2) at the first desk.

"Good morning, HM2. I am HN Brannan reporting to duty at Marine Aircraft Group Twenty-Six."

"Good morning. Welcome aboard. Have a seat and let me get you checked in, and then I will introduce you to Senior and your MAG chief."

The check-in went fast. He had all his data except a phone number. He explained to the HM2 that he would have that within the week and would give it to him as soon as possible.

When the HM2 finished, he escorted Ed to the senior enlisted adviser's office. Ed stood at parade rest, awaiting orders to enter. Ed overheard the HM2 and Senior speaking. He heard Senior tell HM2 to have him report.

HM2 came out and said, "HN Brannan, report to Senior Chief."

"Thank you, HM2," Ed said. He knocked three times on the frame of the hatch and awaited the order to enter.

When Senior announced, "Enter," Ed entered the small office crammed with furniture and every decoration the old man had received throughout his career. Ed despised what he called "I love me walls," and this man had an office dedicated to himself. Ed thought, *This should be an interesting conversation about the senior chief!*

To his surprise, Senior was the opposite of what he had expected. He was a humble man. Ed was not sure of his age, but he was sure he was younger than he appeared. The man who sat before him looked as though he were in his nineties. He was around five foot eleven, one hundred pounds soaking wet, with gray hair, wrinkled sun-dried skin, and hollow eyes sunken into his skull. He could have been mistaken for Skeletor off the old *He-Man* cartoon series.

The man was humble, but my goodness, could he talk. Ed could chew someone's ear off in conversation, but this person must have been lonely, because he would not shut up. Ed listened intently or did his best to pretend to. The last thing he wanted to do was to piss off the boss on his first day, and he wanted a good assignment.

The stories went on for over an hour before his new chief saved him. *Thank you, Jesus!* Ed thought. The chief came in, and Ed rose to his feet. Chief told Senior he was taking Ed back to his desk to brief him and assign him a sponsor to get him checked into the command. The chief asked to which squadron the senior wanted to assign Ed. Ed's ears perked with that remark, and he listened intently.

The old man thought for a moment. "I want him with me. Put him in MWSS 272."

Ed was not familiar with the air wing and had no idea what MWSS meant, but he didn't want to show ignorance in front of his new leaders, so he said, "Thank you, Senior Chief," and left with his new chief.

Chief Taylor was the opposite of Senior. He was direct and to the point. His desk had no clutter, nor did it have any relics of his past service. He did not tell any sea stories and did not care to ask Ed any questions about his past or current circumstance. He provided him with details on what he was to do over the next week and introduced him to his new buddy, HN Gonzalez, his command sponsor.

The navy assigned sponsors to new check-ins to assist them in being checked in and to give them a familiar face for any questions. HN Gonzalez was Hispanic, around five foot nine, one hundred and sixty pounds, with a decent build and a good sense of humor. He was from the Chicago area. He was a perfect sponsor for Ed, and they struck an immediate kinship. They talked about sports and traded some sea stories as they bounced around doing check-in. HN Gonzalez was married and had two children too. Ed asked him if he drank beer and if he would be interested in grilling out with him and the family sometime. HN Gonzalez was more than willing to accept the invitation.

They continued to knock out portions of the check-in sheet the rest of the afternoon, and around 1500, HN Gonzalez told Ed, "Bro, let's get the hell out of here and call it a day. We will meet back here at oh-six hundred for clinic PT and then start again. That sound cool to you?"

"Hell yeah!" Ed said. They headed back to the clinic and snuck out for the day.

Driving home, Ed realized he didn't even ask what MWSS was. *That was dumb. I don't know where I'm going to work. I hope Jenny doesn't ask.* He made it to the house in under fifteen minutes and thought how great it was to have such a short commute to work. Approaching the door, he wondered if Jenny was still going to be upset with him and didn't know whether to apologize or just pretend like it never happened. Acting as if it never happened had worked in the past and was easier for him, so he went with that option.

※❀※

As she expected, he came in talking about checking in, acting as if nothing had transpired less than twenty-four hours ago. *What an asshole. Oh well. Ed is Ed, and he knows he was wrong,* she thought. They talked about his day and inviting HN Gonzalez and his family over. Jenny told him they needed to get some furniture. He said they could go to the Marine Corps Exchange and get furniture on credit.

Not with your credit, dummy, she thought, but didn't say anything. She did not know the Military Exchange System had programs in place for service members in his predicament. Their financial situation was not uncommon, and although it was not discussed frequently, the military was aware of the financial burdens and had programs in place to help alleviate the stress. It was not a perfect system, but they did attempt to take care of their own with or without the assistance of the elected officials.

Over the following weeks, they went about readying their home. Ed continued to check in and meet more and more shipmates. Jenny became familiar with the area and remained on task with her responsibilities as matriarch of the family. They continued to have small spats, as many couples do, but overall they settled into their new lives and were enjoying their new home and lifestyle. Jenny met many of the neighbors and struck friendships with the other spouses. Like the men in their lives, the women were in similar circumstances, and it was easy to form an instant and strong bond. They complained and comforted one another as only they could. They were an extension of each other's family tree.

5

The Military Family Dynamic

~

Jenny came to understand the military lifestyle like most service members do by trial, error, and, most important, friendships. Anyone who has never been in or around the military finds it hard to understand the bond that service members and their families share with one another. Service members refer to one another as brother and sister, and their families think of each other as aunts, uncles, cousins, and sometimes even siblings. That concept was foreign to Jenny at first and may seem strange to someone from the outside looking in, but for families living the military life, it is absolutely the norm.

Thrust into a foreign situation, often alone, Jenny instantly recognized this relationship with her fellow spouses. She formed friendships with the neighborhood girls within the first weeks of arriving. As time progressed and they met more people, her network grew, as did Ed's. They soon found their home was the gathering place on most weekends for other families and anyone who wanted the comforts of home. They both enjoyed hosting and were accustomed to it because of their business experience. Owning a bar in your twenties had its advantages. One was you knew how to throw a party.

Ed's friend from Field Medical Service School, Madden, came over most weekends. He enjoyed getting away from the barracks and loved watching cartoons with Christopher on Saturday morning. Jenny thought it was an amusing sight to see a huge man sitting crisscross applesauce on the floor with a three-year-old, watching cartoons. She could not figure out who enjoyed it more, Madden or Christopher.

Ed's other buddy from the school, Scott, was a frequent flyer at the Brannan abode as well. He didn't make it over as much as Madden, but when he did, they all always had a good time. The holidays were fast approaching; Jenny offered to cook a nice meal for several of the single sailors who frequented their home. They made plans to have a traditional Thanksgiving meal and party, of course. Those in the neighborhood who were staying local all joined in the plan, and a grand event was coordinated.

The day was a huge success, with plenty of food and drinks. The kids and adults both had a great time. The spouses outdid themselves. However, Ed was concerned most of the day. Madden had agreed to come, and Ed had been trying to reach him all day with no luck. He left several messages for him.

Most of the messages were typical Ed-style. "Hey, dude, what the hell? Jenny cooked all this food for your big dumb ass, and you can't even call and cancel. Whatever. Call me back." Jenny could tell there was something more to Ed's concern, but knew asking would only provoke an altercation, and they were having too good of a day for that. She let it be, and they continued to enjoy themselves. Well, she continued to enjoy herself, and so did the others. Ed put on his best front as a host, but he was obviously distraught.

Monday afternoon, as Ed came in the house, Jenny immediately sensed something had happened. He looked enraged, but he was grieving.

"What is going on?" she asked.

"Honey, you need to sit down," Ed said. Jenny went to the couch, sat, and knew she was about to be told something horrible. Ed sat next to her, placed a hand on her shoulder, and said, "Madden killed himself."

Jenny was stunned and couldn't believe what she had just heard. *There is no way! He was always so happy.*

"Babe, he suffered from depression for a long time," Ed said. "Scott, Travis, and I knew about it. We also knew he had attempted suicide before. That's why we always kept an eye on him. That's not the only reason. I obviously cared about him. He was a good friend, but he had a lot going on."

Jenny slumped over and cried as Ed rubbed her back. He tried his best to comfort her as he dealt with his own pain and anger.

Unfortunately, suicide was not uncommon, and Ed had dealt with it more than a few times. He didn't understand the concept. To him, taking your life because life sucked was the dumbest thing you could do, but he understood the people who did this were not of sound mind. Jenny thought it to be a selfish act, but she was too heartbroken to be angry. Ed's natural emotion was anger. If you were to ask Jenny, she would tell you it might be his only emotion.

Madden's suicide was difficult, but it further reinforced the ever-growing family tree. They gathered around one another and supported each other through their pain. They continued to grow as more and more families joined their network. It was a beautiful collage of young people banding together, taking lemons and turning them into lemonade.

As the holidays came and went, a new realization dawned on Jenny. Death was not the only thing that would separate them from their ever-growing network of friends. The military rotated every three to four years, so as fast as people came into your life, they were leaving. The benefit for families who stayed in long enough was that they tended to meet up again. For Jenny, that didn't make it any less painful to say good-bye. Just like saying good-bye to her family, each time she hugged and waved good-bye to a member of their military family, it stung, and she would miss them. They would remain in contact and knew the time they spent together and shared would always be theirs and precious, but it still hurt.

Jenny also saw Ed's relationship with the kids growing. He was more attentive to them than he had been in the past. He was engaged in their development, and his relationship with Clara was definitely blossoming. That struck a chord with Christopher; he didn't like seeing his daddy paying any attention to his little sister and would act up to draw it back to him. But overall, things were settling down and going well for the moment.

※※

Ed had finally figured out that MWSS was Marine Wing Support Squadron. It wasn't quite what he had planned, but he enjoyed working at the clinic and the men and women he worked with. Over the past few months, the United States had issues with an old adversary: Saddam Hussein in Iraq. There were talks of an upcoming invasion if he refused to allow United Nations weapons inspections. Scuttlebutt at work was that MWSS 272 and Second Marine Aircraft Wing (MAW) would be a part of any operation, and that made Ed very happy.

It wasn't Afghanistan, but it was an opportunity to go do what he had reenlisted to do. He knew Jenny had established herself well enough. She had plenty of support, and he knew she would be fine. For some reason, he doubted that would have made any difference in his decision or the military's, if an operation order came through.

※※

Ed was correct in his assumption. Jenny was in fact adjusting very well. She loved her new lifestyle. She wanted more and believed most people do. She didn't think she was being greedy to want to be off government assistance and have a more caring and loving husband. However, for the most part, this was a life in which she could remain content. Her friends were great people. Her kids were her life, and her husband was a pain in the ass most days, but when he wasn't, he was great! Things could be a lot worse, and they were about to get that way.

6

Duty Calls

~

By January 2002, international negotiations with Iraq continued to erode, and the Bush administration built a case for military action against them. With the 2001 terrorist attacks still fresh in the minds of all Americans, and with possible chemical weapons in the hands of a lunatic like Saddam Hussein, it was not a difficult battle. The president mustered support from the majority of both parties and the people to destroy Hussein's capabilities to utilize or sell any weapons of mass destruction. Military leaders began planning operations in Iraq.

※※

Ed's assignment to MWSS 272 was disappointing for him. He missed several opportunities for deployments to Afghanistan and was becoming discouraged with the assignment to the support unit. Tyson, Ed's good friend from home whom he and his brother had encouraged to join the army, had been on the initial invasion in Afghanistan and had already made two additional deployments. This strengthened Ed's resolve to get back in the fight, but it made him begin to question his decision to switch branches again. Tyson called Ed when he returned from duty and told him about his experiences and that he was grateful for the advice Ed and Pat had given him. *I should learn to take my own advice sometime,* Ed thought.

Scuttlebutt continued to swarm around the air station and the clinic about which units would participate in the upcoming action and when the assault would take place. Training and preparation began for the Marine Expeditionary Force at Camp Lejeune and marine bases throughout the world, with commanding officers and their staffs all hoping to get in on the coming onslaught. Of course, their families were not nearly as excited or prepared to see their loved ones readying to board aircraft and ships destined to a foreign land to fight and possibly die for what many believed to be someone else's issue, based on military and foreign intelligence.

※※

Jenny knew there was no sense in discussing this with Ed. He had reenlisted with the intent to go back to war. She knew he had something to prove to himself. She wasn't sure what it was, but she knew anything she said to him contrary to what he believed would be a moot point and not worth the fight. She felt a distance growing between them, and she could tell his focus was solely on work. He spent more and more time at the clinic and with his comrades. When he was home, he was there physically, but his mind was somewhere else. Her focus remained on her daily tasks and on taking care of the kids and him, even if his interest was not with them.

※※

As the days drew on, mission plans were dispensed, and units were given their orders. MWSS 272 was chosen to support Second MAW operations in Operation Iraqi Freedom. They were to leave in March 2003, with an unspecified return date. Ed was ecstatic. This was why he had reenlisted; it was an opportunity to get to the fight. He didn't like going in another supporting role, but accepted the fact that this was as close as he was getting right now. He knew this would be difficult for Jenny to accept, but thought he had explained this possibility and she was prepared to handle his hiatus.

That evening, he returned home and readied to tell Jenny the news. At supper, he began. "Hon, we got our orders and will be leaving sometime in March. We don't know how long the operation will last, but they don't expect it to be very long. This unit is a support unit. I know you don't know a lot about this stuff, but that means we won't be anywhere near the fighting. We will be resupplying airfield operations and convoying supplies."

※※

Jenny was devastated.

"Ed, I know this is what you wanted when you joined, and I support you. I don't want to see you leave, but we will be fine. Please try to spend more time at home with us before you leave. Lately, you have done nothing but work and go out. It is like we are back home again."

She regretted adding the last part as she saw his facial expression change from somber to rage in an instant. He got up from the table and walked to the living room. He said nothing to her the rest of the evening and fell asleep on the couch. He was gone in the morning before she woke.

Their interactions over the next few weeks were much the same. He showed little affection and growing hostility for the slightest imperfection. She thought it must be his way of coping with leaving them. She hoped that was what it was—that he wasn't that big of a jerk—but she really didn't know.

※※

Ed remained vigilant in learning his trade and took every opportunity to train. Predeployment was exhausting for most people, but for him it was exhilarating. He enjoyed the physical and mental aspects of field medicine and was having a blast with the marines. In comparison, he found MWSS to be a cluster bomb of inexperienced support types. Ed was support too and didn't mind admitting it, but these folks were a special kind who believed they had combat skills they didn't. It was Ed's experience that people like that usually got themselves or you killed, and he wanted to stay as far away from them as possible.

Fortunately, it seemed that these folks were only the senior leaders, so it was easy for a junior corpsman to stay away from them. Ed's navy leaders took care of the sailors, but had no pull within the unit. It created a difficult working relationship, but Ed understood that once you got where you were going, those dynamics shifted quickly. Getting there would be the difficult part.

The Marine Aircraft Group surgeon decided to do a base-wide medical training exercise for the corpsmen and flight surgeons to include evacuation and flight-line aid station operations. It was great real-world predeployment training, and he added training in tactical combat casualty care, a newer tactical version of basic life support developed by a group of special operation doctors who focused on tactical medicine/hemorrhage control versus standard American Heart Association protocols. It was a brilliant concept developed from lessons learned after Mogadishu.

The training lasted two days and was outstanding. Everyone enjoyed the interaction with one another, the topics chosen, and the finale. During the after-action report, the group surgeon discussed tactical combat casualty care and lessons learned from Somalia.

He misspoke about the timeline of events and had started to make another misstatement when Ed said, "Excuse me, sir, that is incorrect!"

The commander was obviously annoyed an HN was questioning him, and he asked Ed, "How would you know that?"

"Well, sir, I was there," Ed said. It was dark and cool that evening, but he could see the commander's face flush with embarrassment. Thankfully, the senior chief jumped in and began his debrief. As he finished, he added that they had purchased food and beverages, and everyone could proceed to the flight-line aid station for supper before they were dismissed for the evening.

Ed stood by. He knew the senior chief would want a word with him, and he had a good idea the commander would want to discuss his interruption as well. As he expected, they both promptly marched toward him and told him to follow them to the side of one of the seven-ton vehicles. Ed stood at parade rest and awaited his butt chewing.

The senior chief began with, "HN Brannan, that was highly inappropriate. If you had something to—"

The commander interrupted. "Thank you, Senior, but if I was giving misinformation, I would much rather be corrected immediately than look like a fool later. Thank you, HN Brannan, for having the courage to say something. I had no idea you were in the army or a part of that operation. If I had known that, I would have picked your brain long ago. Is there a reason you have not mentioned to anyone that you were in Mogadishu?"

"Sir, I was a communications guy with the Combat Support Hospital. I coordinated medical evacuations and did internal communications. I know the timeline of events. I know what happened, the casualties, and the after-action report, and in college I did an essay on the failures of the Clinton administration, not the failures of the military during the operation. I do not talk about it because I do not feel it is relevant to being a corpsman. It was not my intent to insult you, but when it comes to that event, I am emotional, and I do not like to hear inaccurate talking points repeated. I apologize for my lack of bearing."

The commander slapped Ed on the shoulder and said, "I think you did the right thing, and I think your experience is relevant where we are headed. I was not insulted. I'm glad you said something. I learned something tonight. Go get something to eat, and I would like to hear more about your time in Somalia sometime if you would like to talk about it with me. Thank you, HN Brannan."

As the commander started to walk away, the senior chief said, "HN Brannan, stand by, please." Ed and the senior chief hung back as the commander headed for chow.

"Brannan, you got lucky," the senior chief said. "You need to learn to keep your emotions in check. You have a lot of potential, but if you mouth off to the wrong person, you are going to get yourself in a situation I won't be able to bail you out of."

"I understand, Senior. That is just a touchy subject for me, and I could not listen to him tell those people any more of that BS. I respect the fact you were trying to cover my butt, and I really appreciate the fact that the commander is a good man. I will work on my bearing, but I have always had a rough time keeping my mouth shut."

Senior smiled and said, "Doc, I believe that! Let's go grab some chow and get home."

Ed headed home that night thinking about what had transpired. If he did not keep his mouth shut, he would end up screwing up his chance of ever accomplishing the goal he had set in motion. His mind drifted back to all the times in the army when he had discipline problems, and focused on a sergeant first class in Somalia who constantly harassed him. The six-foot, two-hundred-pound Hispanic sergeant did not like PFC Brannan's attitude and made an example of him every time an opportunity presented itself. Ed hated the man as much as the man hated him. They were constantly at odds.

Every opportunity Ed had to piss him off, he took a shot at him, and he lost every battle. It was an exercise in futility, but for Ed it was about pride, not winning. He knew the time would come when he would have the last laugh, and that moment came toward the end of the deployment. Ed stalked the man for a few nights. He watched his routine, trying to figure out a way to humiliate him without hurting him and without suspicion. He saw an opportunity the second evening.

Every night at around 2200, the sergeant came out of his office and used the same privy. The privies, constructed of three-quarter-inch plywood, were about four feet square and six feet tall, with a front door and a lower back hatch and fifty-gallon drums cut in half for feces. There were tubes in the ground next to the privies for urine, but most people urinated as they were doing their other business. The privies were nasty-smelling atrocities during the heat of the day, so many people used them at night to avoid the harsh smell.

Ed formulated a plan, gathered material, and awaited his target. At exactly 2200 on the third evening, his mark came strolling out to relieve himself. He would get no relief tonight. Ed had already secured the back hatch of the privy with a padlock, readied duct tape, and was waiting in the shadows to strike. When he heard the man sit down, Ed went into action. He sprang from the shadows. He wrapped the dangling edge of the duct tape around the handle several times and sprinted around the privy like a tetherball wrapping around a pole.

He heard the man inside yell, "Hey, what the hell are you doing out there?" Ed kept running around, securing the door. The man was rustling around inside. Ed wrapped the tape at least ten times before the man's first attempt to push open the door. He wrapped it another ten times as the man struggled futilely to release himself. When Ed knew he was secure, he stopped and went to the rear of the privy. He took several steps back, looked around, and ran as hard as he could toward the rear of the box. He hit the privy like a linebacker hitting a running back coming through a hole made by his linemen.

The box teetered as Ed's feet entrenched in the sand, and he pushed his arms forward with all his strength. He could feel the man attempt to counter the fall, but the center of gravity had already set the object into motion. The privy headed to the ground. It landed with a huge thump on its door, and the contents of the drum sloshed out all over the man as he screamed in disgust. Ed gathered his material and sprinted into the shadows. Mission accomplished!

There was a formation held the following morning, with threats of punishment and false accusations made, but no one knew who did it. Ed never told anyone.

The memory was amusing and gratifying until Ed remembered befriending the man when they returned from deployment. It had been the perfect crime until his conscience got the better of him. One evening drinking beer with the sergeant, the subject came up, and he was still justly upset about it. Ed told him he didn't like him then. The sergeant told Ed he didn't like him then either. Ed confessed to the incident and told him he would understand if they could no longer remain friends. The sergeant was pissed. He told Ed he initially thought it was him. He told him how messed up it was, but that was the past, and there was no need to dwell on it. He added if Ed ever pulled that on him again, he would punch him.

"I understand if you punch me now," Ed said. "I deserve it." They remained friends until he left for his next duty station.

※◈※

It was late when Ed made it home, but Jenny had supper waiting and was eager to hear how everything had gone. They sat down, and she listened intently to his stories about the training and his interaction with the group surgeon.

He is going to chirp off to the wrong person and get in trouble! she thought. The kids stirred around at their feet, and they enjoyed an hour or two before they settled them down and headed to bed.

※◈※

In the morning, they both woke and had coffee to discuss some needed predeployment items. Ed didn't want to talk about this stuff with Jenny. He was worried it would cause some undue worry, and he didn't want to upset her any more than he needed to, but he had to let her know what he was doing, and he would have to give her copies of the documents when they were completed.

He began by saying, "Jenny, I have to go to legal today and do some paperwork that you will need to keep in order to take care of my affairs while I'm gone. Please don't overreact when I tell you what they are. Promise not to freak out, please."

Jenny looked curious, but said OK.

"Honey, I have to get a will prepared and a general power of attorney done. It's just a formality. As I told you before, we are not going to do anything important. This is just a precaution they make everyone do. Do you understand?"

Jenny attempted to hide her distress, but was unable to. "I get it, but I'm worried," she said. "You have done this before. I haven't, and I don't want you to get hurt."

"I understand, baby. Just trust me. Don't worry. This is just a formality, and it gives you access to all my accounts, so you can take care of all our finances. I know you do that now, but this will give you legal access to call and do business on my behalf. I have to go. I love you, and I will give you copies of these two things when I get home. You have to keep them in a safe place and not lose them." He headed to work.

※※

The last weeks went by too fast for both of them. Ed continued to train, get gear, pack, and prepare. Jenny went on with her duties as well. Ed remained distant, but Jenny began to realize this was just a coping mechanism. He was a jerk, but he didn't mean to hurt her. He was just incapable of dealing with more than one emotion at a time. She knew he loved her and the kids, but he had to be focused to go do what he was about to do. It was a delicate situation for both of them.

The night before she was to see him off was a nightmare. He was unbearable. He packed and repacked his gear three to four times, griped the entire night about her moving his stuff, and fussed over everything. She had seen him stressed before, but she had never seen him under stress like this, and she was taking the brunt of it all. She learned a valuable lesson that night. Take the kids in the other room and stay out of the jerk's way.

He managed to get everything the way he wanted it and finally went to bed around midnight. They all were up and in the car by 0330, headed to MWSS 272 headquarters to watch him board the bus for

Cherry Point and then on to Kuwait. She was sad to see him leave, but relieved to be getting a break from the madness.

He hugged her and the kids and said, "I love you all. I will see you soon."

She contained her emotions until he was on the bus and she had made it to the van. Once she secured the kids and she was in the driver's seat, she broke down. Overcome by emotion she could not explain, she sobbed for several minutes. She feared she would never see him again and prayed for his safety. It took several more minutes for her to compose herself well enough to drive home.

※※

The bus ride to Cherry Point was approximately one hour. At 0400 in the morning in March, there was not a lot to see out of blackened charter bus windows, and anytime a service member gets an opportunity to eat, sleep, or drink, he does it, whether or not he is hungry, tired, or thirsty. Ed was not sure why they all did this, but he knew why he did. He had gone without more times than he cared to admit, and even though he knew you couldn't catch up on meals or sleep, it comforted him to have excess of all three of these items when given the opportunity. He also considered the three things sacred, and they were the only things that were off-limits when messing with someone. They may have been the only things that were taboo to him.

Unfortunately, his mind did not allow him to sleep. He did have feelings, and he was sad to leave his family. He wasn't scared to go back to war, but he feared he wasn't prepared to treat a casualty perfectly. He went over different scenarios and injuries in his mind. His mind drifted to his first bus ride to the airport, when he was headed to Somalia, and his chaplain's words.

"Life is a path. Each choice is a fork in the path. If you choose left instead of right, you can never go back. Each choice takes you to a different destination with different people and a different journey, but it is your choice. Make the right one. You can never go back, even if it is a wrong choice."

Ed reflected on those words from so many years ago. *I thought that old man was nuts then. Now I understand. I have taken many wrong paths, but I can't go back, because I wouldn't know the people I love now, and I wouldn't be the man I am. Life is a mystery to me.*

The buses and trucks arrived along the runway at Marine Corps Air Station, Cherry Point, North Carolina's Arrival/Departure Airfield Control Group (A/DACG), and they were escorted by security in line next to the terminal. The group filed from the buses, formed into their platoons, got their counts, and were given instructions to enter the terminal for further instructions. The platoon leaders took charge and filed their platoons into the holding area. As they entered holding, sergeants were plucking E-3 and below from formation for baggage detail. The detail would unload the trucks and load the plane for departure. The norm was to keep your head down and pretend you didn't see the sergeant, in hopes you weren't selected. Ed just stared at him and walked by. He didn't want to do the detail, but he wasn't going to cower from it either.

The 0400 departure was a necessity because the flight left Cherry Point at 1200 that day. Yes, the marine corps loved to be on time. This was how it worked. The unit would get word that the flight would depart at 1200. The A/DACG would tell the unit to be there two hours in advance. The commanding officer would decide the command should be there two hours prior to that, just in case. The executive officer would give them an hour. The operations officer would give them an hour. The sergeant major would give them another hour, and finally the supply officer would give them an hour. Don't forget the fifteen minutes prior to formation the company commander needs, the fifteen minutes prior to that the platoon commander needs, the fifteen minutes prior to that the platoon sergeant needs, and the fifteen minutes the squad leader needs, which makes it a grand total of nine hours prior! Before you sit down on the plane, you have a bunch of disgruntled, tired, and smelly marines and sailors. It made for an unpleasant transcontinental traverse!

The flights were contracted out to civilian airlines that had an amazing staff of patriots who did a wonderful job of making everyone on board as comfortable as possible. They fed them as much as they wanted, kept the drink carts moving up and down the aisles, and had movies nonstop. The pilots and crew were unsung heroes who busted their butts to provide flawless customer service to men and women headed to combat.

The flights had brief layovers in Europe and then continued on to Kuwait. Upon arrival in Kuwait, the unit deplaned and headed to a nearby hangar. The hangar had a gaping hole in the top of it, left over from a bunker buster missile during the Gulf War, but it was structurally sound. The unit formed up and took count. Ed was at the rear of the last platoon and overheard his commanding officer talking with a man in the corner of the hangar. They were having a heated conversation about billeting and who sent them. *How the hell does an entire marine unit deploy without anyone knowing they are coming and their mission?* Ed wondered. It was going to be a long deployment.

Things went from bad to worse as the days passed. They managed to find billeting that evening after haggling with the camp commandant for hours and getting transportation to the marine position. Ed had experienced disorganized messes in the army, but never to this extent. He hoped his buddies with the other units were not experiencing these same cluster bombs. He soon found they were all in the same boat.

After a few days, things started to settle down, and he began to run into familiar faces around camp. The marine corps was known for operating with next to nothing. It wasn't ideal, but it created situations for resourceful individuals and corpsmen to show their skills. Ed had developed these skills in the army and was known for acquiring things at New River. As they all swarmed like wasps after someone disrupted a nest, they discussed the lack of medical supplies and the need to acquire casualty evacuation (CASEVAC) medication, bandages, gear, and aid station medication and supplies. All eyes focused on Ed.

Ed smiled. "Get me a truck and driver, but when I get back, don't ask me how or where I got any of it, and don't tell anyone I did it. If anyone asks, I will lie and tell them I don't know what any one of you is talking about." Everyone agreed to let Ed do some recon and to give him a few days to see what he could do. He started by asking around about where the largest amount of supplies were kept and how you requested the material.

His first priority was the aid station and medication. He learned the air force on base would requisition supplies for the unit. He made a contact with their supply chief and got enough to get his unit by until their equipment made it into country. That was the easy part. He also learned of a huge stash of fully stocked medical bags at the port, but it was run by the army. Unfortunately, they didn't give them out, and he didn't know how he could get to them or how he could get over there without raising suspicion. He would have to involve people higher in the chain of command than he wanted to and then hope they didn't ask too many questions.

The command had a flight surgeon augmented from another command. He was a squared-away lieutenant who was trying to get some supplies from the same base Ed wanted to get to. Ed asked him if he could arrange for a vehicle for him and if he could tag along to see the base and make some contacts for the future, since he was the supply petty officer. The lieutenant was oblivious to his ulterior motives. He probably would have gone along with the plan, but Ed didn't want to get anyone else in trouble if he got caught borrowing things. He set up transportation through Motor Transportation, Supply, and Operations. He let his chain of command know he was making a supply run with the lieutenant and told the CASEVAC guys he was going to try to make a run at their gear.

"No promises, but they have what you need, and I will see what I can do. If I get myself in a jam, someone needs to bail my butt out!"

Ed and the lieutenant met at the motor transportation lot with all their gear early in the morning and met their driver. Ed expected they would head over in a military convoy of some sort, but what he found was three jingle trucks—not ideal for hiding a bunch of borrowed gear, but since he was the only one who knew the true intent of the mission, he should expect Uncle Murphy to show up. Ed believed in Murphy's Law: what can go wrong will go wrong.

The drive was forty-five minutes to the port, all interstate travel on the outskirts of Kuwait City. There wasn't a lot of scenery. You could see the city in the distance, and there weren't many cars on the road at this time of morning. Entering the port, they were searched by contractors and bomb-sniffing dogs and then given directions to the supply depot, where they met a young army sergeant entering the depot. The lieutenant followed him to some containers. Ed got out of the vehicle and looked around, reading the cargo contents. He opened a few containers before he found what he was looking for. He ran back to the jingle truck and told the driver to pull up to the container.

The lance corporal, reading his magazine, attempted to blow Ed off by saying, "I just drive."

Ed went off. "Listen, pull this piece of crap up to that damn container, get out, and help me load that shit, or I am going to mess you up. You read me, Lance Corporal ?" The lance corporal got the message loud and clear. He pulled the vehicle up, and they frantically loaded as many boxes into the truck as they could.

They both were dripping sweat and breathing heavily as Ed told him, "Listen, this stuff is for CASEVAC. They don't have supplies. If they don't have it, marines will die. We just saved marines' lives. I'm sorry I yelled. Thank you for helping, and do not say anything to the lieutenant or anyone else about this. Please."

The lance corporal smiled. "You got it, Doc!"

The lance corporal backed the vehicle into its original location as Ed positioned the boxes. When he had hidden the plunder the best he could, he got out of the truck and waited for the lieutenant. Minutes later, the lieutenant and the sergeant came back to the jingle truck with a small box.

"Sergeant, I'm HN Brannan, the supply guy for the unit," Ed said. "Can I have your contact information for the future? We will be operating out of Kuwait, and our supplies may not be in country for a while. I would like to be able to contact you if we need some help in the future. I used to be in the army too."

"Absolutely," the sergeant said. He gave Ed his information. Ed thanked him, and he and the lieutenant jumped in the truck to meet their convoy for the return to base. During the ride back, the lieutenant noticed the added cargo and asked Ed what it was.

Ed gave him a wry smile. "There are some things you are better off not knowing, sir, but if you want to know, I will tell you."

The lieutenant gave him a puzzled look and said, "HN Brannan, I would rather not know anything you are up to."

Upon their return to base, the driver and Ed dropped the lieutenant off at the aid station, and Ed asked the driver to take him and the supplies over to the CASEVAC tent. When they pulled up to the front of the tent, Ed jumped out and ran inside.

He found the chief and said, "Santa Claus dropped off some presents for you guys. They're out in that truck. The driver and I already handled them once. Now it's your guys' turn."

The chief laughed and asked, "How many did you get?"

"Chief, I honestly do not know. I grabbed as many as I could. There should be enough for everyone on your team and resupply, though."

"Really?"

Ed just pointed. "Please get your guys to get that stuff off the truck, Chief. I need to get the driver and the vehicle back. The lieutenant already knows I am up to no good." They expedited the transfer and did a quick count of the merchandise. He and the driver had acquired thirty-eight fully stocked bags for the team. As Ed climbed in the jingle truck, he told the chief, "The only thing on those that can be traced is the national stock number on those bags. If I were you, I would take everything and ditch the bags."

The chief chuckled. "Thanks, Shipmate."

Ed smiled and said, "You could do better than a thank you by getting me out of MWSS and on CASEVAC, Chief."

The supply efforts gained Ed a lot of credibility within his unit and the Marine Aircraft Group, but it did nothing to help him out of MWSS. If anything, it hindered his efforts. Unfortunately, the better you are at your job, the more of an asset you become, and that's what happened. Ed's leaders in MWSS liked him. He did as told and did a good job at it. Dependable and hardworking are qualities you want to keep, not give to someone else.

His leaders knew they had to reward his efforts in some way or they would lose him, so they decided to put him on convoy operations for the initial invasion. Operations were to kick off in the coming weeks, and everyone was busy prepping. They were also preparing for the biannual advancement examination. Ed was studying. He lost rank coming into the navy and needed to promote for added money and responsibility.

The exam setup was less than ideal: a tent in the desert with no air-conditioning, adjacent to a busy airfield, with enough tests for half the sailors and seating for less than half of those. *Well, I guess another six months as an E-3 will not kill me,* Ed thought. He finished the half of the exam he was given in under thirty minutes and sat there sweating for another hour before he was given the second half, which had been torn away for the other corpsman. It took him about twenty minutes to complete the second half of the test. He checked his answer sheet for completeness and turned it in.

"How do you think you did?" the chief asked.

Ed looked at him strangely and said, "Oh, I am sure I did great, Chief!" He walked away pissed off and couldn't believe the navy subjected sailors to this.

True to their word, his leaders had Ed on the first convoy operations behind the initial invasion into Iraq. He gathered his equipment, formed up with the marines and a senior corpsman, and received their operation order. They departed in their convoy to the staging area at the border of Kuwait and Iraq.

They rode through Kuwait. When he knew they were in a secure area, Ed daydreamed about his interaction with the marines in Somalia and how he had developed such a profound respect for them. He remembered being on the airfield in Mogadishu. They were doing a turnover with the Marine Expeditionary Unit. He had just completed a twelve-hour watch and fallen asleep minutes prior to being awoken by a bunch of marines entering the compound, singing at the top of their lungs. He jumped out of his cot and ran to the door of his tent. As he was getting ready to yell at them to shut up, he realized what they were singing. It was the "Marines' Hymn." He stopped and wondered, *What are these knuckleheads doing?*

The next day he asked one of them what all the commotion was about. The young marine "devil dog" (a name given to the marines by the Germans in World War II) explained they had been through a horrible area named K-4 circle the night prior and had been in a firefight. They lit the place up and came back with no casualties. They were just pumped up and sang. Ed was amazed at the *esprit de corps*, and he respected them. It didn't stop him from busting their balls, but he always remembered that moment, and it drove him to where he sat. It was one of the paths in the road his chaplain spoke about.

He drifted back to reality as they approached the staging area. It was a massive gathering, with rows upon rows of America's finest waiting to charge into the desert and finally take down the enemy. The scene was awe-inspiring. Ed's unit would be one of the last to cross the line of departure, so they staged at the rear. *Here I am, a supporting combat operations again instead of at the front. I guess this is my lot in life.*

More attempts at diplomacy were made prior to the invasion. Germany, France, and Russia were opponents of any military action, while most of the rest of the world was more than willing to see another brutal dictator gone. Talks broke down, and plans proceeded. When Saddam saw the end in sight, he launched Scud missiles. The concern was that they were loaded with chemical weapons, so every time one came toward the line of departure, the troops went into Mission

Oriented Protective Posture, level 4. Nuclear, biological, and chemical protective levels were designed to protect troops against attacks by weapons of mass destruction. Wearing that type of gear in the desert was *hot!* Add in the fact that some madman may be loading the weapon with chemical agents that could melt your skin, and it was intimidating.

Ed found humor in the strangest situations, and leave it to him to find it during an attack. They staged, Scud alarms went off, and people went running to bunkers. Ed saw a lieutenant junior grade physician assistant come running through the tent with a look of terror on his face. He had his gas mask in one hand and was zipping his suit with the other. When he tripped, he landed on his face, but he executed the perfect combat roll while he finished zipping his suit, came to his knee, and placed the mask on his face. He cleared and sealed it in one move like a ninja. He then pulled and secured the straps over his head and threw his hood over the mask.

Ed was on the ground laughing so loud, he couldn't breathe. The lieutenant junior grade did not stop to look back. He just kept running as if everything that had happened was all a part of his ninja plan. It was priceless. Ed didn't bother to put his gear on. He stayed on the ground, trying to contain himself until the all-clear was given, and didn't let the lieutenant junior grade forget it until they crossed the line of departure.

Orders came, and they crossed the line. They followed the main and secondary forces through the line of departure. Two main battles were fought on the way to Baghdad. There were many small battles, but for the most part, the coalition forces marched into the Iraqi capital with little opposition.

Ed's bad luck and Uncle Murphy stayed with him. His convoy remained out for three weeks. Every time they had orders to return, they were sent on another resupply mission. Ed loved it. His senior corpsman apparently did not. He decided to return to base at some point and left Ed alone with a fifty-vehicle convoy. Fortunately, they saw no significant action, and no one was hurt. They returned to base weeks later and began plans to return home.

Leaving the country was as big a mess as entering it. The only benefit was that everyone knew they were headed home, and no one was hurt or killed during operations. It was frustrating and a pain in the rump, but the goal was to remain calm and get back home to their loved ones with as few issues as possible. Ed's biggest problem when they arrived was finding supplies and equipment. It was amazing how different it was when people were leaving. No one wanted to take anything home. Containers full of things started showing up in Ed's supply tent, in such quantity that he had to requisition a second tent to house everything.

The larger issue was that the people dropping things off were just throwing everything in a box and then dumping it in the tent. There was no way of knowing what he had or turning over anything to someone else without a full accountability. That meant Ed was going to be busy organizing and counting other people's supplies. At least he would have something to do. He sorted, counted, and organized all the supplies, and had planned to donate them to a Kuwaiti hospital. Instead, he turned everything over to their replacements, and they took care of it.

Ed spent any downtime writing letters to Jenny and the kids. As before, he honed his poetry and drawing skills. He started to practice the alphabet, and he drew pictures of the stars he saw at night for the kids. He wrote Jenny his thoughts about wanting to work on his faults and promised he would try harder. He told her how much he loved and missed her and that she and the kids were his priority in life. He wrote little about what they were doing. He did write about funny things and anything that made him mad. He had some good news. Finally he received word he was being promoted, based on the exam he took. He would be frocked prior to leaving and would return to her wearing his Petty Officer Crow. He was proud of himself and hoped she was proud of him too.

7

Daily Grind

~

The drive back home was excruciating for Jenny. She sobbed as she drove the Red Rooster, with her children fast asleep in the car seats behind her. She couldn't believe she had thought this would be a nice break from Ed, and she hated herself for imagining it would be in the first place.

She remembered the first night they reconnected. She knew who he was in high school; most people knew who Ed was. He was a little pain-in-the-butt freshman who hung out with all the seniors. Everyone knows everyone in small towns, and their parents grew up with everyone else's parents. It was an endless cycle of rumors and who's who. She recalled Ed strutting in the bar and talking to everyone, laughing and joking and looking like he was the happiest man on the planet. *He could fool everyone*, she thought. *He really had me.*

They all played euchre, a common Midwest card game similar to spades. Ed played with a good friend whom Jenny was working for part time. They kicked everyone's butt that night, and Ed was not humble in his triumph. She remembered thinking he was cute, successful, and fun. When they were playing, he told her how beautiful she was and that he was going to marry her. She knew he was full of crap, but he was flattering and made her feel special, and she was coming out of a crappy relationship with a real loser.

The night drew on, and their friend and Jenny's mom encouraged her to go out with him sometime. As the drinks flowed, so did his charm. She found herself across the street at his bar, drinking more with him, listening to his stories and watching him interact with everyone. She had a wonderful time with him that evening. After she had fallen in love with him, she realized that everything she had seen was a magician's sideshow, all smoke and mirrors. He was living a nightmare, and she would become another character in his dream.

She cleared her head and dried her eyes before making the turn into the Tarawa Terrace II gate. She didn't want the guard to question her about crying. The last thing she wanted to do was explain to a sentry left to guard base housing while marines and sailors went to war that she lost control because her husband was headed to Iraq. She knew that would devastate the young marine and probably piss him off, ending in a vehicle search or possible cavity search—which, she thought, might not be too bad, considering the lack of affection the last few weeks. And the guards were all young, physically fit marines. The thought made her giggle, and she laughed aloud, because she knew it would piss Ed off.

The marine at the gate checked her tags and military identification and cleared her through, and she headed home. He looked puzzled seeing a woman who had obviously been crying now smiling like a madwoman and looking at him like a piece of sirloin, but he had learned early on in his duties that spouses were as special as their military counterparts. He brushed it off, probably thinking, *What the hell is wrong with these people?*

Jenny returned to the house and rustled the children inside. She prepared breakfast, got herself coffee, and did some cleaning before initiating diaper duty. The daily grind for her was efficient, routine, boring, and exhausting all in one. It was difficult with Ed at home. He didn't help a lot, but he did do some things around the house. He mostly got in the way, but he managed to entertain the kids in the evening long enough for her to get things done for the following day. She realized that not having him around was going to be difficult. She also knew she was going to miss his grumpy butt. With all his faults, she loved him. He had the ability to make her so mad, she could want to punch him in the face, and then he would do something so sweet that she would forget he was such an asshole. He also played an important role she didn't like: disciplinarian to the kids. Jenny wasn't looking forward to assuming that duty.

The hours grew into days and the days into weeks. The routine grew into monotony, and the exhaustion turned into depression. She managed all of this by staying busy and putting all her efforts into the kids and waiting for phone calls and letters. She got mostly letters, because she knew her husband well enough to know he was not going to stand in a line to call home. The man would not wait in line for anything. He would not wait for more than fifteen minutes for a table at a restaurant.

Just as during his training, they received letters frequently. He wrote about everything but what he was doing. He drew pictures, wrote poetry, and started writing the alphabet for Christopher. She was amazed that her tin man had a heart. It was a small one, but it was in his chest.

She found herself thinking, *I'm the mother, father, caretaker, and accountant, and I spend less time with my husband now than when we were dating. Was this the right choice?* She didn't know the answer, and it scared her. She was still deeply in love with Ed, but she didn't know if this was a life she could lead for any sustained period, and she felt selfish for having these thoughts. The only comfort she had were her family and friends. Her friends were going through the same thing, so it was a lot easier to talk with them about the frustration, and the bonds they shared grew stronger as the time away from their spouses grew longer.

Jenny had her friends over for the evening. The house was full of kids running around like animals, playing and trashing the home. The women were enjoying their company, talking about their latest letter or phone call from their loved ones. Jenny assumed it was a nightly ritual throughout Camp Lejeune and every military base in the world. As the night wound down and her friends departed with their hellions, she thought, *I have great friends who have become like sisters to me. They support me, and I support them. We share everything, maybe out of necessity, but more out of pure love. This is the hardest job I have ever had, and no one appreciates what I do. How long can I keep doing this, and is it worth it?*

Again she found herself hating feeling like this, and she prayed for strength. She wanted to ask her friends if they felt the same, but she didn't want to look weak. They all looked to her for strength because she was older, and she didn't want to disappoint them. The kids were still so young; they had no concept of time, and other than the occasional cry for Daddy, they had no idea how far away he was, but she felt alone and afraid. She wanted her honey bunny home.

She finally received the phone call she was waiting for. She knew it was good news by the excitement in his voice.

He began with, "Baby, I got promoted! I can't believe I made it off that test. They must have graded it wrong."

She laughed at him and said, "I'm so proud of you, honey. That is great news. I wish the kids and I could have been there to see you get pinned."

"I do too, babe. I had the guys pin me, and we took some pictures so you can see them when we get home. Oh, I almost forgot. We will be home in two weeks."

How the heck do you almost forget you are coming home in two weeks? she thought. *Is that really less important than being promoted? What a freak!* She was so excited, she didn't give him the butt-chewing he needed.

"Oh my goodness," she said. "That is great news. The command hasn't told us anything about you coming home." Ed wondered aloud if the rear detachment was as jacked up as the forward element and guessed it most likely was.

"Who cares?" he said. "I told you. I'll let you know when and where to pick me up. We won't stick around with these morons afterward. I'm ready to get you and the kids in my arms and get home. This sand sucks, and I want to soak in a bath for a day. I think it is stuck so far up my butt, it will take a few weeks to get it out." She didn't think it was possible for him to get any more crude, but she was sure he had over the last few months. She didn't care at this point. She just wanted him home.

Jenny continued to get letters and phone calls for the two weeks leading up to Ed's homecoming. Each time, he talked about wanting to go on a family vacation, spending quality time together and working on their relationship. He sounded sincere and convincing, but she had heard these promises before and wasn't going to get her hopes up again.

She was paying attention to the other things he was saying about his career as well, and her fear grew when she heard him make statements like, "I need to get into a flying squadron when I get back, so I can get back over here and do something more next time. Not soon, honey, but I will need to come back to further my career."

This seems like he has traded one addiction for another, she thought. *Alcohol for revenge. Is he driven by hate, or does he want to improve himself?* She feared he was taking the wrong path again and worried she was going to accompany him.

※※

The entire country was impressed with the speed and overwhelming strength with which the United States and its allies overtook Iraq. People celebrated the return of navy vessels and army, marine, and air force units across the world. Since the Gulf War, the nation had taken great pride in welcoming home her warriors and made certain not to make the mistakes made during Vietnam. Those men and women had been treated unnecessarily cruelly by many Americans for failed policies they had no part of. It was decades too late, but they were finally being welcomed home vicariously through their children.

Ed saw the earlier treatment as a slap in the face to the men he loved and respected. He never missed an opportunity to thank an older veteran for his service and to welcome him home. The gesture often generated an odd look, a smile, and then an immediate kinship. Sometimes the older veteran would know immediately what the young man was referring to, and his eyes would mist as he recalled being spat at or receiving some other form of humiliation from fellow citizens who knew nothing of the horrors he had witnessed in the service of this great nation. Ed found it amazing that people still wondered why veterans kept to themselves.

As the day approached, more and more of the spouses were returning, and the excitement grew. The women discussed what to wear, what to cook, and what they would do when they had their loved ones home again. Jenny wanted to wear something special, and she wanted the kids to look good too. The deployment allowed them to catch up on some bills and put a little money back, but she didn't have enough to go out and buy anything too expensive. Ed would not get his promotion money for several months, so she would have to make do.

She had picked up extra money cleaning houses on base for families that received Permanent Change of Station orders and were leaving the area. She and a friend would go in, clean, and scour the housing unit for a minimal fee. It wasn't a lot of money for the effort, but she did an outstanding job, and they had developed a great reputation with the housing office. The extra money gave her enough to get a nice shirt from a clothing outlet instead of the dollar store or yard sale, and that felt nice for a change. She was excited.

Ed contacted her the day he was leaving to give her a time frame when they would arrive. Jenny did not hear from the command during the deployment. The night before his arrival, a friend who was still waiting for her husband to return came over to help her with her hair and to talk about what to expect. They made a welcome home sign and had a drink while the kids frolicked around the house, destroying their rooms and toys as usual.

※※

Ed's return flight was as disorganized as his departure, with the exception that they were on the Freedom Bird, as they all called it. Heading home was refreshing, and no amount of discomfort could ruin the mood. They did the normal stop in Europe and got back in the air. The pilots and crew were as kind and accommodating as they were before, if not more so. Ed was watching a movie when the pilot announced they would have a brief layover in Bangor, Maine. The name drew his immediate attention. He had a layover in Bangor on his return from Mogadishu. He remembered it like it was yesterday.

Nineteen-year-old, pimple-faced PFC Brannan strolled down the empty corridor with a group of his buddies at the Bangor, Maine Airport after an international flight from Shannon, Ireland. Still a little buzzed from the Guinness the commanding officer allowed them and the Irish whiskey they bought in the duty-free shop, he wondered, *Who the hell are all those people up there in the terminal?* In a small airport at 0300 in the morning, the last thing he expected was to see a huge group of geriatrics whooping and hollering, waving signs, shaking hands, and welcoming people home.

I'm either still asleep, I drank some laced whiskey, or I'm a lot more buzzed than I thought. He was none of the three. The mix of old and young patriots awaiting them were the Maine Troop Greeters. Ed was amazed by the gesture of patriotism. He once received a letter from his grandma during Christmas telling him about a woman who asked why she had a yellow ribbon on her tree. His mom's mother was a handful on a good day, and he imagined the woman got more than a mouthful for the question, but Ed thought people back home just didn't know they were over there after the events in October, and this was April the following year.

How did these folks know we would be coming? He didn't care how. It felt good to be recognized, and he high-fived, shook hands, and hugged old women. He ate up the attention. The group had food and drinks and had opened the bar for those of age. Ed mingled with them in the bar and chatted with an elderly woman. She told him about losing her son in Vietnam and that she never missed a flight. He was impressed and saddened. If he were alone, he would have cried.

He hugged her and said, "You are an amazing and beautiful woman. I'm sorry for your loss, ma'am, but thank you for what you do."

She smiled. "You are quite the charmer, young man, and you are a handsome devil. How old are you?"

Ed gave her a devilish grin and said, "I am old enough, darling!" When he winked at her, she laughed hysterically.

"Sit on my lap," she said.

"Ma'am, I weigh two hundred pounds. I might crush you."

She laughed again and said, "I'm a lot tougher than I look, son. Now take a seat." Ed gently sat down, propping himself up on the table as she talked about her life in Bangor. She noticed he wasn't having anything to drink and asked, "You're not drinking?"

"No, ma'am, I'm only nineteen."

"Well, I don't give a damn how young you are. If you are old enough to go do what you just did, you are old enough to have a drink with me. Get up. What are you drinking?"

Ed hopped up and said, "Beer." She went over to the bar, ordered two drinks, and returned.

She took her seat, slapped her knee, and told Ed, "Sit down, young man, let's have a drink."

Ed was amazed. He sat down and said, "Thank you, ma'am." They sat talking for the rest of the layover like old pals. When it was time to leave, Ed hugged and kissed the wonderful woman on the cheek. He never expected to return to Bangor until he heard that announcement.

Ed wondered if he would see his old friend. He wondered if the Maine Greeters were still in action. He wondered if he would consider them as old as he had so many years ago. Time was odd like that. He remembered thinking people his age were old then. He knew teenage guys in the unit who thought he was old, and he was only twenty-nine. *Has it really been ten years since I was first here?* he thought. The pilots announced that they were on final, and the crew readied the aircraft and passengers for landing on American soil. Ed thought that *American soil* was a beautiful term for a returning warrior. It was poetic, like a beautiful song.

For the second time, he returned at zero dark thirty in the morning to American soil in Bangor, Maine, and the Maine Greeters did not disappoint him. In rank and file, with signs, flags, cheers, high fives, hugs, and handshakes, they stood, proud Americans welcoming home their warriors. An immense feeling of gratitude and pride swept over Ed.

As before, he felt and acted like a rock star entering a concert. He played to the crowd, and they loved it. He scanned the crowd hoping to see a familiar face, but didn't see his old pal. He couldn't help but wonder what had happened to her and prayed she was well or with her son. The layover was brief, but the Greeters had all they had before and more. This time they had a phone center, cell phones, food, and drinks. These folks were true Americans.

They had a short flight to Cherry Point. The Wing commanding general waited to personally greet everyone who exited the plane with the sergeants major and command master chief. Working parties formed to unload the plane and to load the trucks and buses. The marines and sailors filed into the A/DACG for count. When the counts were correct, they all filed onto the buses for the ride back to headquarters and their waiting families.

Jenny and the kids arrived at the headquarters' parking lot where they had dropped Ed off, and waited in the van, patiently listening to the radio while the kids played with toys. The van was full of nervous energy. The kids were oblivious to what was going on, but Jenny was a mess. She kept looking in the mirror and fussing over her clothes. She had no idea when they were going to arrive, but there were many other vehicles in the parking lot, and people were mingling around. She wondered if anyone had been notified, because she had not received any information from the command. She would say something, but knew Ed would lose it if she did. He just wanted to be transferred immediately.

She saw the first bus pulling in, and her heart nearly skipped a beat. When the second pulled in, her heart felt like it was going to come out of her chest. She grabbed the sign, looked herself over, and gathered the kids. She speed-walked up to the gathering area with the mob of families swarming from the parking lot. *Oh my, what are these girls wearing?* she thought. *They look like hookers.* She settled to the back of the mob, because she knew Ed would want to get out of there quickly.

Standing there, she was a nervous wreck until a friendly face came into view. HN Gonzalez, their friend from the clinic, came over and gave her a hug. He had stayed in contact with her throughout the deployment. He was there to welcome Ed home too. She calmed down a bit when she saw him and made small talk.

The buses staggered in and waited for the last to arrive to open the doors. The marines and sailors began to exit the buses to cheers as they formed into their platoons. There was a brief ceremony with speeches. Each person talked about how great a job the marines had done, and they all should be proud of them. Jenny wondered why they didn't mention the sailors, but remembered Ed complaining about that before. At the end of the ceremony, the commanding officer dismissed the unit, and Jenny and HN Gonzalez looked for Ed.

Finally, HN Gonzalez said, "There's the big prick!" Ed came walking over with all his gear in tow. He was the only person who went to get his bags before he came to see his family. HN Gonzalez grabbed his bags and welcomed him home.

"Thanks, bro, good to see you," Ed said. He looked at Jenny and said, "Hi, hon." He grabbed Christopher, who was grinning from ear to ear, and tickled Clara, who just smiled at him. "Let's get the hell out of here. I have spent way too much time around these idiots." He started for the parking lot, telling them about the flight home and how screwed up the unit was.

When they made it to the Rooster, Ed shook HN Gonzalez's hand, thanked him for coming, and told him he would give him a call in a couple of days. Jenny asked if he wanted to drive.

He laughed and said, "I don't know if I remember how to drive. You better, or I might kill us on the way home." They loaded up and headed to the house.

8

You Just Got Back

As promised, Ed spent time with Jenny and the kids, and he was a different man. They took leave for two weeks and drove back to Illinois to see their family and spend time at the lake. Ed had some souvenirs he wanted to give to his buddy CO, an old Vietnam marine and a mentor of his. CO gave Ed a bunch of crap when he heard he joined the army in high school, and he started to give him hell for joining the navy until Ed said one word: *corpsman.* CO had been wounded in Vietnam, and like most marines who were patched up or treated by a doc, he loved them. CO's only complaint was that he thought Ed would have made a good marine.

Going home on leave was never relaxing. Everyone has good intentions, but their plans manage to interfere with others, and someone's feelings always get hurt. Ed didn't give a damn. He told people where he would be, and if they didn't come to him, then he considered it their own fault if they didn't see him. Jenny tried to appease everyone and take the kids to each family. It was a stressful nightmare for her. Ed just sat at the lake, drank beer, and fished. That was when he started to slide back into his old self.

Ed's brother Pat had reenlisted while Ed was in Iraq. He was stationed in Italy now with the 173rd Airborne Division. Pat and his girlfriend, Angie, married after their son, Stephen, was born, and they had all moved when Pat accepted orders. Those two Brannan boys were cut from the same cloth. Their brother, Andy, would have made one hell of a warrior too, but he wanted no part of the military. He was not scared of a soul and would fight at the drop of a hat. He considered the marines after high school, went to MEPS, and participated in Delayed Entry Program, but he realized it was not for him and told them no.

Ed thought it was a good choice. He knew Andy could make it physically with no problem, but he also knew the first time someone pissed him off, he would knock him out and end up in Leavenworth, Kansas, making big rocks into little rocks at the federal penitentiary.

It was a nice leave for Ed, but Jenny came home more stressed than she had left. Their family loved seeing them and the kids. CO was initiating a local chapter of the Marine Corps League and paid for Ed's membership as a charter member. His wife, Carol, enlisted Jenny and Ed's mom in the Ladies Auxiliary.

When they returned home, Ed went back to work, and Jenny went back to her daily routine and continued cleaning houses. Ed immediately submitted a special request chit/paperwork to transfer to a flying squadron. His chain of command knew he was eager to leave MWSS. His performance in Iraq left them no doubt he could handle the responsibilities of a squadron aviation medicine technician. Ed didn't realize his performance was so good that they were considering him for a higher position, and that is exactly where they placed him.

Ed was working in the aviation medicine department when he heard an announcement for him to report to the senior chief's office. He didn't remember doing anything stupid that morning or the day before, so he figured he wasn't in trouble, or he hoped he wasn't. He moved with a purpose to the admin offices and directly to the senior's hatch, where he knocked three times and waited.

Ed heard Senior say, "Enter." He went to the front of the desk and reported. Senior Chief told him he was now the leading petty officer for Marine Medium Helicopter Squadron (HMM) 261.

Ed wasn't sure if he had heard the senior chief correctly, so he asked, "Say again, Senior Chief?"

Senior gave him an annoyed look and said, "You got what you asked for, HM3. You are the LPO of a flying squadron. Get out."

Ed said, "Yes, Senior," and then turned and moved out. As he was leaving, he realized what was going on and stopped. He turned back around, poked his head in Senior's office with a huge smile, and said, "Thank you, Senior Chief!"

Senior shook his head and said, "Get out of here, goofy, and do not make me regret this."

As Ed was walking on air leaving the admin office, he yelled over his shoulder, "Aye aye, Senior Chief. I guarantee you will not regret the decision."

Delighted by the news, Ed went directly to his chief and said thank you before he returned to work. When he finished his clinic duties, he went directly to MWSS and got his check-out sheet. He set a land-speed check-out record that afternoon. It felt like being paroled or set free from jail. Walking out of headquarters, he wanted to skip to the Rooster and to give the one-finger salute to the squadron, but knew if he got caught doing either, he would end up in trouble, so he decided to do it in his mind and call it even.

Ed returned to the clinic and went back to his chief's desk. He asked if the chief wanted to take him to the flight surgeon, or if Ed should just go speak to him on his own. The chief was busy, so he told Ed to just go talk to him on his own.

"He doesn't have any corpsmen right now, so you should be a welcome sight," the chief said.

Ed headed over to the doctor's office.

Lieutenant Thomas Gallagher, a twenty-nine-year-old doctor of osteology from New York City, was five foot eleven, one hundred and forty pounds. He had dark hair, glasses, and looked like a college professor. Ed knew very little of him. He had interacted with him through aviation medicine, and he seemed thorough with his physicals and easy to work with, but that was all Ed knew. He had checked in while Ed was gone, and some of the other corpsmen said he was a pain in the butt.

Ed didn't care. He wanted a flying squadron, and he wanted a CH-46 helicopter platform, which the HMM was, because that was what the CASEVAC mission was utilizing. Ed knocked and walked in as the doctor swung around in his chair. Ed told him he would be his new leading petty officer. The lieutenant told Ed he wanted an HM1.

"Well, sir, that is something you will need to address with the senior chief, but either way, I am being assigned to the squadron," Ed said. "I am an AVT, so I can check in and get to work on readiness and help you get things squared away."

Lieutenant Gallagher looked at Ed and said, "Have a seat. I will be right back."

※※

The lieutenant stormed off to the commander's office to complain about getting an HM3 assigned as his leading petty officer. When he reached the clinic director's office, the director and the senior chief were sitting in the office. The commander saw the lieutenant lurking at the door and told him to come in.

"Sir, I have an HM3 in my office saying he is my new leading petty officer," Lieutenant Gallagher said. "I am supposed to have an HM1, and I would like to get an HM1."

The commander looked at the senior chief and asked, "Senior, would you like to explain our decision to the lieutenant?"

"Yes, sir. Lieutenant, you are getting HM3 Brannan, but if you want an HM1, you can wait until November. I will tell you this, though. He will do a better job for you. You are judging him on rank without asking any questions about experience or maturity or without having a clue to his capability. That is insulting and demonstrates a lack of experience on your part."

The conversation was not going how Lieutenant Gallagher had planned, and the commander intervened. "Tom, we gave you HM3 Brannan because he is damn good. He was a rock star in Iraq. He has ten years of combined service. He was in the army, knows supply, sick call, trauma medicine, and is a leader. We are not trying to screw you. We are giving you one of our best corpsmen, because we know you guys are pushing out in a few months."

Lieutenant Gallagher's apprehension was appeased for the moment, but he asked, "Does he know we are going back to Iraq in four months?"

"No, he does not, but the guy is an animal," Senior said. "He reenlisted to serve. He volunteers for every mission that comes up, and I have told him no too many times. Do not worry, LT, when you tell him you are taking him back, he will work even harder for you. That is why we wanted you to tell him. We also suggest that you get him on flight orders. He wants to be an aerial observer/gunner on the Forty-Six, and he wants to do CASEVAC. I could not afford to give him up in Iraq, but he will be an asset to that mission."

Lieutenant Gallagher quickly realized he was either getting a great deal or these two were the best salesmen he had ever met.

※※

Ed sat in the doctor's office, thinking to himself, *This sucks. I bust my butt to get the orders I want, and the guy doesn't want to work with me. My luck sucks.* He heard footsteps coming down the hall and sat up in his chair. The lieutenant entered the room, and Ed stood up.

"Sir, I understand your frustration, and I am sure they can find another squadron for me," Ed said.

"HM3 Brannan, I made a hasty decision to discount your experience and our leadership's assessment to put you in the position. I should have discussed that with them without saying anything to you. If I insulted you, I apologize. After talking to Commander and Senior and discussing your background and experience, I understand their decision. You should know we are deploying again in four months to Iraq."

"That's awesome," Ed said. "We have a lot to do, sir." Lieutenant Gallagher could not believe he was so eager to return that quickly, but he thought the senior chief must know the sailor pretty well. He told

Ed he would take him over to the squadron in the morning to meet the commanding officer, executive officer, and the sergeant major and begin his check-in.

Leaving the clinic, Ed realized explaining this to Jenny was going to be difficult. His brain went into overdrive trying to come up with a good spin on how best to break the news to her. He knew the broken promises to stay home and clean up his act were eating at her, and this would fuel the fire. He thought it would be best to just tell her he had orders to a new squadron and tell her about the deployment when they had orders. Not technically a lie, just an omission of a fact. At least, that's how he justified it in his warped mind.

He got home and started playing with the kids as usual. He loved messing with them. He and Clara formed the typical daddy's girl bond, and he and Christopher roughhoused all the time. They both had unique personalities. Christopher had been through his terrible twos. He was a pain in the rear. He pushed Jenny to the limit and tried Ed, but didn't get far.

Ed had the temperament of his father and lacked the patience for a disruptive child. He rarely spanked the kids, but he would pick them up and go sit with them in the van at restaurants or put them in their room in a split second at home for misbehaving. Jenny thought he was too strict, and Ed thought she was too lenient. Somehow they were raising two well-behaved kids. Christopher could recite the Pledge of Allegiance by three, loved patriotic music, and stood at attention with his hand over his heart for colors and the national anthem. Most of the kids on base knew more respect for their nation than 90 percent of the country. Clara loved pizza, had a raspy voice, and big bushy eyebrows. She was a bit conceited. When she was told she was pretty, she would say, "I know."

It was potty training time, and Ed was trying his hand at being a dad. Christopher had the number one down. He loved going pee. He went pee anywhere he wanted to, usually outside in front of the house. Unfortunately, for number two, he wanted to go in a pull-up and would ask for one. Jenny would eventually give in and let him do his business.

Ed was not that easy. He would sit him on the potty until he went. It may not have been the Dr. Spock way of parenting, but Ed managed to get him trained in a short period—at least, that's what Jenny allowed him to believe. She spent most of the day working with Christopher.

As Ed played with the kids that evening and Jenny cooked, he told her, "Baby, I got some good news today. I checked out of MWSS."

"Awesome," Jenny said. "Where are you assigned?"

"HMM 261. It's a flying squadron. They gave me the leading petty officer position. Cool, huh?"

"That is great. Do you get more money?"

"No, hon, it doesn't work like that." Ed laughed. *Damn, I wish it did.*

"What will you be doing?"

Ed thought about telling her all the details, but decided to stick to his plan. "I will be the leading petty officer, aviation medicine technician, and I'll stay in the aviation medicine department at the clinic, but they haven't had a corpsman in the squadron for a long time. I imagine I'm going to have some long days ahead of me, baby. I know that's not what you wanted to hear, but it truly is good for our career."

※❈※

Our career, my butt, she thought. *It's our career when you need help with those damn correspondence courses, uniforms taken to the cleaners, ribbons picked up, boot polish from the store, or some other crap, but it's your career if I need anything.* She kept the comment to herself to keep the interaction civil and let him have his moment. He knew she played a huge role in his career. She did help him study for advancement, Enlisted Fleet Marine Force Warfare Specialist, and do correspondence. She took his uniforms to the cleaners every week and picked up everything from the Exchange so he didn't have to wait in lines. She was good to him, and he knew it. He just didn't have the emotional capacity to show her.

※❈※

Ed checked into 261 the following day. He and Lieutenant Gallagher went to work on readiness, medical records, and administration. It was a nightmare. The lieutenant received a poor turnover from a group that neglected its duties postdeployment because the members knew they were transferring. It was common. The two men spent several hours each evening getting everything in order. It was maddening for Jenny and Lieutenant Gallagher's wife, but it had to be done in order for the squadron to be prepared to deploy. When the squadron received orders for Iraq, Ed knew he had to break the news to Jenny. Fortunately, the time line had shifted, and he had been home for four months. They were not scheduled to depart for two more months, at the beginning of 2004.

Unfortunately, things in Iraq had taken a turn for the worse after the initial invasion. Insurgents had infiltrated the country, and groups of terrorist cells were operating throughout Iraq, conducting insurgent operations. They attacked convoys with improvised explosive devices, used rockets to assault bases, shot rocket-propelled grenades and sur-face-to-air missiles at aircrafts, and were coordinating small ambushes against foot patrols.

The press destroyed the president and his administration for the operation and because there were no weapons of mass destruction found, so they questioned the reasoning behind the invasion and the credibility of the president and the cabinet. Politics 101 was in full force, but boots were on the ground, and the infighting was putting lives at risk. Not that the press corps gave a damn about anything but ratings.

The other issue Ed had to contend with was that he had violated Jenny's trust again. He had let the pendulum swing fully back to his old ways over the last few months. When he was not at work, he was out with his friends partying and had little time for his family. Jenny was at her wit's end. He knew this news could mean the end of their relation-ship. He didn't want that, but as usual, he knew he had put himself in the predicament and was prepared to lie in the bed he had made. He returned home expecting the worst.

✳✳

When he told Jenny what was going on, she asked him how long he had known about it. He told her the truth. She couldn't believe how deceitful he had been. *Since he returned from deployment four months ago, I've spent just as little time with him as before. Every letter I received was a promise to change when he got home, and none of it has happened. He volunteered to go back to Iraq in two months, and he will be gone for eight months this time. This will never end. I need to consider my options. I have to decide what is best for the kids and me, because he is not going to change.*

Jenny was enraged. She looked him dead in the eyes and said, "You lied to me. You say you love us. You say you are going to change. You say you want to work on being a better husband and father, but all you care about is yourself. Ed, I'm done." Ed knew this time would come. He had expected it a lot sooner. He couldn't imagine how she put up with it for as long as she did.

"I understand," he said. "I do love you. I do love the kids. I know you don't believe me, and I know my actions are contrary to what I say, but I do. Do what you think you have to do, and I will support it. I don't want you to leave. I want to be a part of your life and the kids' lives, but you're probably right. I will just mess your lives up, like I have messed up mine. I will pack my crap and have one of the guys come get me."

Jenny didn't know what to expect, but this wasn't it. She couldn't believe his reaction. "You're just going to pack your bags and leave?"

"I guess. I don't know what else to do, Jenny. I know I screwed up, and I don't want to fight with you. I wanted to tell you before, but I was afraid this is how you would react. I don't know what to do. I think we're doing better. Things aren't perfect, but I'm trying. I just want you to be happy. I am selfish, but this was not all about me. I saw this as an opportunity for all of us. It definitely benefited me. I'm not going to bullshit you. This job and going over there is what I like to do, but doing it puts me in line for another promotion and more opportunity for us.

You don't want to hear that, though. You believe I'm so self-centered, I only think of me."

"Ed, what the hell are you talking about? I have given you everything you've asked for over the last two years. The only thing I want is for you to spend time with us and be a husband and father. That is not a lot to ask. You need to grow up."

"Grow up? Really? You want to talk about growing up to a guy who turned eighteen in basic training, nineteen in a foreign country, and six days later saw things no one should have to see."

"That's not what I meant. You're married and a father now. You're not a twenty-one-year-old or a bar owner anymore. Quit acting like one. We don't have the money for you to go out and spend like you used to, and you have other priorities besides your friends. That is growing up!"

"Like I said, Jenny, I know all of this. That is why I said I would pack my shit and go. You have access to all my accounts. I will leave you access to everything until I get back, and we can finalize whatever you want to do."

Jenny started to cry. "I don't know if that is what I want or not, but you have to quit doing this. I can't take this crap anymore."

"Jenny, I'm trying. I love you. Please don't cry. I don't want to hurt your feelings. I don't know what to do. I'm doing what I think is right. It will work out."

Two months went by like two days. Ed had friends over to party instead of going out when he was not at work. Jenny kept it together as she had in the past by maintaining her routine and focusing on the kids. Lieutenant Gallagher had Ed placed on flight orders and put in the Aerial Observer/Gunner training syllabus. He completed aviation water survival training at Cherry Point and safety training within the squadron prior to their scheduled departure. They received two additional corpsmen for the deployment. One was an HN from the clinic, a new check-in, HN Baptiste. He was a tall, skinny, African American, totally undisciplined, always brushing his hair. The other was Hospital Corpsman Apprentice (HA) Fernandez, a short, stout, African American from Atlanta who didn't know his butt from a hole in the ground. Ed knew he was going to have his hands full with these two knuckleheads.

Jenny and Ed invited the two corpsmen over for supper and drinks so they could get to know them and Jenny could get their families' contact information. She wanted to make sure she let their parents know when they got to their destination, plus any pertinent information and when they would be coming home. She knew from experience the sailors were not a priority in a marine command, and she didn't want their families to worry. They also went out to eat with Lieutenant Gallagher and his wife, Bug. She was a hoot. Bug was a beautiful, short blonde from Long Island whom Lieutenant Gallagher had recently impregnated, so she was going to have a miserable first deployment. They all hoped they would be home in time for the birth of the child.

※※

The night before departure was upon them, Ed was a stress monster, just like the last time. Jenny had learned her lesson from the previous deployment. She didn't need prompting this time. She grabbed the kids when he got home and exited stage right to their room as the sea bags, kit bags, and gear filled the living room. She heard him cussing and bitching from the room, and she couldn't help laughing. He finished after two repacks this time. He was becoming more efficient. They all watched TV, and he played with the kids before they went to bed.

The following morning was not nearly as disorganized as the prior deployment. The squadron had scheduled flight times from New River to the awaiting Landing Helicopter Deck class ship waiting off the coast of North Carolina. They had loaded the planes and dropped off all the gear the day before, so all they had to do was load bags and personnel and depart. There was a brief ceremony, the planes started, and they were off.

Jenny and the kids sat with Bug in the bleachers, watching the ceremony. The kids loved seeing the planes start up, taxi, and take off. They were too young to understand that their daddy wasn't going to be home for a long time. Jenny was once again alone with her little ones and friends. Her big oaf was off to go do whatever it was he did and loved so much. She didn't shed a tear until she reached the van again. She now had another routine.

❊❊

The squadron made its way to the waiting vessel and landed safely for the voyage across the Atlantic, Mediterranean, Suez Canal, Indian, and then the Gulf. Ed had been in the navy for three years when they touched down on the big gray ship, and that was the first time he had stepped foot on a navy vessel. *I wonder how many sailors have never been on a ship*, he thought. He wasn't about to tell anyone he didn't have a clue about shipboard life.

They off-loaded and went to the armory to turn in their weapons, and then stowed their gear in berthing. Ed mustered the men in medical and met up with the ship's medical personnel. He introduced himself to the senior chief and the senior medical officer. They gave him a tour of medical and offered operating room six to them as a work space. It doubled as the aviation medicine work space, so it was a good base for them to work out of.

Ed set a duty schedule and coordinated with operations and the maintenance master gunnery sergeant to continue his training for the aerial observer/gunner syllabus. He did several flights on the transit and met most of the crew chiefs. He loved flying and became familiar with the aircraft. He didn't have a maintenance background, so he had to prove himself in other ways. He just showed up early, did what the crew chiefs asked, and took care of the planes the best he could. The marines were good to him, and he took care of them.

The pilots enjoyed having him around as well. They were doing deck landings one afternoon, and the helicopter aircraft commander (HAC) was training his copilot. The crew all communicated via internal communications systems, and the pilots could switch to the tower for external communication by pushing a button on their controls. The navy and marine corps had a great working relationship, but they still talked a lot of crap back and forth. The air boss gave the HAC a command he didn't like. It didn't matter if he liked the command or thought it was right; the boss was in charge of the air space, and the HAC had to follow orders.

The HAC came over internal communication and said, "Damn squids are all idiots."

Ed thought it was freaking hilarious, but said, "Damn, sir, you have a sailor on your plane."

The HAC didn't skip a beat. "Docs are different. I didn't mean you." It wasn't the first time Ed had heard that from a marine.

The lieutenant and Ed took the opportunity to train the guys in sick call, trauma medicine, and CASEVAC during downtime. Ed had them all set up their medical bags the same in case they grabbed the wrong one, and he did drills blindfolded, so they knew by memory where everything was.

The lieutenant was impressed, but it wasn't an original idea. Ed had learned this from his own training with the CASEVAC chief in Iraq. The corpsman methodology was "see one, do one, teach one," and it worked. It was what separated corpsmen from medics, and was why navy corpsmen hated being called medics. They respected their counterparts just as other services respected one other; they just believed they were a cut above the rest.

They passed the Rock of Gibraltar entering the Mediterranean Sea. It was a beautiful sight. Ed didn't like the ship. He went to the flight deck as often as he could and hung out in flight operations just to see what was going on. The odd thing about being a sailor on a ship with marines is you don't fit in with either group. The sailors don't see you as a peer, and the marines don't either. Ed felt like he was just stuck in a difficult situation most days. If the chow line for the navy was short, they told him to go to the marine line, and if the marine line was short, they would tell him to go to the navy line. Oddly enough, it was usually the sailors pulling this crap on him. Ed finally had enough of it down at the ship's store. He went down to get envelopes. He was standing in the navy line. The storekeeper first class came out and told him to get in the marine line.

Ed pointed to the US Navy tape on his uniform and said, "I am in the navy, SK1, and I will be staying in the navy line."

"HM3, get your butt over in the marine line, or do not come in my store," the SK1 said. A major overheard the exchange and walked up.

"What is the issue?" he asked the SK1.

"He needs to be in the marine line," the SK1 said.

"He is a sailor. He and the other two sailors with us have been putting up with this crap for two weeks. Enough is enough. You all are playing games, and they are over right now. Do you understand, Petty Officer?"

"Yes, sir," the SK1 said.

"Thank you, sir," Ed told the major. When he finished getting his envelopes, he told the SK1, "I don't understand why you all want to treat us any different than any other sailor on this ship, but I am going to go talk to the command master chief about this."

Ed headed directly to the command master chief's office. Ed knocked and waited until he heard the master chief say, "Enter."

Ed entered his office and introduced himself. "Master Chief, we have been onboard for a couple of weeks. Your crew has been shuffling my sailors and me from one line to the next, depending on which one is shorter, and I do not understand why other sailors would treat us like this. Could you please tell me what line we are supposed to be in so we can quit getting screwed?"

The master chief was astonished.

"HM3, I had no idea my crew was pulling that crap. You are sailors. You stand in the navy line. I will address the crew. Thank you for coming and letting me know. I am sorry you and the other sailors have dealt with this, and I wish you had mentioned it sooner. Is there anything else I can help you with?"

Ed thought for a moment and remembered they had two missing medical bags from storage. He questioned himself before adding, "Yes, Master Chief. We are missing two medical bags from storage. I do not know why anyone would want those bags, but we need them back."

The master chief was pissed. "When did that happen?"

"I found them missing two days ago from our trifold, but I should have known better than to put them in a nonsecure container."

The master chief turned red and said, "Bullshit. I do not tolerate thieves on my ship. You will have your bags back by the end of the day, or we will do a sweep of this ship."

"Thank you, Master Chief." Ed turned and bugged out of there. He knew all hell was about to break loose and wondered if it was worth bringing up, but knew the gear was essential to their mission. Soon the ship-wide intercom came to life.

"Attention on deck, attention all hands, this is the master chief. It has come to my attention that two medical bags are missing from storage. Return the bags by seventeen hundred today, or we will lock this ship down and do a complete sweep. Every one of you know where we are heading and know the mission of the passengers we have on board. Those bags are essential to that mission. Whoever took them is putting lives at risk, and if you do not put them back immediately, the skipper has guaranteed me the harshest punishment for the person or persons responsible. That is all."

The bridge notified Ed forty-five minutes later that two medical bags had been located in storage. He and HN Baptiste retrieved the bags, did an inventory, and found they were missing two head lamps. *I can live with that,* Ed thought. *I don't think we will have any more bullshit from this crew.* The rest of the cruise was smooth sailing. They passed through the Suez Canal and the Indian Ocean and anchored in the Gulf.

The squadron and sailors readied the gear, planes, and personnel for departure. They transported equipment and supplies to port the day prior to the main body's launch. On the final day, Ed mustered his guys and did a final sweep of medical. They made sure to leave the space cleaner than they had found it and to thank the staff for their help.

Ed ran by the command master chief's office to say thank you as well, but he wasn't in. He imagined the old master chief would tell him to get the hell out of his office, since he was just doing his job anyway, so it was probably for the best. The squadron mustered in the hangar bay, filed right, and waited in the tunnel to board the planes. When cleared to board, they looked like ants leaving an anthill in search of food. They boarded each plane to its full capacity and did a running takeoff because of the load. They were off to Iraq to fight Operation Iraqi Freedom II.

Ed's transatlantic trip took around three weeks, and he called home frequently. The ship's medical staff gave him and the other sailors access to the DSN line. They used it to contact the Lejeune morale line. The morale line would in turn connect you with a local number for free or with any long-distance provider.

The service had been in place for years. Ed had used it in the army. He would call bases in Indiana and Southern Illinois and be connected with the operator for cheaper long-distance calls. He didn't understand why the military and exchange service allowed the phone service providers to put those damn phone centers in when they had a military system in place that saved the service member thousands of dollars. He knew guys who spent paychecks on phone bills, and he knew why the military allowed the centers on base. The almighty dollar bill was more important to a politician than a young service person, unless there was a camera around.

※※

Jenny and the kids loved hearing Ed's rants about the ship and hitting his head or shins. She loved hearing about the master chief taking care of them. She was glad Ed was enjoying his job. She missed his grumpy ass. The kids missed him too. Clara could just tell something was missing, but Christopher knew his daddy was gone. Occasionally he would ask Jenny when Daddy was coming home, and she would tell him soon. It crushed her when he asked for his daddy. They looked at his pictures often. She didn't want them to forget him. Clara was speaking well now, but she was shy, so she would just listen to her daddy talk and smile.

Jenny settled into her routine and was busy with her business. Ed was being paid for E-4 now, and his deployment pays were back in effect, so they were doing better financially. Christopher was out of diapers, and Clara was in pull-ups, so their expenses were lower. She got off government assistance, and that alone made her feel ten times better. She had told Ed how deceitful he was about keeping Iraq from her, and she had kept this from him for years. *That is what the programs are for,* she thought, *to help people in need to get back on their own feet and to help those who can't help themselves.*

She knew there was a lot of abuse in the system. *Every system has it, but it does a lot of good for a lot of kids, and you can't punish kids for their parents' mistakes.* She also knew Ed would never let the kids or her go hungry, but he would never ask for help. He would rather not eat himself or work three jobs than use the system. *For someone so smart, he is a damn fool. I wonder where my honey bunny is tonight.*

※❈※

There is a seven-and-a-half-hour time difference from Iraq to the East Coast. Ed was up early, sitting outside the tent and staring into the desert sky at the stars. He and Christopher decided last deployment that the constellation Orion would be theirs and anytime they were looking at it, the other would be looking at it too. Ed knew how ridiculous it was, but it was cute and comforting. He stared at the sky, missing that little boy as he had never missed anyone in his life.

Something was changing in Ed. He was fighting it every step of the way, but his heart was growing as he spent more time around Jenny and the kids. The love he felt for his grandmother Peg was resonating again and transferring to the three of them. It scared him. The loss of his grandma had nearly destroyed him, and he wanted no further pain in his life, but he knew there was no fighting or running from this. He just looked to the sky and asked for help.

The next day, the planes loaded, and combat crews flew them into western Iraq. Ed and the main body of marines boarded Air Force C-130 Hercules airplanes and departed for the same airfield. Ed's group made it there quite a bit faster than the squadron's CH-46 flying phrog helicopters did. The advance party met them with transportation, and everything moved seamlessly. The difference between a cluster bomb and a perfectly executed mission is the five Ps (proper planning prevents poor performance).

Ed loved 261. He knew he was going to love it the first time he saw the squadron logo and heard its call sign: a raging bull and Elvis. *Holy shit, it is me. I love Elvis,* Ed thought. *I am home.* The command and marines were good to him and the sailors.

The planes and Lieutenant Gallagher arrived several hours later. The lieutenant looked tired. Ed had warned him that he might want to reconsider taking the C-130 and putting a corpsman on the plane for two reasons. One, it was dumb to risk the medical officer's life on the first mission in country, and two, it was going to be a miserable flight. Doc was going to do it his way, and he told Ed the commanding officer wanted him on the flight.

Ed laughed and said, "Sir, if you want to sweat your ass off for nothing, have fun, but that is why you have three corpsmen."

Ed saw a lot of that crap in Operation Iraqi Freedom I. The flight surgeons wanted to jump on aircraft and be corpsmen instead of doing their job. It happened a lot in the military. Everyone wanted to be a cool guy, and no one was satisfied with being himself. Ed was just as bad; why else would he be doing the aerial observer syllabus? It is just the alpha male thing. Except it was not a predominantly male trait in the military; it was a gender-neutral trait. Females in the service were just as bad.

The squadron got billeting, office spaces, a runway, and a maintenance hangar. Everyone went to work readying the spaces and living quarters for the coming months of operations. Assigned to Third Marine Aircraft Wing, Marine Aircraft Group Sixteen from the West Coast, Ed took his medical readiness information to their chief so he could meet him and give him the status of the squadron.

Two Sixty-One was 100 percent medically ready on everything. Dr. Gallagher was as anal about readiness as Ed was, and their work ethic matched perfectly. It was unfortunate for their two junior corpsmen, who lacked both the desire and knowledge to keep up with them.

Ed contacted MAG Sixteen's leading chief by landline prior to walking down to their headquarters. He was surprised the man had an English accent. When they met, Ed was expecting a slender Caucasian with bad teeth, drinking tea or doing something that fit the stereotype he formed from British Broadcasting. Chief Andrews did not match Ed's stereotype, and Ed learned a valuable lesson: do not stereotype people. It was something he already knew not to do, but the thought of his boss being a tea-drinking Brit with bad teeth was humorous to him.

The man had moved to the States when he was a young adult. He joined the navy, became a US citizen, and would retire following this tour. He was African American, five foot nine, around two hundred pounds of muscle, and a great chief.

The MAG leading petty officer took Ed's medical readiness information while the chief and Ed discussed what was going on in the coming weeks. Ed asked about the CASEVAC mission and if he and the lieutenant could help with any of the training or mission. The chief explained that the CASEVAC crew was working in the combined aid station and was not being utilized until a mission evolved. The leading petty officer came back in and told the chief that 261's medical readiness was the highest in the MAG.

"Great job, HM3!" the chief said. "We look forward to working with you. If you need anything, give us a call. We will be out once a week to check on you and would like you to send us your readiness data each week."

"Yes, Chief." Ed shook hands with the chief and the leading petty officer, and headed back to the squadron.

On the way, he thought, *I can't understand why they would have the CASEVAC team over doing sick call. I'm going over to see if I know any of them.* He headed over to the aid station to snoop around and see if he could borrow anything for their medical space. *I'm twisted. I just got that ship in trouble for taking our stuff, and I'm going to go liberate someone else's supplies.*

He found the aid station with ease. The Marine Logistics Group ran the aid station for the base. Ed went to the front desk and asked the HN where the CASEVAC team was working.

The HN didn't know what he was talking about, so Ed asked, "Where is your LPO?"

"His office is down the corner to the left, HM3."

You just let the fox in the hen house, moron, Ed thought as he made his way to the spoils. Ed slowly crept through the aid station, poking his head in offices, looking around and trying not to look suspicious. He identified a few items that would look good in their office, but he didn't have the cargo pocket space to carry them this time. He decided he would bring a bag back for them next time.

As he was lurking around, he heard a familiar voice. He was sure it was a friend of his from New River with whom he had deployed with 272. He hastily moved to the sound of the voice. As he poked his head in the office, their eyes met, and HM2 Munshower smiled.

"What up?" Ed said.

"Holy crap, man," HM2 Munshower said. "What are you doing here?"

The two shook hands and did a quick man hug, with three pats on the back.

"Is there somewhere to go talk, bro?" Ed asked.

"Yeah, man. Let's go out to the smoke deck and chat." The two old buddies headed out back, catching up on the way. When they reached the smoke deck, their conversation turned to business.

"Why are you guys working in the aid station if you are here for CASEVAC?" Ed asked.

HM2 Munshower shrugged and said, "They don't know what to do with us."

Ed laughed. "OK, well, I think I can help fix that problem. Give me a couple of days. I need you to get me a few things I saw lying around in there that no one was using."

HM2 Munshower smiled. "I see you are up to your old tricks again, bro."

Ed giggled. "I'm not up to anything now. You are. Here is what we need." Ed wrote down what he wanted and passed the list to HM2 Munshower. "Grab that stuff if you can, but don't get caught. I know you guys are not as gifted as I am! It doesn't matter if you get it or not. I will get you up with us." They gave each other the man hug, and Ed headed to the squadron.

When he reached the squadron, he found the lieutenant immediately to discuss talking to the MAG about what he learned from HM2 Munshower. The lieutenant was as baffled as Ed at the decision to waste the CASEVAC asset in the aid station instead of doing air operations with things heating up. He and Ed discussed how best to approach the issue. Ed suggested that the lieutenant take it to the operations officer as a training opportunity for the squadron. They had all the medical training developed for their corpsmen from the float over, and they could utilize the crew chiefs and pilots to teach safety and the aircraft. Then they could schedule some flights and put the corpsmen on flights.

Ed knew if the operations officer bought it, he would sell it to the executive officer and commanding officer, and they would push it to the Marine Aircraft Group. Ed and the lieutenant could work the idea with the group surgeon and chief on their end. Unfortunately, Ed knew the smart thing to do in the military was not always the easiest thing, so he was skeptical.

With the increasing operational tempo and the common sense of the training plan, everyone approached took interest. It was put into play immediately. The CASEVAC team withdrew from the aid station and began classes at 261. The courses went great. The team interacted with the squadron well, and they integrated into the flight schedule.

Ed maintained a heavy schedule. He did his daily duties as the 261 leading petty officer, worked an eight-hour shift, and managed to get on the flight schedule as an aerial observer. The lieutenant worried he was working late, but he seemed to be energetic and able to maintain the schedule. Ed loved it. He was exhausted at the end of each day, but it made time fly. He made time each day to write and draw something for his family. He tried to call home at least once a week.

As operations intensified to the south, the MAG moved the CASEVAC team to another squadron closer to the base of operations in case of a need for their services. The squadron, medical, and Ed said their good-byes as the team thanked them all for what they had done. Ed and HM2 Munshower stood to the side.

"Well, punk, I guess I will see you later," Ed said.

HM2 Munshower laughed and said, "You really are a prick, man, but thanks for hooking us up. If we get into anything, I will try to get you down there to help out."

Ed laughed. "It's OK, bro. I have finally accepted the fact that it is what it is. Be safe. I'll see you when I see you." They gave each other a man pat and said good-bye.

❊❊❊

Timing is everything in life and in combat. Fortunately for everyone involved in Operation Iraqi Freedom II, timing was on their side with the CASEVAC training and placement. They were in place prior to a major battle early in 2004. They didn't have the number of corpsmen or supplies to sustain continued operations, but the leaders within Marine Expeditionary Force made it happen quickly, and the CASEVAC team was reinforced before they were too strung out to operate effectively. Two Sixty-One sent a detachment to link up and reinforce the squadron operating missions in the region, and a reserve squadron was in place doing the same.

Ed liaised with the team as soon as he arrived, and coordinated with his detachment officer in charge and the squadron to allow him to assist the team in CASEVAC operations and to maintain the detachment's medical needs. He brought a secondary corpsman with him to maintain medical when he was not on base. When he was not flying CASEVAC missions, he flew as an aerial observer on 261's flight schedule. He didn't know which job he liked better: the gunner job or his own. *I may be a lot more messed up than I admit,* he thought.

Operations continued for several weeks until the marines finally secured the city. The battle was brutal and left many good men and women dead and injured. The city reeked of death and looked like it from the air. Ed continued to write home daily but never mentioned what he was doing or that he was in any added danger. He would look to Orion in the evening and wonder if he would have the opportunity to see it with his family again.

❈❈

Jenny was home watching the news every night, as she had the first deployment. Ed told her and his parents not to watch the news; they did nothing but report bad things, because bad news sells. She tried, but she knew he would never tell her what was going on. She prayed he was OK, but he hadn't called in a couple of weeks, and she imagined the worst. She could feel he was in the middle of all the horror going on. She finally got a call late in the evening when the kids were sleeping. She anticipated calls, but she dreaded them as well. She didn't want any bad news.

She answered and heard the static of the morale line and his voice. "Honey, are you there?"

"Hi, baby," she said. "Why haven't you called?"

"Hey, some of us work for a living," he said. As he laughed, she was instantly annoyed. "Babe, we are busy. Quit watching the damn news. I told you those clowns only report bad stuff. You are worrying about nothing. I am out with the Air Wing at an air base in the middle of nowhere, so chill out."

"I think you are full of it," she said.

"I am full of it, but I'm doing good. I don't have a lot of time. I have to get back to work. I just wanted to call and check in. I love you all."

"I love you too. Be careful." She hung up and put a pillow over her face as she sobbed.

The detachment finished operations and rejoined its squadron, where Ed assumed his normal duties and regular schedule. Months drew on with little action, which was welcome to everyone involved. A month prior to leaving, the lieutenant approached Ed and asked to speak to him.

"HM3, Bug is scheduled to deliver in two weeks. I have discussed with the commanding officer about going home on advanced party if you are willing to assume responsibilities as the senior person in medical." Ed was amazed the lieutenant had such confidence in him after his initial experience.

"Sir, you should be home for the birth of your baby," Ed said. "I can handle things. The only thing that concerns me is that without an officer in charge, they may try to push me around."

"We thought of that, and the operations officer would be your chain of command. You handle all the medical decisions and report to him. He takes care of the meetings and anything you need."

"Awesome. I got it. When are you rolling out?"

Lieutenant Gallagher smiled. "Thank you. We will be leaving in a week."

The advanced party gathered their gear, staged, and headed for the A/DACG a week later. Lieutenant Gallagher gave Ed a list of things to do and contact information if he was stumped on any medical issue. He also gave him a letter authorizing him to administer care and medication under his name and license.

Ed smiled when he gave him the document and said, "You are probably going to jail."

The lieutenant knew Ed was full of it and would never do anything to hurt a marine or jeopardize his career. "You will be there with me." They shook hands as the lieutenant headed for the Freedom Bird.

Over the next three weeks, each section began inventory and turnover plans. The squadron would turn over all equipment and supplies to the replacements and leave the country with only their personal gear. Ed was grateful for this. He had no desire to do a wash down and pack everything up again. He and the corpsmen did a complete wall-to-wall inventory with expiration dates and cleaned the spaces. Ed had HN Baptiste wash the writing off the walls.

Over the deployment, Baptiste had worked on his enlisted Fleet Marine Force warfare specialist badge. The warfare device consisted of a personal qualification sheet, written exam, oral board, and practical application. The intense process took up to eighteen months to complete and gave the individual great knowledge of the Fleet Marine Force operating platform. Ed had earned his in Iraq the first deployment among gathering supplies, advancing, convoys, and regular duties. His board was six hours long, and four of the six corpsmen who attempted failed. Ed was so confused when he left the board, he didn't know if he had passed.

When he and a first class were called back into the room of chiefs, he thought he had failed until they said, "You two did an outstanding job, and it is clear you put a lot of effort into studying. Congratulations on earning your Fleet Marine Force device."

Ed knew HN Baptiste would not put the effort into it on his own, so every time he pissed Ed off, Ed would have him get a dry-erase marker out and start writing the study guide on the porcelain tile wall. Ed thought it was brilliant. It forced him to study, and they all saw it every day. By the time HN Baptiste took his boards, he had written the entire guide on all four walls.

When Ed told him to wash it off, he was devastated and said, "HM3, are you kidding?"

"Does it look like I'm joking? I am not turning this space over to another squadron with your graffiti all over the damn place. What would they think of us?" Ed started laughing as he chucked a sponge at HN Baptiste and said, "Go get your buddy HA Fernandez to help you out."

The replacement squadron arrived, and they did turnover with them. It went very smoothly. The unit that replaced them was their sister squadron from New River, and Ed knew all the corpsmen and the doctor. He gave them all the tour, provided information, and answered questions as they needed. Ed was pulled off the flight roster at Lieutenant Gallagher's request when he left country. Doc didn't want Ed flying with the added responsibility. Ed didn't like that portion, but went with it because he had no choice. The benefit of completing turnover was that he could jump on some flights before they left. Unfortunately, the operations officer could only get him on one.

The commanding officer decided the only way to properly turn over the squadron was to ensure all planes were up and flying. That was a maintenance nightmare. The planes had been beat to hell over the last several months from endless combat operations, and so were the marines and sailors, but everyone thought it would be cool to see a formation that size flying over the base. The marines busted their butts getting those birds ready to soar, and they did.

Ed was scheduled to crew with the commanding officer on plane number double zero. The plane was an old piece of crap. Her airframe was Vietnam era. She had been upgraded, of course, but that girl had so many bugs in her, Ed wondered if they would get in the air, let alone make it to the ground in one piece. She did her part, and the formation was a sight to see. Ed stood at the left gun in amazement as they flew in perfect formation around the air base, landed, and taxied back on line. Raging Bulls, baby!

The main body loaded up and rolled out to the A/DACG three days later. The return home was the same as his previous route. The Bangor Greeters did not disappoint him, and he called Jenny to let her know he was headed her way. She surprised him with news that she knew he was on the way and that Christopher had fallen and hurt himself. *Well, if he isn't in the hospital, he should be OK,* Ed thought.

They reboarded, headed to Cherry Point, and bused to the squadron. All their families were waiting for them at the flight line. The Marine Band was there to welcome them, and they had a brief ceremony and speeches welcoming them home and thanking them for a job well done. When that was complete, the commanding officer dismissed them. Ed once again headed to retrieve his bags and avoided the crowds.

When he found his gear, he walked over, scanning the crowd for Jenny and the kids. He saw Jenny holding Clara and saw a little boy running up to him. He didn't recognize him. He looked like a little mutant. His forehead was swollen the size of a watermelon and was a deep shade of purple.

It took Ed a minute to recognize the voice he heard screaming, "Daddy, Daddy, Daddy!" Ed's stomach churned, and he felt the rage ready to burst out. He dropped his things and grabbed his son. He looked at his poor little head and couldn't believe this was his boy. He glared at Jenny. Jenny could feel his eyes burning through her and knew this was not going to be a pleasant homecoming.

Thankfully, the lieutenant and Bug saw them standing there and came over. Lieutenant Gallagher had already seen Christopher and knew his injury was not as bad as it seemed, but he also knew Ed wouldn't react well to seeing his son like this. He told Ed it was just a hematoma and it would go away in a week or two.

"That is comforting, sir." Ed looked at the Gallaghers' baby and complimented them. "She is beautiful. What did you name her?"

"Reilly," Bug answered.

"Pretty. I don't want to be rude, Doc and Bug, but I'm ready to go home. I'll be in tomorrow. You all have a good day." Ed grabbed his things and headed to the gate. He didn't say a thing to Jenny.

When they got to the gate, he only asked, "Where are you parked?"

"Over there," she said. They loaded the van and headed home. On the way she asked, "Are you going to talk to me?"

"Not until I calm down, I am not."

"That is just great. I haven't seen you in eight months, and you are going to act like this."

"Jenny, I just got off a bus expecting to see my family and had my son run up to me looking like someone has been beating the shit out of him. You need to chill out before I lose my cool."

They went home and unloaded the van. Ed took a shower, ate, and took a nap. When he came out of the bedroom, he asked what had happened to Christopher.

"He was over at Kristen's while I was working," Jenny said. "He was on her coffee table with his hands in his shirt and fell off onto his head. He is OK."

"He looks OK. Reminds me of how he looked when he was born. Kristen doesn't watch her own kids. Why are you leaving our kids with her?"

"You don't know what the hell you are talking about. She is a good mom, and I leave them there because we can't afford a babysitter. Try staying home for a change, and you would know more."

"Get crazy, and see where that gets you, Jenny."

"Enough with the threats, Ed. If you don't like the way I raise the kids, then leave."

Ed started laughing like a madman and replied, "Welcome home! I sure missed this. You talk about me being selfish? You should look in the mirror. You were right, this crap is not going to work."

9

Friends Come and Go

⁓

The tension within the Brannan house eased the following day, but Jenny and Ed knew if they wanted their marriage to survive, they needed to work on it together.

"I accept the fact I am to blame for most of our problems," Ed told Jenny. "I don't communicate well, and I have been an absent partner and father. I'm trying to better myself, but you have to work with me, Jenny."

"Eddie, I want what is best for the kids. I don't want them growing up as we did, but growing up in a home with parents constantly fighting is just as bad. Our relationship needs a lot of work. I want it to work, but if it doesn't start to improve, we need to consider getting help." They agreed to work on their relationship and see where things went. If things began to erode, they would seek help through the programs offered through the base chaplain. They had friends who went through rough patches in their marriages, and they went to marriage counseling and Chaplains Religious Enrichment Development Operation retreats to build stronger relationships. Those friends strengthened their marriage and developed great communication skills because they used the chaplain's service.

Ed had a few days of postdeployment training to complete prior to leave, and they were planning a trip to Tennessee to his aunt and uncle's campground to link up with his brother Pat and his friend Tyson, and to spend time with one another. They decided to avoid the hassle of going home so they could spend time together without worrying about satisfying everyone else. The campground was half the drive too, so it was a lot less stressful for them both.

While Ed completed his training and work, Jenny packed their things and prepared for the trip. They called Ed's aunt to let her know they were coming for a visit and to reserve a cabin. Ed had not been to the campground or seen his aunt and uncle in many years, so he was looking forward to the visit. He had been close to them growing up. Every summer when Ed was a kid, he went with his grandma and grandpa to visit them when they lived in Southern Illinois. His memories of those trips were some of the finest of his childhood.

They loaded up the Rooster and got on the road early in the morning so the kids would be asleep for most of the ride. Jenny drove the first part of the trip, and Ed planned to drive through the mountains. Ed didn't like being a passenger on long trips, especially with Jenny driving. She was a good driver; she just made him nervous. He managed to keep his comments to himself, and it was a peaceful trip. They decided to stop for gas and switch positions outside of Winston-Salem.

After fueling, using the bathroom, and grabbing drinks and snacks, they were back on the road with Ed at the wheel. He was not a patient driver and cussed other drivers a lot. He didn't go more than five miles an hour over the speed limit, and it drove Jenny crazy. She thought he drove like an old person.

As they approached the mountain pass, he enjoyed the view and began daydreaming about the last visit to his aunt and uncle's campground. He was twenty-two then and had been experiencing the worst part of PTSD. He recognized the symptoms he was having but didn't know what to do. He withdrew from classes at college and decided to take a vacation to sort things out. He was not sure where the road was taking him, but he knew he needed to get away for a while. His aunt and uncle had purchased the campground after his uncle retired from coal mining a couple of years prior to his trip. Ed just showed up at the campground.

He remembered driving into the Kampground of America. It was a gorgeous little campground set off on the side of a small mountain near Lookout Mountain, Chattanooga, Tennessee. The entrance was lined with tall pine trees. It included four kabins (everything in a KOA starts with a *k*), a beautiful pool, a large pavilion, a playground, and an A-frame office building with an apartment above. Ed parked in front and went to the office. The door entered into a game room with a laundry facility to the rear and the office/gift shop and store to the left.

He opened the door to the store, hoping to see his aunt. The woman at the register did not look familiar. She was much older than he thought Aunt Harriet should be and didn't look anything like her.

He laughed and said, "You don't look like my Aunt Harriet."

"No, Harriet is off today. Can I help you?"

"Yes. Can you call my aunt and tell her that her nephew Eddie is down here?"

"Yes. Give me a second, darling." The woman picked up the phone and made a call. She told Ed's aunt her nephew was in the shop. A few minutes later, the rear door of the shop opened. It had been several years since he had seen her, but he recognized the woman walking in. It didn't take long for his aunt to recognize which nephew was standing in her shop.

"Well, it's Eddie B," she said. "What are you doing here?"

"I came down to pester you and Uncle Jerry for a couple of days. Hope you don't mind. I brought a tent."

She laughed. "Well, you know we're glad to have you, but you are not sleeping in a tent. You'll stay upstairs with us." She went up to him and squeezed the life out of him, just like his grandmother used to. She couldn't have known how much he needed that then.

She gathered him up and gave him a tour, and then told Ed to pull his truck to the back and bring his bag to the apartment. His uncle was sitting on the couch, having a beer.

When he saw Ed, he jumped up with a huge grin, came over, hugged him, and said, "How the hell are you, boy?"

"I am good, but damn, you are looking old and worn out, Airborne. What has my aunt been doing to your flatfooted ass?"

Jerry just laughed. "You're still a pain in my ass like your daddy! You want a beer?"

"I'm not much of a drinker, but if you're having one, I guess I will too." Jerry was a Vietnam vet. He was Airborne Infantry, had a couple of Purple Hearts, and got out as a sergeant. He was an M60 machine gunner and didn't make it a full year with the 173rd Airborne before he was wounded so bad, he couldn't return and couldn't remain on jump status. When he left the army and came home to the entire BS, he had nothing to do with the military and never spoke of it. Ed knew he was in from stories his dad had told and remembered Uncle Jerry giving him his sergeant stripes when he was a kid.

Aunt Harriet, like Ed's grandma, couldn't have someone in her home without forcing food down his throat. She insisted on cooking and insisted that he eat. The only thing he wanted to do was have a few beers and catch up with them, but he was not about to be rude to two of the people he respected most in the world. While his aunt cooked, Ed and Jerry sat and talked as they threw back several beers. When she had finished cooking, they ate and chatted until Aunt Harriet called it an evening.

Ed and Jerry were enjoying the beer and company. Conversation turned from family and old times to the military. They laughed about good times and told stories about their adventures. Neither brought up any bad events. The night turned into early morning quickly, which was the norm for Ed. For a man twice his age who had to work in a couple of hours, it was an issue, and Jerry finally had the sense to call it a night. Ed fell asleep on the couch shortly after.

The morning came quickly. Aunt Harriet was not happy with the two of them, but she contained her anger, made breakfast and coffee, and harassed them for staying up so late. Ed ventured out on the town that day and located the VFW and Elks Club. He met the VFW commander and a few people, had some beers, and then headed to the Elks and met a local business owner for a couple more drinks before heading back to the campground to cap off the night like the first. This time, Harriet and Jerry's kids, Maggie and John, joined them for supper.

Thankfully, the night was much briefer than the first. The next day, Ed went to Lookout Mountain and then back to the VFW and Elks, and spent the evening talking with his uncle. Ed spent a lot of time at the VFW, and in the afternoon would meet the business owner for drinks at the Elks. He was an older man whom Ed found hilarious. Ed sat with him, joking and making fun of people. They talked about business, his family, and golf.

Ed was telling his uncle about the man and that he was supposed to go golfing with him, when Jerry said, "Damn, Eddie. That is the wealthiest guy in Chattanooga."

Ed laughed and said, "You would never know it. He is a nice person. He probably enjoys talking to someone who doesn't want anything from him."

The next night, Ed took his cousin to the VFW with him to meet all his new friends. They had a great time. Ed spent the entire night introducing John to everyone, talking about their childhood adventures and about Jerry. Ed's dad told him later that John called him and told him, "It was like walking into Cheers with Norm. I have lived here for two years. Eddie comes here for a week and knows half the town."

Ed spent another night at the campground before moving on. He wanted to stay, but felt like he needed to keep going. His aunt later told him that the day he left, his uncle said, "I wish that kid was staying. I'm going to miss having the crazy little bastard around. He always did shit too close to the house, but I love that boy." Ed's Uncle Jerry had a way with words only he understood.

Just as his childhood visits had been, that visit was refreshing. It was the beginning of his healing. Jerry had unknowingly helped Ed realize it was possible to lead a normal life with the baggage of war, and that's what he was looking for on this journey. He loved his aunt and uncle and couldn't wait to see them again. As he watched the mountains pass, he thought, *I wonder if that old fart can still stay up till the crack of dawn.*

※※

Jenny and Ed and the family made their way to the campground from North Carolina as Pat and his family drove in from Illinois, and Tyson and his girlfriend came in from Georgia. Ed, Jenny, and the kids arrived first. They met Aunt Harriet and Uncle Jerry in the office. Jenny had heard a lot about Ed's aunt and uncle and looked forward to meeting them. She wasn't disappointed. She immediately loved Harriet. She could tell she was a kind and loving person. She grabbed the kids, instantly gave them drinks and candy, and handed them souvenirs.

Aunt Harriet introduced herself to Jenny and gave her a hug as if she had known her for years. She made her feel at home. Ed told her on the ride in that his aunt reminded him of his grandma. Jenny knew how much Ed's grandma had meant to him before her death and the influence she had had on his life. She now understood why.

His uncle Jerry introduced himself and asked, "What did you do wrong in life to end up with this prick?"

Jenny laughed and said, "I don't know! It must have been horrible."

Jerry chuckled. "He has been a pain in my ass for years and just keeps coming around. He's like a stray dog that you feed once and he keeps coming back."

Ed laughed. "I'm the only one in the family who still likes your old ass. You shouldn't push it, Chief Washum Your Bottom." They all laughed, and Ed's aunt suggested they head down to the cabins she set up for them.

Aunt Harriet and Uncle Jerry climbed in their golf cart and escorted Ed and the family to their campsite. The cabins they chose were new additions Jerry had installed the year prior in the back half of the campground. The site was secluded and perfect for their planned rendezvous. Ed unpacked the van and readied the site as his family got to know one another. Uncle Jerry threw an insult his way every now and then to

135

let him know he cared as Ed finished up. The last thing to come out of the van was the most important: the cooler full of beer.

Ed grabbed Jerry and himself a beer and asked Jenny and his aunt if they would like one. They declined since it was still early, but Uncle Jerry thought it would be rude to decline his nephew's offer. They popped the tops, toasted to absent comrades, and had a drink. Their vacation began. Pat, his wife, and his son were the next to arrive, followed by Tyson and his girlfriend. They both did as Ed had and set camp before joining Ed and Jerry by the cooler. The women gathered with the kids, talking about what they wanted to see as the boys were busy talking crap to one another.

※※

It was midafternoon and time to do some grilling. Ed planned to cook burgers and dogs, but Pat busted out steaks and olive oil he had brought from Italy. Ed was willing to sit back and enjoy the beer as his brother did the cooking. When the food was prepared, everyone sat and had dinner. They all shared childhood stories, where they were living, and what they were doing. They enjoyed one another's company. The kids were running around, the women chatting, and the boys being boys. As the evening drew on, the kids grew restless, and the mothers decided to head to the cabins. Aunt Harriet headed to the apartment, and Tyson's girlfriend called it a night. The boys had other plans.

When everyone had settled, Ed, Pat, Tyson, and Jerry grouped closer, and the conversation turned to the military. They all had waited for this. The young veterans wanted to hear Jerry's stories, and he wanted to hear theirs. They were separated by generations, but they were brothers in arms. The beer flowed as they laughed about the silly things they had done and seen. The night was getting chilly, so they decided to start a fire and continue their conversation. As Ed expected, the conversation turned to him leaving the army for the navy and serving with the marines. The harassing started. Ed could take as much as he could give, and he thought it was funny they carried on and on.

"I'm done with you army idiots," Ed said, picking up his lawn chair and moving to the opposite side of the fire pit. "This side of the fire is the NARMY. You guys stay over there and play with yourselves. I will be over here in the NARMY. The NARMY is better." They kept talking crap and trying to get him to respond, but he just sat there as if they didn't exist. It was too much for Tyson.

Tyson got up, grabbed his chair, moved over to Ed, put it down, sat, and said, "I'm in the NARMY too."

"Hey, Tyson, how have you been doing?" Ed said. "Did you go to the head or something? I haven't seen you in a while." Tyson laughed so loud, he nearly fell out of his chair. It didn't take long for Ed's brother Pat and Uncle Jerry to follow suit and join the NARMY side of the fire. They all decided that since they had just formed a secret society, they should have an initiation, bylaws, a salute, and a history. After a few more drinks, they came up with a plan of action and began to implement the plan.

First order of business was initiation. They decided to burn a chair. In the Airborne, you burn in or burn out, so it made sense to all of them. They burned a lawn chair. Next, they needed some ceremonial wine to toast new members. All Ed had was Boone's Farm, so Boone's it was, and they chugged the bottle. The bylaws were easy. They decided you needed one member to vouch for you and two members to give a thumbs-up, and you were allowed to initiate. The rules were simple. The NARMY was a place of healing. There were only a couple of rules: no liars and no bullshit. They also decided you didn't have to be a veteran to be in.

Earlier in the evening, Uncle Jerry had told a story about his stay at a hospital in Okinawa. He kept leaving the hospital without permission, so they took his clothes. He wanted to go to a movie on the ward, but didn't have clothes. He remembered a mental patient who walked around with his finger on his head, so he wrapped a towel around his waist and a sheet around his head. He put a finger on the sheet around his head and acted catatonic as he walked to the movie. Every time he moved his finger, he put his other finger up. They decided they could modify that as a salute. The only other thing they needed was a greeting. Jerry talked about the lizards in Vietnam that made a noise that sounded like "eff you," so their greeting became "Fook you." The NARMY was born.

They had an excessive amount of fun with the NARMY that night. Ed's question about whether or not the old man could still hang was answered; they had to walk him up to his apartment around 0400. They all went to bed as soon as they got back. That morning, all of their significant others made sure to make plenty of noise to show their appreciation for them staying up drinking all night. The boys were smart enough not to complain. Each of them looked and smelled like bums, but they managed to get up, eat, and collect themselves for the day.

The rest of the trip was not nearly as exciting as the first night, but they continued to muster in the evening and refine their new organization as their loved ones slept. They enjoyed the time with their families and one another. Despite the NARMY gatherings, Jenny and Ed enjoyed family time together, and they had several outings. When they were packing, Jenny had the same feelings Ed did: she wanted to stay. Harriet and Jerry had that effect on people. They were just outstanding people to be around. Everyone said their good-byes, loaded vehicles, thanked their hosts, and headed home exhausted.

When Jenny, Ed, and the kids made it home, Ed still had a week of leave to spend with them. He stayed home. For the first time in many years, Jenny had time to go do things on her own as Ed took care of the kids. The house was always worse than she left it, and she wondered if it was wise leaving him alone with the kids unsupervised, but he and the kids seemed to love it. *Maybe he is going to make it work this time,* she thought.

The week went by fast, and Ed returned to work. He came home the first evening looking depressed.

"What's wrong, honey?" Jenny asked.

"HN Gonzalez got orders. They're leaving in a couple of weeks." Jenny knew how close Ed and HN Gonzalez were, and she loved him and his wife too. She hated that part of the military. *As soon as you become close to people, they get transferred. That sucks.*

This wasn't the first time either of them had experienced it, but it didn't make the pain any easier. Many of Jenny's friends had come and gone. She hated it. Ed didn't show his emotions, but she knew it affected him too. He wasn't close to a lot of people. He hung out with many people, but there were only a couple he routinely called. HN Gonzalez was one of the friends he spent a lot of time with, and she knew he didn't want to see him leave. Ed told her the benefit of staying in was that you always end up stationed with people again. It was hard for her to understand, because all of this was still new to her. Other people told her the same thing, so she knew he was telling her the truth.

Over the next months, it seemed the entire neighborhood changed. All Jenny's original friends received Permanent Change of Station/ transfer orders, and she was starting over meeting new people. Ed was doing the same at New River. Neither of them liked this part of their new life, but it was a huge part of the lifestyle that they had to adjust to. As time wore on and stress crept in, Ed began to slip into his old pattern.

10

You Can't Keep Doing This

~

After Ed left for work, Jenny sat having her morning coffee, thinking, *All I want is the man from the letters. He consistently makes promises he doesn't have the capability to carry out. I know he's trying. He's staying home more and is maturing. Our life is better, and I know he loves his job, but I fear he loves his work more than he loves us.*

She felt alone in that kitchen, alone in her home, and alone in a state far from her family. All she had to comfort her were two small children, still fast asleep. *Am I the only wife who feels like this?* She couldn't imagine going through this at a young age like many of her friends, and all of them had just left.

⌘

At work, Ed received word to report to the admin office. Once again he had to replay the previous days and ponder if he was about to walk into a butt-chewing. Walking into admin, he was surprised to see all the chiefs gathered near the senior chief's hatch.

The new MAG Twenty-Six chief said grouchily, "Get over here, Brannan." *Damn, I wonder what I messed up,* Ed thought. He moved to the center of the chiefs and stood at parade rest. They all looked sternly at him, shaking their heads in disgust. Ed tried to think of what he had done to receive such harsh treatment, but couldn't think of anything.

Finally, Senior Chief spoke. "Congratulations on your command advancement to hospital corpsman second class. You will be promoted immediately." All the chiefs started laughing and slapping him on the back as Ed stood in shock at the news.

"Is this a joke?" he asked.

Chief Miller laughed. "No, HM2, it is not a joke. MAG Twenty-Six, based on your performance as the LPO during your last deployment, submitted you to Second Marine Aircraft Wing for the command advancement. You won. We will be promoting you in formation today. Call your family and tell them to come over for the ceremony here at the clinic at fourteen hundred hours. I also need to speak to you in private."

"Holy shit! Thank you. That is awesome." Ed shook everyone's hand and left the office with Chief Miller. They headed back to Chief Miller's office to talk.

As they walked down the passageway to the office, Ed recalled the first time he met Chief Miller. Ed and HM2 Munshower had gone out to a local bar across from Tarawa Terrace II. Ed had too much to drink and didn't pay attention when HM2 Munshower said his old chief worked there. They sat at the bar, and a big barrel-chested, stocky guy with big, white Bugs Bunny teeth walked behind the bar. Ed assumed he was the bouncer. He came over and started talking trash to HM2 Munshower.

Ed looked at him and said, "You say another word to my bro, and I am going to knock those big teeth down your throat, muscle head." Chief Miller had no idea who Ed was and tried to explain they were friends and just playing, but Ed said, "I don't give a damn. Just go pick up some bottles or take out the trash and leave us the hell alone. We were not messing with you."

HM2 Munshower jumped in. "He is pretty messed up, Chief."

Chief laughed and said, "That happens in bars. You guys be safe."

"Dude, are you kidding me?" HM2 Munshower said to Ed. "That guy is a chief, and you are going to threaten to beat his ass. What the hell are you thinking?"

Ed laughed hysterically and said, "I didn't know he was a chief. Screw him if he can't take a joke. He shouldn't work in a bar if he can't handle drunks." When Ed learned Chief Miller was reporting to MAG Twenty-Six, he thought it was funny. One of the other chiefs heard the story about Ed meeting Chief Miller. He was trying to stir the pot by telling Ed he was going to pay for his comments that night.

Ed laughed. "Chief, if you think I am scared or I have not dealt with repercussions for something stupid I have said before, you are mistaken. If Chief Miller has a problem, I am sure we can handle it."

Ed wondered as they walked toward the office if they were about to handle it. He and the chief had never discussed that evening, and he doubted they would. Chief Miller was much like Ed. He worked hard and partied hard. What happened off-duty was exactly that: off-duty. If you asked either of them about their first impression of the other, the answer would be simple: "Jerk!" Now that impression was much different. They respected each other, and that's why Ed couldn't figure out what was coming. He never expected what came next.

Chief brought him in and closed the hatch.

"Sit down, Ed. I have an offer for you. I know you just got back and you have already done two tours in Iraq. I also know you and Lieutenant Gallagher put together a damn good training syllabus for CASEVAC. You also have many hours on the plane and plenty of contacts within the squadron flight equipment shops that will help us secure and build flight gear. I want you to be the Marine Aircraft Group Twenty-Six headquarters leading petty officer and deploy with the CASEVAC team."

Ed was stunned with the confidence that the chief had in him and knew this was another great career opportunity, but he knew his marriage was teetering again. If he said yes, he might lose his family. *Is all of this worth it? I want to go back. This is an opportunity to make a difference and save lives. This is why I came back in, but I don't want to lose my family trying to fill a void left from Mogadishu. What kind of choice is this?*

"Chief, I am humbled and honored you would consider me for the position. I want it, but I have some things going on at home that may not allow me to accept the offer."

"I know it is a hard decision. I have been through three wives in my career and understand your concern. You know what this position can do for you career-wise. I do not expect an answer today, but I need one soon. We are submitting for individual augments to increase our staff from other commands throughout the navy/marine corps and will deploy in four months. We need to get a lot of things planned and ready before anyone arrives. Call your wife and let her know about your promotion and discuss this with her. Let me know after you talk to her."

"Thank you, Chief. This opportunity means a lot to me." He stood, shook the chief's hand, and left the office. He headed across the passageway to the lieutenant's office, shut the door, and called Jenny.

※※

Jenny was cleaning the house as the kids were watching cartoons when the phone rang. She picked up, thinking a family member or friend was calling to chat, and she was delighted to talk to an adult.

"Hello!" she answered cheerfully.

"Good morning, love," Ed said. Jenny's mood swung back down as she thought, *I wonder what he wants.*

"Hi."

"Hey, I got some really good news this morning. We got a meritorious promotion to HM2, and they are pinning me this afternoon at fourteen hundred hours here at the clinic. Can you and the kids come?"

Jenny was happy to hear the news and said, "Absolutely. We'll get ready and be over there this afternoon. That is incredible. Did you know they were going to promote you?"

"No, I thought I was in trouble when they called me into the office. They got me good. I need to talk to you about something else too. Can you come over early so we can talk?"

"Sure."

"Great, thank you, and I will see you later."

When Jenny hung up the phone, she wondered what he wanted to talk about. *He just gave me good news, so I am sure he'll have some bad news. I wonder what he did or is planning to do.* She decided to finish cleaning and get herself and the kids ready for the promotion ceremony. She had no idea what to expect. This would be the first time she saw him promoted and was elated they finally could participate. Unfortunately, she was concerned he was about to drop another bombshell on their relationship.

At noon, Jenny loaded the kids in the car and headed to the air station. She planned to meet Ed at the clinic, go to lunch, and then attend the promotion. On the drive over, she couldn't help the dreadful feeling that something bad was about to happen. She hoped it was just nerves or her overreacting to the emotional roller coaster Ed kept her on, but she knew he was up to something. When she arrived at the clinic, Ed stood at the ambulance breezeway and waved them over.

He climbed in and said, "Let's go over to the bowling alley for lunch."

They all went in the bowling alley and sat down in the corner. Ed went to the counter, ordered, paid, and brought back their lunch. He gave everyone a meal and prepared the kids' food as he and Jenny talked about the promotion.

When he sat down, he said, "There is obviously something else. Chief offered me the MAG headquarters leading petty officer position this morning."

"That is good, right?"

Ed smiled. "It's a really good opportunity for a junior HM2, but there is a problem. The Marine Aircraft Group is deploying back to Iraq."

Jenny's tone changed. "When?" Ed said in four months. Jenny stared right through him and said, "That is just great, Ed. We do well, then start having problems, and you run off again. Perfect. Typical, but what did I expect?"

"You know you just jumped to the conclusion that I've already accepted the position. I understand I'm hard to deal with. I ask myself how you have managed to stay, but this is exactly why I avoid talking to you about shit. I just get pissed off. I end up saying something that hurts your feelings, so I try to avoid the situation, and I know that doesn't do any good. I don't know what you want. You complain about money. I work harder to make rank. You complain about me not being home. I stay home. You complain about my attitude when I'm home. I can't seem to make you happy."

Jenny felt horrible for jumping to conclusions, but he was right. He did say hurtful things. He just did it and didn't even know he was hurting her.

"You could have just left it at 'I didn't take the job,' but you had to make me feel like crap," she said.

"You're right. You always are. I'll make it easy for you. When I get back, I'm going to tell Chief I'll take the job. If you are here when I get back, great. If not, then we'll figure it out." Ed got up, kissed the kids on the head, and left.

❈❈

Ed was steaming when he walked out of the bowling alley. He didn't know what had just happened. He had intended to have a civil discussion about what they should do, and it turned into a fight. He didn't know if he had just ended his marriage. *I don't want to be like these people I meet who have been married two and three times. I cannot figure out if it's the career that destroys these relationships or the people. It's more than likely a mix of both. Either way, I'm going to deploy. It will set me up career-wise, give me an opportunity to lead people in combat, and save lives.*

When Ed reached the clinic, he went directly to Chief Miller's office.

"Chief, I will take the LPO job if it is still on the table, and I look forward to helping train and execute this operation."

"Great. We will get your orders today and have you check out of Two Sixty-One and into MAG this week. Is your wife coming to the promotion ceremony?"

"I don't know, Chief. I am not sure I will be married after this, but I am making the choice, and I will deal with whatever consequence comes with the choice I have made."

Chief could tell Ed was distraught. "Is there anything I can do?"

"No, Chief. I have put myself in this position. It has nothing to do with the command or the navy. I just suck at the whole marriage and father thing."

Chief tried to encourage him by saying, "Keep your head up and hope for the best, but if all else fails, I know some good attorneys. I have been through this and don't want to see you get hammered."

Ed laughed. "Thank you, but for everything I have put her through, she is entitled to whatever she wants. I have started over before, and she will use anything to take care of the kids if it comes to that. She is too good for me."

As Ed left the office, he was confused about many things. He didn't understand how he managed to turn everything good in his life into complete crap. He didn't want to let all of his personal problems reflect on his work or interfere with the ceremony, so he sucked it up and hoped Jenny would show up with the kids. He wanted to share this with them, but his pride refused to allow him to go find her. He also thought, *Where the hell am I going to stay if she doesn't come?*

At 1345, an announcement was made to report to the lobby for the promotion ceremony. As Ed entered the lobby, his eyes scanned the crowd, searching for his family. Jenny and the kids were dutifully sitting to the side of the lobby. Ed's face flushed with embarrassment, and he fought back the tears forming in his eyes.

He walked to Jenny and said, "Thank you for coming. Please come up here and meet the chiefs and commander before we get started with the ceremony."

As they walked toward the formation, Lieutenant Gallagher approached. "Hey, I just heard. Congratulations."

"Thank you, sir, but you will not like the other news. I will fill you in when we get done."

The lieutenant looked puzzled, but said, "OK, come find me when you are done. Jenny, you look great. Congratulations to you too. I know you do all the work!"

"Thank you," Jenny said. They continued through the crowd and made their way to the gaggle of senior personnel.

✳✳

"Excuse me, ladies and gentlemen," Ed said. "This is my family, Jenny, Christopher, and Clara." Everyone introduced themselves and shook Jenny's hand, congratulating her on the promotion. Jenny found it odd that they all considered it a promotion for both of them, but she had always felt like a part of Ed's career. It was amazing for her that leaders recognized spouses were an integral part of the service members' lives and careers.

When introductions were complete, the senior chief and commander went over the plan with Ed and his family and proceeded to the front of the formation.

"Person to be promoted, center move," said the senior chief. Ed marched to the center and reported to the commander. Chief Miller read the promotion.

When he finished, Senior asked Ed whom he would like to pin him, and he said, "My family, Senior Chief."

"Mrs. Brannan and family, please come to the front," Senior called. Jenny and the kids moved to the front center of the formation, where Ed was standing at attention. Jenny was nervous, and as she pulled the Second Class Crow out of her pocket, her hands were visibly shaking.

Senior Chief leaned over and said, "Calm down, Jenny. You are doing great. We will be done soon." Ed smiled, seeing how nervous his wife was. Christopher and Clara were at his feet, looking up at him and talking while Jenny was trying to get the rank ready. She pulled his HM3 rank off his collar and began to place his HM2 Crow. When she had it on, she stepped back. Ed knelt down. The kids touched his rank, acting as if they had helped, and he returned to the position of attention. Commander made a brief statement about the command advancement program and Ed's performance.

Senior Chief commented and congratulated him, then said, "At the command of fall out, fall out, congratulate HM2, and carry out the plan of the day. Fall out." Everyone clapped. Ed hugged Jenny and the kids and thanked them. Then they stood by as the clinic staff came through, shaking their hands and congratulating them. When they had finished, Chief Miller asked to speak to them in the breezeway.

In the breezeway, he said, "Jenny, I know how upset you are with Ed about going to Iraq again, but I hope you understand that I put him in a difficult position. He didn't agree to go until he had a chance to talk to you. I don't want this to cause you two any problems, but I would like to have him. His experience will be an asset to the MAG and the CASEVAC team, and it will help his career in the future, but it is not worth losing his family. If you don't want him to go, I will keep him in Two Sixty-One."

Jenny was heartbroken and could feel the struggle Ed must go through every time someone asked him to do something that would put him in a no-win situation with one of the parties. He never complained to her. He just got frustrated and sucked it up. She understood.

She looked at Chief Miller. "If you need him to go, I understand, and I will support him as I always have. We will figure it out. We always do." Ed couldn't believe what he was hearing, but he loved her for it and appreciated the chief's thoughtfulness.

"Chief, it has been a long day," Ed said. "Do you mind if I bug out and go home with my family? We have a lot to talk about this afternoon."

"Go home, Shipmate, and figure this out. I will see you in the morning, and we will get your orders."

Ed, Jenny, and the kids met back at the house. The kids were excited they got to participate in their daddy's promotion and were running around the house like monkeys. Jenny and Ed knew they needed to talk but didn't want to ruin the kids' mood. They decided to order pizza, get a movie, and enjoy the rest of the day together.

That evening, Jenny put the kids to bed early. She came back into the living room to sit with Ed and talk.

"Jenny, I understand how difficult this is for you," Ed began. "I know how hard you work. I appreciate what you do for all of us. There are opportunities you can't turn down, and this is one of them. I'll stay home if that's what you want, but I'm moving fast, and this will help us in the future. I won't lie to you and say I don't want the opportunity. I want to go. It's a good mission, but it isn't worth losing you and the kids. Nothing is worth that. I'll get out of the navy, and we can go try something else if that is what you want."

Jenny was crying before he had finished. Ed was confused and asked, "What did I say wrong?"

"Ed, you didn't say anything wrong. I know you love us. It doesn't feel like you do sometimes, and it doesn't feel like I am appreciated, but we need to stay in, and you need to go on this deployment. You are good at this job. It's the job you like. You can do anything, but this is who you are. I love you. We'll make it work."

※※

The next day, Ed caught up with the lieutenant and broke the news. The lieutenant was not thrilled with the idea, but he knew it was a good opportunity for Ed, and he understood he had little choice in the matter. Ed checked out of 261, said his good-byes to the marines and leaders, and proceeded to MAG Twenty-Six headquarters to check in. For Ed, that afternoon began a four-month whirlwind of planning, training, and predeployment administrative headaches that no one foresaw. For Jenny and the kids, that day was when Ed's deployment began. He was rarely home, and when he managed to get home, it was to sleep. He had little time for them and was a bear to live with. She felt bad about it, but she thought, *I cannot wait till he leaves!*

The MAG received corpsmen from throughout the operating forces to reinforce the CASEVAC detachment. They were to deploy with forty CASEVAC corpsmen and MAG Twenty-Six headquarters' core assets. You would think with a high-profile mission that leaders would send their best and brightest out to represent their commands. If you thought that, you would have thought wrong. Some did, but most saw an opportunity to give their problem to someone else for a while.

Ed hoped they would get a first class in to relieve him of some administrative duties. That didn't happen. They did get several second classes, and they all were good to go, so he was able to focus on the MAG and the training as the senior second class assumed the role as the CASEVAC leading petty officer and took care of the team's administrative duties.

When Ed was not instructing, he was busy ensuring MAG headquarters was medically ready to deploy. A commander from Cherry Point checked in to deploy with the MAG. The commander, an older man who attended medical school after he was a naval aviator, was a resident in aerospace medicine. He was an eccentric man—intelligent, quiet, and more interested in aircraft and weapons than medicine. Ed thought that was unusual, but they got along well, and he allowed him to run things the way he saw fit, so it was a good match.

Chief Miller attended the training and left the predeployment duties to Ed. The MAG headquarters was much different from a regular squadron. It reminded Ed of the MWSS, and the interaction he had with the marines was similar. Ed knew it didn't matter how long you served with the marines or how well you performed; at every new duty station, you had to prove yourself again. It frustrated him, especially with young marines who had never deployed. He appreciated self-confidence and could tolerate a little arrogance from people who had earned it, but these kids had not done anything. He believed they had earned the title *marine* and should be proud of it, but that didn't give them the right to be little pricks to sailors. He would pull them to the side and explain that to them often.

Chief Brown, a search and rescue corpsman who flew CASEVAC in Operation Iraqi Freedom I, took the training Ed and the lieutenant had developed, added classes, and developed a program. This allowed them to train a great team with the support of the MAG, flight surgeons, and other instructors. One of the best additions was the tactical combat casualty course. Ed, Chief Miller, and an HM1 went to the training at Eglin Air Force Base prior to the team to see if it was worth the cost. Their experience verified the need and the value of the training. Ed and the commander had the MAG headquarters and CASEVAC team medically ready to deploy, and they were on standby for deployment.

Like marines, sailors with too much downtime are dangerous. They start doing dumb things, and that is what the team did. They were all away from their commands, living in open-bay barracks, so the likely place to gather was a bar. They frequented many local establishments in the evening and started to make phone calls at inappropriate times to Chief Brown, telling him of their exploits and talking trash.

One morning, Ed discussed this with Chief Brown and told him, "I would not take that crap from them. I heard them say you were a punk and would not do anything about it."

Ed hadn't heard them say anything, but he knew he could spin the chief up enough to go PT the hell out of them and put a stop to the BS. That is exactly what happened. As he walked by the breezeway entrance, he looked outside and saw a mass of bodies on the deck doing flutter kicks, with the chief standing over them yelling. He started laughing so hard, he fell to one knee.

When he had composed himself, he walked outside and asked, "What are you all doing on the deck?"

"They think I am a punk," Chief Brown said. "I am teaching them that I don't like getting woken up by drunken sailors, and I am not someone to mess with."

Ed pointed to one sailor. "He just rolled his eyes. I do not think they are taking you seriously, Chief." Ed walked off as the chief went ballistic.

That afternoon, Ed talked to Chief Miller and the commander about putting the team on leave for a couple of weeks. They both agreed that would be a good idea. They brought them all in and made plans for a two-week predeployment leave period. All the sailors were relieved to get out of there and let Chief Brown cool down.

Ed took two weeks of leave to spend time with Jenny and the kids. He stayed home and enjoyed their company. Jenny took care of them, as she always had. They enjoyed the time off and went to the beach. Ed was not a fan of the beach, because of the sand. Jenny loved it. She and the kids loved hunting for megalodon shark teeth at Onslow Beach on base. She had a huge collection. Ed couldn't find them, so it didn't interest him. Jenny and the kids spent hours out there and enjoyed every minute.

When the two weeks concluded, everyone returned to New River. They finally had word on a departure date. They all prepared records, gear, and personnel for deployment. As usual, Ed began to detach and focus solely on deployment. The night prior, Jenny, who was now a pro, gathered the kids and headed for the security of the room. Ed had become just as proficient with laying out his gear and packed once. They were both ready.

The following morning, they set off on their third trip in less than three years to drop Ed off, not knowing how long it would be until they would see him again. Jenny wanted no part of the departing ceremony, and Ed was grateful. They said their good-byes at the van. They hugged, kissed, said, "I love you," and he grabbed his gear. When he walked off toward the group of marines and sailors, that sinking feeling came back to Jenny, but this time she was prepared, so she fought off the tears as she headed home.

The team assembled, and the chief passed on all the pertinent information. The squadron formed for the departure and remarks from the commanding officer and the sergeant major. They boarded the buses and headed to Cherry Point. At Cherry Point, they off-loaded, formed baggage details, and awaited orders to board the plane. When they boarded, they got a final count, the doors closed, and they were treated to the same hospitality that Ed had experienced each time before. Their flight path was the same. It was getting so routine for Ed, he felt like a businessperson on the red-eye flight.

They arrived at the same base Ed had departed seven months ago. The squadron that had replaced him was still in place. It felt like a second home. As they were bused to their holding tents, Ed pointed out the areas of the base and explained where everything was. He told them they would not remain on this base. When they reached the area where the tents had been, Ed was surprised to see modular living structures the marines called *cans* in their place. The base had grown quite a bit in seven months. The cans were a huge step up from the tents. Ed thought it was five-star living, but sailors could always find something to complain about, and their complaint was that the heads were too far away. Ed just laughed at them.

Everything was going smoothly. They were there for two days and had done a turnover with MAG Sixteen. The team helped get everything set up in the MAG offices and prepared for transport to their base of operations. Ed was sitting in the MAG office, completing a request to have supplies moved to their site, when Chief Miller came in.

"Ed, I need you to stay here and take care of the MAG," he said.

Ed looked bewildered. "OK, Chief. When will I meet up with the team?"

"I am going to get everything set up, and then I will pass word."

"Good to go, Chief." *That is some BS, but what can I do about it?* Ed thought.

He continued to prepare the team for departure and to run the small aid station, moving from the cans to the MAG headquarters' E-5 and below, billeting and starting a twelve-hour-day schedule. They got computer access and a DSN line, so he contacted Jenny and the kids regularly. He also continued to write letters and poetry and draw. The kids were getting older, but they still enjoyed his cartoons.

The day finally came to see the team off. Ed and the commander escorted them to the A/DACG for departure and wished them luck and safety. Ed was upset he wasn't accompanying them, but he had other duties to attend to.

On the way back to MAG, Ed asked the commander, "Sir, how long will I be here?"

"I am not sure, HM2." Ed got the uneasy feeling that not everyone was onboard with this choice. He overheard the command master chief, Master Chief Johnson, and Chief Miller arguing about something the day prior, and saw the master chief storm off. Ed nicknamed the master chief "Dark Helmet" after the *Spaceballs* character, but never dared call him that to his face. He was a force reconnaissance corpsman around five foot nine, one hundred and ninety pounds, with a big fat head and an evil smile and laugh. He liked to call Ed "Blackhawk" because of his Somalia deployment, and because he knew it pissed Ed off. Ed respected the man, but he could only take him in small doses. He was a handful. He was a great man and good to his sailors, but he was a pain in the ass.

Ed remembered the first time they met. The MEF sponsored a corpsman competition annually, before the endless deployments. The Wing rarely had a team enter, and when they did, the team didn't do well. Ed and five of the sailors from the clinic decided to form a team and train on their own. A first class, HM1 Bradway, offered to coach them. Ed was sure the man was a sadist, because he just enjoyed PTing the hell out of them. They trained for a month before the competition.

When they arrived, they found they weren't the only Wing team. A team from Cherry Point was there as well, but they had gear and a guide-on (unit flag), and the command master chief was hanging out with them. As the competition drew on, New River was doing well, and the master chief started to migrate over to their camp. The fact that he had failed to acknowledge them until they were doing well did not escape Ed's attention. They were the only team without a guide-on, so Ed ripped a pine sapling out of the ground and pulled his nasty skivvies off. He used a Sharpie marker to write "Shit Stains" on the underwear, tied it to the sapling, and marched around their camp. They had a guide-on. Master Chief saw this, came over, and asked how his team was doing.

Ed laughed. "Your team is sucking wind. We are kicking their ass."

The master chief turned red with fury and said, "I have two teams in this competition, Brannan."

"Really, Master Chief? Because this is the first time we have seen you."

"Brannan, why don't you do everyone a favor and go hang yourself?"

Ed laughed. "I am pretty sure if I followed that order, you would get in a lot of trouble." Master Chief turned and left. Ed's teammates were not as amused as he was. They all asked him what was wrong with him. They went on to take fourth place—not a great finish, but better than the Wing had ever done, and they had proved to the rest of the Marine Expeditionary Force that the Wing could hang with the best of them.

※◈※

The routine at the MAG sucked for Ed. He was doing minimal sick call and mainly administrative duties. He had to report medical information from the MAG to Wing, and getting information from the squadrons on time was a pain in the butt. He would ask for the data, ask again, and then have to threaten them by e-mail, with a courtesy copy sent to the commander, to get the information. It was growing old fast, and Ed voiced his concern to the commander.

Chief Miller remained incognito for a month with minimal communication, and Ed knew how this was going to go. The master chief hammered him daily, and it was a running joke that he was the MAG chief. ED knew this was a no-win situation. When there was a supply mix-up with one of the containers, Ed took an ass-chewing from the master chief.

"Master Chief, do you think it is right to keep me in this position?" Ed asked. "You are taking your frustration out on me. Chief is chewing my ass, and I am stuck in between you two. I lose either way, so I am not sure what I should do."

Master Chief was not one to have a civil conversation with, so the attempt was futile. "You wanted the job. Do it."

"Roger that, Master Chief."

What Ed did not know was they had already requested another chief. They wanted Ed to assist with a different issue before they sent him back to the team. Ed just kept doing his job the best he could.

Commander finally told him a chief was inbound, and he would be heading out soon.

Ed was relieved and said, "Thank you, sir. I am tired of dealing with these flight surgeons. I do not know how you do it."

Commander laughed and said, "I drink. I drink a lot." Ed smiled and thought, *Me too. I guess you're not as weird as I thought.*

Chief Stahl showed up a week later to relieve Ed and assume control of the MAG. Chief Stahl was ready to retire, but he had extended his time to cover the operation. Ed couldn't believe the dedication. His first impression was that he was old and just riding out his time. He should have learned his lesson on first impressions.

The two did their turnover, and Ed escorted him around to the squadrons. Chief Stahl explained to each squadron that he in no way would be waiting for information like HM2 Brannan had.

"Turn it in on time or do not," he said to each lieutenant. "I don't care. I will report to the Wing surgeon the numbers I have, and he will report those to the commanding general. When your commanding officer is explaining to the general why your numbers were not on the report, you will answer to him, not me." *Damn, he's good,* Ed thought.

When they finished the squadron rounds, Ed knew he needed to take him over to the master chief. Ed was dreading this interaction. He knew it was going to be a shit-slinging contest, and he needed to keep his mouth shut. He and Chief Stahl headed to the Wing headquarters building.

They entered the old Iraqi air base officer's club turned Wing headquarters. The building was directly across the paved street from a beautiful desert oasis pool complex that unfortunately had not operated in years. The converted building had an enormous walnut-lined wall with marble floors. The busts of the former dictator had been replaced by plants and the Iraqi flags by the national ensign and USMC flag. They called it swinging with the Wing for a reason!

Chief Stahl was impressed as they wove through the maze of offices. As they approached the master chief's hatch, Ed heard him before he saw him. Ed was sure everyone in the room heard him. Ed knew it was going to be an interesting meeting; the old prick was in a fine mood.

Fortunately, Chief Stahl noticed Ed's apprehension and said, "I will deal with the master chief."

"Thank you, Chief. He has been beating me up for weeks. I am ready to get far away from him."

Chief Stahl chuckled and said, "Give me a week, and I will too." He knocked, and they were called into the office. Master Chief and Chief Stahl shook hands and talked.

Master Chief just stared at Ed and said, "Blackhawk, step outside." Ed did not bother to address the master chief. He knew he was in a foul mood and exited his office. He overheard their discussion about Chief Miller and Ed running the MAG. Ed expected all of this. Then he heard master chief say something unexpected.

He complimented Ed's performance and said, "I would keep him on, but we have some issues that I think he can help with, and those damn flight surgeons are jacking with him. He doesn't have the experience of a chief. Hell, the kid just made second. I was worried he would tell one of them to go screw himself and get into trouble. He is not afraid and has come close to telling me to shove it."

Chief Stahl laughed. "Master Chief, someone needs to tell you to shove it on a daily basis, or you'll walk all over people! I've got this. What are you going to have Brannan do?"

"Let's call him in. I know with those big-ass ears of his, he can hear what we are saying, and he is a nosy bastard. Brannan, get in here."

"Yes, Master Chief," Ed said, and popped back in the room.

"Were you being nosy?" Master Chief asked.

"Yes. It is hard not to hear your loud voice."

The master chief gave his evil troll smile and said, "You are going to Ramadi to MEF headquarters. I want you to assess the patient evacuation team and see what the hell is going on there."

Ed looked puzzled. "Is this about the aircraft being put in holding patterns waiting on urgent patients?"

The master chief's menacing smile grew larger. "Yes. How did you know about that?"

"I have been keeping up with the team, Master Chief, and that is a huge complaint."

"Why do you think that is happening?" Master Chief asked.

"I have some ideas, but I need to go and poke around for a couple of days to verify them. It should be an easy fix if it is what I think it is."

Master Chief said, "Good. Now get out and go pack. We have chief things to discuss, and we don't need your big ears hearing them."

"Yes, Master Chief." Ed walked out of the office and headed directly to the MAG to call Chief Miller. He was pissed at Chief Miller, but remained loyal and wanted him to know what was afoot.

As usual, Chief Miller was not in the office, so Ed sent him an e-mail with the details. He packed his bags for his departure. He hoped he would be traveling soon. When he secured his gear, he headed back to the MAG and waited for Chief Stahl to return to brief him.

"You need to get your gear in order and pack," Chief Stahl said. "You will leave for MEF headquarters tomorrow evening."

"I packed when I left the master chief's office. Chief, not that I do not like your company, but I am ready to roll. You are going to want to shoot one of these doctors. They have made my life miserable."

Chief Stahl laughed and said, "I will be fine. I can handle myself. You are going to do well in the navy if you can keep yourself out of trouble. You will make a damn good chief someday. Take some advice from an old salt and pay attention to everyone, even the dipshits. There is a lesson in everything. The master chief is a rough old prick, but he thinks you did a damn good job. That is a compliment. You are walking into a bad situation in Ramadi. That is not our house, and you are going to be pissing in somebody's Cheerios. Be careful how you do it."

"Yes, Chief, and thank you." They stopped for the day.

The following day, Ed checked out of MAG headquarters and bounced around to the squadrons, saying good-bye to corpsmen he liked. He had lunch with the commander and the chief. Then he headed down to be briefed by the master chief and his Marine Wing

Headquarters Squadron's leading chief petty officer, Chief Dean. Chief Dean reminded Ed of Dustin Hoffman in *Rain Man:* a wealth of useless knowledge. He was a nerdy guy with a goofy mustache, but with a great sense of humor and a quick wit. Ed liked him, but he insisted on calling Ed Blackhawk, like his mentor, the Dark Helmet.

"I allow you and Master Chief to get away with that crap because I respect you," Ed once told Chief Dean. "If people start trying to use that as a call sign, I will black some eyes. That shit is not a fond memory for me, and it's not a joke." When he arrived, the chief and master chief were waiting in the master chief's office. They called him in and briefed him.

The master chief explained the situation and whom he would contact, and then said, "I called Chief Smith and told him I was sending a second class to fix him."

"Why would you do that, Master Chief?"

The master chief grinned. "If you want to be a chief, it is best you learn to swim in shark-infested water. Now go fix that shit."

Ed shook his head as he left the room. He heard Chief Dean ask Master Chief, "You did not really tell Tom that, did you?"

"Damn right I did," Master Chief said. "Those idiots are going to get someone killed. That kid can handle himself, and he has the support of the commanding general, the Wing surgeon, and me. Tom can pound sand." Hearing that gave Ed more confidence, but he thought, *I'm going to be walking into a hornet's nest.*

That afternoon, he finished cleaning up his area in his room and ensured he and Chief Stahl had turned over everything. Commander and Chief escorted him out to the A/DACG for his flight to Ramadi. They said good-bye, and Ed waited on his plane. When the CH-46 Phrog helicopter rolled up, he wished he was on the gun instead of climbing in the rear, but thought, *Different mission this time.* The ride was rough, and the landing shook the spine. Ed had flown into the landing zone many times, a tight landing zone that would fit two 46s at a time. *This pilot is fresh out of flight school, damn boot!* He grabbed his gear and exited the aircraft. He headed over to the bunker and dropped his bags as the planes roared off.

As Ed gathered his bags, he was verbally assaulted by two figures. His initial reaction was to grab his pistol until he realized they knew his name. He didn't recognize either of them and stood there in shock, looking at them strangely, until he finally had enough of the abuse.

"Who the hell are you two?" Ed said. "How smart do you think it is walking up to someone you do not know in the middle of the night, chewing his ass when you know he has a loaded weapon on his side? Step back, let me get my shit, and we will go talk about why I am here, gentlemen. Thank you."

Ed snatched up his things and stomped off the landing zone and around a concrete wall. He threw the bags against the wall, stripped off his protective gear, and stood waiting for the men.

When the other two men came around the wall, Ed stuck out his hand and said, "I am HM2 Brannan. I do not know what that miserable-ass master chief of mine called and said that fired you two up, but I am just here to watch how things operate and see if I can help. If you do not want me here, I will grab my shit and get right back on the next flight out of here, but both you and I know this is not our call."

The tense situation lightened immediately. The men all shook hands and introduced themselves.

Lieutenant Morris was in charge of the PET, a nurse corps officer, and former air force enlisted. He was a reasonable man who escorted Ed to his quarters and gave him instructions to meet him in the morning at the Combat Operations Center (COC). Ed billeted with the communications marines. He grabbed an empty rack close to the door so he wouldn't disturb any of the sleeping marines, pulled out his sleeping bag, and grabbed a few hours of sleep.

At 0500, Ed woke, grabbed his head lamp and shaving kit, and ventured out to find the nearest head. Hesco barriers formed walls around the perimeter of the base and the interior of each compound, making the path anywhere a maze for any newcomer. Ed wandered aimlessly for several minutes until he saw waterlines on the ground and decided to follow them. The guess proved to be accurate, and he found the heads, where he shaved, brushed his teeth, did a quick washcloth bath, and applied deodorant. As he finished, he thought, *I hope I can find my way back to that hooch, or this is going to be a long morning.*

He left the head and backtracked his way through the Hesco maze to his rack. The quarters were lit and alive when he returned. He quickly realized why no one was occupying the rack he slept in. It was filthy. *I am glad I've had all my immunizations or I would surely get a communicable disease from sleeping on that thing!* He introduced himself to the marines. Like most outfits, they were not friendly and wondered why someone from a different command had invaded their space, but Ed didn't bother with them and finished getting ready for his meeting with the lieutenant.

After he dressed and secured his gear, he grabbed his weapon, vest, and helmet, and headed to the chow hall. As he walked outside, the sun was rising in the east, and he could see the Euphrates parts of the city and the base across the river. The smell of raw sewage filled the air. Ed thought it was either a honey wagon or waste from the river. As he made his way to the chow hall, his eyes scanned the dust-filled street and palm-lined sidewalks. It was early, and few people were roaming. The place looked like a Saharan city from an *Indiana Jones* movie, with clutter blowing from one end to the next. He wanted to finish his business there quickly and get to the team.

When he reached the chow hall, he cleared his weapon, walked through another maze of barriers, and washed his hands before signing in and moving into line. The chow halls were contracted out to corporations instead of being run by military cooks. Ed remembered the good old days of army chow and kitchen duty and thought this was a much better option. The food was better, and it was one less duty to pull. He got eggs, bacon, and coffee, and took his tray over to a corner table. He watched the mix of civilians and military come through and listened to their conversations. He still enjoyed listening and watching people interact.

A group of security contractors came in with their high-speed gear, beards, and attitude. Ed didn't like them. His brother talked about applying once, and Ed's advice was simple: "You do not know who you are working with. You have no support, and for the right price, I am pretty sure most of them would shoot at us." He wasn't sure about the last part, but he didn't want Pat doing it, and he knew that would sway his decision. Ed finished his coffee and meal and headed to the COC.

At the COC, he stopped at the entrance by the guard and waited for the lieutenant to escort him in. When they verified his clearance and gave him a visitor's pass, they proceeded. The lieutenant showed Ed around and explained the operations to him before they met Chief Smith at the PET desk. They all sat and discussed the standard operating procedure. Ed learned another team member would be joining him that afternoon. HM2 Johnson, no relation to the master chief, was flying in from their CASEVAC base. He would assist them in determining how to adjust operations to better suit the mission.

Ed welcomed the extra eyes and knew it would take some of the heat off him. He liked HM2 Johnson and knew he wasn't afraid to speak his mind. As they were going over the standard operating procedure, a call for CASEVAC came in, and Ed watched in real time how the process went and how everyone responded. He immediately recognized the issue after the first drop, and a second request came in immediately for the same patient they had just brought in to that location. The problem was not the PET or the COC. It was the requesting units. The unit that had just received the patient was requesting the CASEVAC before the patient was even in their facility, let alone stable. Ed knew they were sending a request before they had the patient in the operating room.

"Did you hear that?" he asked the lieutenant and chief.

"What?" they both replied in unison.

"The requesting unit just called in a nine-line casualty evacuation request for the patient they just received." Both men looked stunned.

"I do not think so, HM2," the chief said.

"I guarantee that is what is going on, Chief. Check the request time, flight time, holding time, and when that patient comes out of the facility when this is over."

"I think you may be right," the lieutenant said.

"I do not blame them for doing it," Ed said. "I would think it was the right call too, if I did not know the response time was less than fifteen minutes on an urgent. I think we just need to track a few of these and do some training for the requesting units."

Unfortunately, nothing in the military is that easy. It took Ed and HM2 Johnson a month of tracking data and submitting it through the chain of commands to get any positive feedback and a go-ahead to push the training. When they got the green light, the patient evacuation team did an outstanding job relaying to all the commands the necessity of properly requesting CASEVAC and why it was dangerous to spin planes early and have them in the air for long periods of time. It took another week for the two corpsmen to get a flight back to the team.

When Ed finally reached the CASEVAC team, he was on cloud nine. All he wanted to do was get on the flight schedule and start doing his job. To his dismay, other issues needed to be addressed, and if they were not taken care of immediately, it would mean trouble for all of them. The teams had developed a rivalry, and there was a lot of infighting. There had been some fights, and for whatever reason, a couple of the second classes didn't think they should tell Chief Miller. The last thing you want to be in the navy is the person with a secret. Ed knew this issue could bite them all in the butt, and he knew he had to tell Chief Miller.

He found the chief, and they discussed the Marine Aircraft Group, Patient Evacuation Team, and the CASEVAC team. Ed told him of the issues within the team. Since Ed was the only one readily available, Chief Miller was irate and started cussing Ed out.

"Wait a second," Ed said. "You left my ass at the MAG. Then Master Chief threw me to the wolves at the PET, and now you are blaming me for crap here. That isn't happening."

"Go get every second and get back here now." Ed left and gathered all the seconds.

As they walked back, he told them, "I don't know what the hell you all were doing, but it ends now. He is pissed, and he has every right to be. We're all going to get an ass-chewing, and I just got here."

"He is never around," said one of the HM2s. "What were we supposed to do?"

Ed glared at him. "How about be a damn leader?" No one said anything else.

When they reached Chief Miller's tent, they all filed in, and he started raging. He reassigned the team's leading petty officer.

"HM2 Brannan will handle the master-at-arms duties. Any disciplinary problems, he will deal with directly and report to me. When you leave here, go discuss this among yourselves. Does everyone understand?"

Everyone said, "Yes, Chief." They all departed and headed to their tent.

At the HM2's tent, Ed began. "Listen, there are some serious issues. We need to end the mommy and daddy games the sailors are playing on you folks and start leading these sailors. I wanted to come here and fly, but apparently that is going to be secondary to this situation. I didn't ask for this responsibility, but I need your help."

They all agreed, and the new overall team-leading petty officer, HM2 Johnson, said, "Ed is right. Let's all work together and get shit done right."

All went well for several weeks. The team got back on track. Turnovers went smoothly. No one was late. Sailors quit losing gear, medication, and logs. They thought they could see the light at the end of the tunnel. They had three weeks until their replacements arrived and five weeks until they headed home.

Ed woke early and completed his morning routine. He returned to the tent, dressed, and headed to chow. On the way, he passed HM2 Shocker's rack. HM2 Shocker moved to his side as Ed passed, and it reminded him of his first day in the tent. He and HM2 Johnson had arrived from the A/DACG. HM2 Johnson was showing him around the tent, explaining where he could put his gear and where everyone's things were kept.

Ed asked HM2 Johnson why everyone had sheets up around their sleeping areas, and HM2 Johnson just smiled and said, "HM2 Shocker.

He's hard to take." *I will show him hard to take*, Ed thought. When HM2 Shocker came in that night, Ed had a surprise waiting for him.

Ed was nude, lying on Shocker's rack, and said, "Come here, big boy. You're little spoon, and I am big spoon." HM2 Shocker hated people touching his things, but he was scared of Ed, and seeing him naked on his cot confirmed his belief Ed was insane. Ed continued to mess with HM2 Shocker until he lightened up. *It wasn't all HM2 Shocker*, Ed thought. *He was a trucker for twenty years before he joined the navy and is old enough to be these people's dad, and they are pigs. He is weird, but I like weird.*

Ed continued to chow and did his normal routine for the morning: eggs, bacon, and coffee at a corner table by himself, watching and listening to people he didn't know. This was morning entertainment for him. His tentmates joined him as he finished. He talked briefly and then excused himself to utilize the head. Ed didn't have to use the head, but as he did every morning, he made an excuse to be alone to go over the plan of the day, write, or call home.

※※

Jenny was home doing chores and tending to the kids. She was relaying to the families all the information Ed was passing to her about the team. She stayed in constant contact with a few of the sailors' wives who were experiencing their first deployment. She knew the discomfort they were experiencing and did the best she could to lessen their pain. A major obstacle to deal with was rumors and overreaction. She had one fellow spouse who constantly felt the need to cause problems. The woman could not go a week without causing a new problem, and it was growing old for her and the team leaders. Ed asked her the last time they spoke to try to talk to the woman and get her to quit contacting the command and causing trouble.

Jenny didn't like talking to the woman, because she was dramatic and a pain in the butt. She attempted to discuss the issue with her, but the conversation went nowhere and frustrated her. *I will be glad when they all get home safe and this one is over*, Jenny thought.

Jenny was also dealing with new dramas with the kids. Both kids had reached an age where they understood their daddy was gone, and they missed him. Clara cried for him often, and Christopher knew Ed was the enforcer of the rules. Christopher had taken full advantage of that opportunity over the last several months and was creeping on Jenny's last nerve. They both would cry for their daddy anytime they were disciplined, in an attempt to make their mommy feel bad. Jenny had enough work to do just managing everything else within the home; the added difficulty of a disruptive little boy and a heartbroken little girl only complicated things more.

❈❈

Ed made his way over to the CASEVAC shack on the flight line for turnover. He talked to the offgoing team leader and went over the evening's runs. They prepared for the daily shift change, had coffee, and BS'd until everyone arrived for muster.

The muster chief passed the plan of the day, shared redeployment news, and handed over the formation to the blue and gold team leaders for turnover. The teams were blue and gold in honor of the navy colors. Turnover consisted of personnel, gear, and medication accountability. When the offgoing team accounted for everything and signed the log, the oncoming team would sign for the equipment and medication and begin their twelve-hour shift. The normal turnover would last approximately forty-five minutes from muster to departure of the offgoing team, depending on how smoothly everything went.

The turnover went well, and the offgoing team was heading to breakfast within thirty minutes. The ongoing team was ready to go. Ed loved to fly, and he loved medicine. The problem with the job was that someone had to get hurt for him or the team to work, and none of them liked that aspect of the job. Ed learned early in his career that people assume that combat is an endless battle. The reality is the majority of the time, service members are patrolling, convoying, flying, training, or standing by, bored out of their minds. Then when something happens, and they are experiencing the horror of war, they wish they were bored.

That morning, the team was completing training when the CASEVAC bell rang. The bell, located outside the squadron's operations duty officer's office, was an eight-inch brass ship's bell. When sounded, it was the alarm for all the crews on alert to report to their aircraft and begin start-up procedures for launch. During daytime operations, the crews spun three planes: a primary, secondary, and tertiary. The secondary and tertiary planes would just start up and stand by until the primary was in the air. If the primary had any issue, then they could be used as a backup. Each plane consisted of a pilot, copilot, crew chief, two gunners, and two corpsmen. They all reported to the plane and prepared for immediate takeoff.

It was approximately fifteen minutes from the time the bell rang to the time the plane taxied. Daytime operations were dangerous due to the enemy's enhanced visibility of the aircraft, so it was necessary to have a gunship escort if a CASEVAC launched. Standard operating procedure dictated that a daytime launch would only be initiated if there was a true point-of-injury urgent casualty/life-or-death situation.

The marines and sailors leaped into action. The teams on call reported to their aircraft and began start-up procedures as the other personnel stood by for maintenance and safety and to taxi the aircraft. Everything went smoothly. The primary plane spun and taxied, meeting its escort at the runway. The primary took the lead and taxied to the main runway for takeoff. The support crews all stood on the squadron's taxi runway with the spinning secondary and tertiary planes until the primary and escort had exited the air space. When they had left the air space, the planes and crew that remained on the ground performed their shutdown procedures, replaced covers, and buttoned up the aircraft as the support crews returned to their duties.

Ed and Chief Miller reported to the operations office to get information about the ongoing CASEVAC mission and to monitor what was going on. Missions had decreased significantly, so it was a welcome break from the routine, and there was a full house. Everyone listened intently to the operation. The room was tense, because of the daytime operation and how close the squadron and team were to going home. No one wanted something bad to happen this late in the deployment.

Things started to go wrong quickly. The original request was for one urgent casualty, but radio traffic relayed there were three on the deck, with two priority. *That is a lot for two corpsmen to handle, and the area is obviously not as secure as they have reported if they are taking more casualties,* Ed thought.

The gunship reported taking fire and seeing surface-to-air-missiles or rocket-propelled grenade fire directed at the aircraft on approach. The aircraft waved off the first landing attempt. The mood in the room grew more tense, and you could have heard a pin drop. The primary pilot radioed they were attempting another landing from the south. Five minutes later, they heard another radio call from the primary reporting ground fire and rocket-propelled grenade fire, then silence.

A frenzy of radio traffic followed, reporting an aircraft hit by small arms fire, a surface-to-air missile, or a rocket-propelled grenade, and the aircraft went down. Everyone in the room let out a gasp and immediately started discussing recovery operations. Ed and the chief were visibly distraught. Ed felt like he was going to be sick. He knew the risk of flying around in a two-ton fuel tank, but had never put a lot of thought into the true danger of it.

He hoped and prayed for the best, but deep inside he knew they had just lost seven of their comrades. Without all the details, no one in that room was going to leave and cause any undue concern for the rest of the squadron, but they all expected the worst. Their fears were soon confirmed by reports from the gunship and the quick reaction force on the ground. The aircraft and crew were a total loss. Ed was devastated, as was everyone standing there.

Ed looked at Chief Miller and asked, "What the hell are we going to tell the guys, Chief?"

"We need to calm down, get all the information, and wait for orders from the commanding officer," the chief said. It was obvious that he was as upset as Ed. He had lost friends before too, and it didn't get any easier.

As they were speaking, the commanding officer said to the group, "We have just experienced a tremendous loss. The marines and sailors need us to remain strong, lead with compassion, and keep the faith. I need to see the executive officer, maintenance officer, operations officer, Doc, and the sergeant major in my office immediately. Everyone else, stand by here for further word." The commanding officer exited to his office, with the leaders he requested following.

They all returned forty-five minutes later. "I want everyone to return to your shops, gather your marines and sailors, and send runners to get the night crew," the commanding officer said. "We will have a squadron formation on the taxiway in two hours, and I don't want any information passed prior to that formation. Does everyone understand?"

Everyone answered, "Yes, sir." The sergeant major called the room to attention as the commanding officer announced, "Carry on." Ed and Chief Miller proceeded directly to the CASEVAC shack and did exactly as the commanding officer directed.

Two hours later the squadron formed on the taxiway. The sergeant major called the formation to attention and turned the formation over to the commanding officer, who told everyone to form a school circle around him. The commanding officer delivered the news as only a man with many years of leadership experience could have. He was direct but compassionate.

"We have been delivered an awful blow by the enemy today, but we have to continue the mission. The crew's sacrifice was not in vain, and our continued success will ensure that. That is what all of them would want, and that is what we will do. We will maintain an operational pause for the remainder of the day, and a memorial service will be conducted tomorrow. We have already begun the decedent affairs process, with the families contacted per procedure. Do not discuss this matter with anyone. This will be hard enough on the families. They will receive this information in a timely manner and through official means. Do not hurt them further by allowing them to receive this information through any other nonofficial channel.

"The chaplains, medical officer, and grief counselors will be available for anyone having trouble, and I expect you to utilize them if you have any issue. The corpsmen can direct you to the appropriate care too. Thank you. Are there any questions?"

The squadron stood silent in mourning. After a few moments, the commanding officer asked the chaplain to say a few words. When he had finished, the commanding officer said, "Fall in," and released the sections to their respective officers in charge.

Chief Miller directed the team to return to the CASEVAC shack. The sailors somberly entered the shack and took seats. Chief came in and spoke to the crew. He spoke eloquently as the commanding officer had about the crew and specifically about the two members they had lost. Tears filled the eyes of the men and women in the room. Ed stood silent in the corner, wondering, *How the hell did this happen?* He was sad, but he was more pissed off than anything. He couldn't handle seeing these sailors destroyed like this, and hurt deeply from the loss of the two men. He also knew Jenny was close to the younger sailor's wife. He felt horrible about putting her in this position and had no idea how she would handle it.

The following day, the commanding general flew in for the memorial service, and most of the base attended. Ed thought the service was beautiful, but it was heart-wrenching. The squadron, Wing chaplain, and religious program specialist prepared the chow hall for the service. A single table covered with a white cloth sat centered at the forward portion of the hall. The table had seven photographs of the fallen men. To the portside, as you looked at the table, stood a small podium, and a PA system played soothing music. As people entered, they received small programs with biographical data on the fallen warriors.

The service consisted of a prelude, posting of the colors, national anthem, invocation, memorial tribute, CO's remarks, benediction, and last roll call. The last roll call was a final tribute paid by service members to their fallen comrades. It was an accountability roll call, painful to listen to. The last roll ensured all were accounted for, and none forgotten. It was followed by the firing of rifle volleys and the playing of "Taps."

During the last roll call, the squadron prepared seven battle crosses, one for each fallen comrade. The cross consisted of the helmet and identification tags to signify the fallen member. The inverted rifle with bayonet signaled a time for prayer, a break in the action to pay tribute to their comrade. The combat boots represented the final march of the last battle. For these men, the pilot's naval aviator wings and the air crew's combat wings were added.

When the ceremony ended, all members in attendance formed lines and walked past each of the photos and battle crosses to pay respect to the fallen warriors. Some knelt and prayed. Others touched their helmet or tags, and some just paused briefly. No warrior wants to admit the possibility of death, and these ceremonies were difficult on everyone. Ed was not handling the situation well. HM2 Shocker, the man he frequently pestered in his tent, the man he had threatened to make his little spoon—his old trucker buddy—was now gone forever, and so was a young man with an even younger wife and child at home. *This is war. This is the shit you don't see in a damn movie, and there is nothing glamorous about this. I hope and pray Jenny is OK.*

Anytime there was a death or a significant action against the base, communication was limited to official business only. The marines called it "river city." They were in river city, and Ed could not reach Jenny. The condition alleviated the chance some knucklehead would leak information about a death to his family or the news media, or call the family of the deceased. It was inconvenient but necessary.

※※

Jenny's reaction to the news was devastating. When she first heard reports of an aircraft from Camp Lejeune being shot down, her thoughts were horrible. She couldn't stop imagining Ed being on the plane. As time drew on, she realized she would have been contacted had it been him, but as reports came through, she had no doubt it was Ed's unit, and he had lost two of his men. She knew he was hurting, and she couldn't do anything for him. She was more worried about who had lost their loved ones. It was difficult for her to feel good about not losing Ed when she knew someone had lost her spouse.

She soon learned whom the unfortunate young woman was, and she had no idea how to comfort her. Jenny realized there was nothing she could say or do to ease the pain, and she had no way of relating to the woman's disaster. The woman was a widow at twenty, with a one-year-old daughter. How could she possibly know that level of pain? Jenny went to Andrea's home and helped care for the baby. She helped clean the home and listened to her. She didn't attempt to tell her she knew how she felt. She could not know. It was hard on Jenny, but she remained vigilant in her efforts. Andrea's family and her fallen sailor's family made their way to Jacksonville. When Andrea's mom arrived, Jenny was relieved. Jenny stayed in contact and checked on her often.

✹✹

Ed, the team, and the squadron resumed operations. They proceeded to perform their duties with conviction and without fear. When they were finally relieved and finished their last shift, it was a bittersweet moment, and all of them let out a sigh of relief. They began their preparation for redeployment. As they had entered, they would return. They were transported to the MAG, staged, and awaited their Freedom Bird home. Reunited with the commander and Chief Stahl, they all enjoyed a couple of days before their departure.

"I know why you were pulling your hair out," Chief Stahl said. "These flight surgeons are a pain in the neck." The day they departed, Ed hoped he would never return to this hellhole.

11

Career Choices

~

Jenny, the kids, and the other spouses awaited the team's arrival at Marine Aircraft Group Twenty-Six headquarters. Standing beside Jenny were Andrea and her child, who had reunited with their loved one weeks prior under much different circumstances. Jenny admired Andrea's courage and commitment to the team. She didn't believe she could muster the strength to participate in a welcome home so soon after losing a loved one, nor did she believe she could ever forgive her nation for a loss so significant if she were the young woman. Andrea's presence made the others feel guilty about how happy they were their loved ones were returning today. *All the times I have wished Ed would just leave, and this poor girl will never be with her husband again. I will never think that again.*

As the buses arrived, the women were careful not to show too much excitement until Andrea spoke.

"All of you were there for me and my baby girl in our darkest hour. I did not come here to make any of you feel bad. I came here to celebrate the return of our team and to be with you to welcome home your husbands. Quit acting like a bunch of Sallys. Cheer up and get ready to show your men some love, dammit, or you are going to piss me off, and I will leave!"

The women were all shocked. Then they huddled around her with smiles on their faces and tears streaming from their eyes as they hugged her and her little one.

"Get off me, you crazy wenches," Andrea said. "Save it for them."

Jenny laughed and said, "Thank you for coming. We all appreciate you being here and setting us straight. We love you!"

The action was a clear reminder to all of them that their loved ones were not the only ones who shared deep bonds.

The buses all filed into the circle and halted. As the doors opened, marines and sailors filed out into their respective platoons for the ceremony. The commanding general, commanding officer, chaplain, and sergeants major made brief remarks about their mission and had a moment of silence for the loss of the crew. The MAG dismissed.

Jenny expected Ed to follow his normal postdeployment routine of grabbing his bags first so he could make a quick exit, but instead she heard Clara say, "Daddy." Ed swept his kids up into his arms instantly and hugged them tightly. He moved to Jenny and rested his head on her shoulder, with the kids in his arms. Jenny thought he looked ten years older. He was thin, his eyes dark, and his hair more gray than when he departed. She knew the loss took as much of a toll on him as it had taken on her. She wanted to cry, but didn't want to upset him any further.

"I missed you and love you all," he said. "Thank you for coming." Ed saw his friend's wife and set the kids down. He walked to her and the little girl.

"I am so sorry for your loss," he said. He bent over and hugged her as she wept in his arms. "Thank you for coming. I cannot imagine how hard this must be for you, but we appreciate you being here. If there is anything we can do, please call." They stood holding each other for a few more moments before Ed patted her on the back, rubbed her shoulder, and said, "There are some other folks who want to say hello." The entire team had formed a line to greet and thank her.

The moment took a lot out of Ed. Jenny could tell he wanted to cry but wouldn't allow himself to do so in front of his team. He moved to the pile of gear, retrieved his bags, and moved to the parking lot. Jenny and the kids met him on the way to the van.

"Are you ready to leave?" she asked.

"Yes. I'll call them all later, but I need to get out of here." Jenny loaded the kids as Ed tossed his bags in the vehicle. They piled in and headed home.

Jenny attempted to talk to Ed a few times on the ride home. His answers were short. The kids asked him about the helicopters and if he had fun flying. He did the best he could to answer their questions and not to be mean, but she knew he didn't want to talk. There was no traffic, and they made it home quickly. When they reached the house, Ed took his gear to the porch. Jenny unloaded the kids and brought them inside.

"I'm going to jump in the tub and soak for a while," Ed said.

"Let your daddy get cleaned up, and then he will play with you," Jenny told the kids. She hoped that would give him some peace and time to calm down.

Ed went to the small bathroom and stripped out of his grimy uniform. It reeked from days of travel. He threw it in the corner, ran a bath, and climbed in the small tub. *I need a house with a tub I fit in. I can barely sit in this thing. I know how a child feels getting bathed in the kitchen sink!* He smiled at the thought. His mind drifted to seeing his friend's widow earlier, and he couldn't contain his tears. He sat in the tiny tub, weeping like a child. *Maybe I should put some soap in my eyes in case Jenny comes in, so I don't look like a little girl.* When he saw No More Tears was the only shampoo on the shelf of the tub, he laughed aloud. At least he still had a sick sense of humor.

Is all of this worth it? he thought. *I came back in for many reasons. I have fulfilled most of them. Maybe it's time to move on before I lose my family or they lose me. I thought coming back in would fill the void left from Somalia, and it has just made a bigger one. I knew deep down that vengeance was never the answer and should have followed my faith. My dreams are not gone. I just have more faces in them. My faith is growing stronger. My family is better off financially, but I have missed my kids' childhood, and I don't know where my relationship with Jenny stands. What am I going to do?*

Ed sat in the tub, praying for an answer, a sign, or a revelation on what to do next. Nothing came, so he got out, dried off, and decided to spend time with the ones he loved.

❋❋

Jenny sat in the living room, watching cartoons with the kids, waiting for Ed to finish and wondering what he was thinking. She was worrying he would stay in there all day so he wouldn't have to be around them, when she heard the bathroom door open. He came out wearing a towel and went to their room. After a moment, he walked into the living room in shorts and a T-shirt. He plopped down in between the kids and started wrestling with Christopher. Clara jumped on him as he submitted to their brawling. Jenny sat smiling until he grabbed her leg, pulling her to the floor. A cage match ensued in the middle of the living room. The kids tag team was victorious over their parents, and they relished the moment.

For the rest of the afternoon, the family enjoyed their time with one another, drawing, watching television, and eating snacks. Jenny was glad Ed snapped out of his mood so quickly and took advantage of the moment.

That evening after supper, when the kids were asleep, Ed asked, "Jenny, do you want to keep doing this?"

"What do you want to do?"

"Babe, I asked what you wanted."

Jenny, shocked by the question, asked, "Ed, are you OK?"

"I'm fine, but with everything that happened, I think we should take some time to evaluate if this is what we want to keep doing."

Jenny looked puzzled. "I don't want to lose you, but we are doing well. We need to work on our relationship. I would like to have you home more than you have been the last few years, but you're doing what you wanted to do."

"I still love this job. I just don't want to be like so many people at the end of their careers: broke, married three times, with their kids hating them for never being there for them. I also don't want to come home in a flag-draped coffin."

Ed's last words hit Jenny like a ton of bricks, and she crumpled from the weight. She looked at him as tears filled her eyes.

"Please don't talk like that. If you don't want to end up like that, then don't. We can make things work. We just have to work together. We love each other, we love the kids, and we have faith. That's all we need to raise a family and have a strong marriage. I will support whatever you want to do. I always have, and I always will. I love you even when you are an asshole."

Ed laughed and said, "I'm good at being an asshole. Dad told me to stick to things I'm good at!" They hugged and enjoyed the rest of the evening together.

※※

Ed and the team completed postdeployment training in the following days. Ed and Chief Miller coordinated leave for the sailors returning to their permanent duty station and ensured all of them checked out of MAG. When all the administrative tasks were complete, Ed submitted for and checked out on leave. He and the family decided to head home to Illinois again. Ed knew his brother Pat would be home on leave from Afghanistan the same time, and Ed looked forward to seeing him.

Pat had recently received the Silver Star for combat actions in the Uruzgan Valley. He, his team, and a group of Afghan National Police fought a tremendous two-hour battle with a local militia. Pat's group was severely outnumbered and barely managed to survive before a not-so-quick reactionary force came to their aid. Ed thought Pat should have received a higher award, but knew all too well the politics of the awards system.

Jenny packed their gear and readied the children for travel. The kids were troopers in the car by now. They had logged more miles in their short lives than most adults do in a lifetime. Ed dreaded the ride, but could not wait to get home, fish, and see Pat. He also wanted to see Pat's new addition to the Brannan clan. He and his wife had shucked out another baby boy, a darling little redhead.

They loaded the van and hit the road. Jenny dreaded the ride too. Ed was still insane when he drove. He gave new meaning to the term "road rage." It didn't take long for him to lose his patience. Five hours into their trip outside of Winston-Salem, a new SUV kept swerving in and out of traffic, dueling with another car. Ed eased back and let the man in front of him. Jenny could tell he was growing frustrated with the driver. The man kept switching lanes and nearly clipped the front of the van. Ed lost it. He pushed the accelerator to the floor as an endless stream of curse words flew from his mouth. He pulled beside the SUV, glared at the man, and gave him a one-fingered salute. The man returned the gesture, which infuriated Ed as he maneuvered the van toward the SUV.

"Ed, this is not NASCAR!" Jenny yelled. "You have babies in the car."

"That prick is going to kill someone," Ed yelled back. He realized he was taking things too far and backed off the SUV. He stayed on the vehicle's rear end, shaking his fist at the driver as the man kept flying him the bird.

When they approached a tollbooth, Ed's demeanor changed immediately. He smiled widely and let out an evil laugh as he pointed to the stopped traffic ahead. The man must have realized he was about to meet someone crazier than he was, because as they approached the stopped vehicles and Ed undid his seatbelt, the SUV swerved all the way to the right of the traffic, nearly hitting four vehicles in the other lanes. He sped over to an emergency lane and exited the interstate.

Ed looked crushed. "Shit. I didn't see that coming."

"You're an idiot," Jenny said. "What if that crazy bastard had a gun?"

Ed grinned. "Damn shame getting shot with your own gun."

Thankfully, the rest of the day was not exciting. They decided to stay in a hotel at the halfway point for the evening. They chose one with a pool for the kids to play in. When the kids were worn out, they returned to the room for their favorite meal—pizza—and some much-needed rest. In the morning, they proceeded to the lake.

When they arrived, Pat and his family were already there. The NARMY brothers greeted each other with a "Fook you," hugged, and BS'd as their wives laughed at them. Ed found his nephews and grabbed the new addition. They all enjoyed the company. Karen, Ed's mother, joined them and explained she had planned a welcome-home party for them both, so they didn't have to worry about going to see everyone. *That is considerate, but you didn't think to ask and you planned it at your hangout,* Ed thought. *Now I have to deal with everyone's bullshit anyway. Not that I wouldn't be out here anyway. Oh well. Good job, Mom.*

The kids flocked to Grandma and Papa, the moms talked, and the brothers found some beer. It didn't take long for Ed and Pat to disappear. They grabbed a couple of fishing poles and headed out to a dock with a cooler of beer. They talked about their deployments. Ed knew Pat had to return in two weeks, and that scared him. He told Pat he was considering leaving the military again.

Pat laughed and said, "Yeah, because you were such a good civilian."

Ed giggled and replied, "Good point, asshole." They decided to wear their uniforms for the first part of the welcome-home party so their parents could get pictures of them together, and then they proceeded to drink.

The next morning, they headed to Karen's to clean up, shave, and get into uniform. They made their grand entrance an hour late after stopping at three different bars. They would have been much later if Jenny and Pat's wife had not called them every five minutes and threatened divorce. Ed couldn't believe how many people showed up. He didn't know that many people still liked him, but then he realized they were most likely there to see Pat. He laughed to himself and thought, *Oh well, I'll still have more fun than anyone else.*

※※

If looks could kill, Ed would have dropped in his tracks. Jenny stood there with a beady death stare trained right on him. Ed looked around and pointed at his brother, shrugging his shoulders as if he was not responsible and smiling from ear to ear. His humor was not lost on her, and her mood lightened with his childish behavior.

That asshole always knows how to get out of trouble, she thought. *He is worse than a child.* Ed's grandma gave him a tongue-lashing for being late, and he did the same thing to her. He just sat on her lap, and she melted. Jenny realized that the people he allowed in couldn't stay mad at him.

※※

The family got their pictures, although the Brannan boys always managed to get a middle finger in their pose. Ed's cousins came to see them, and they took a picture together. It was the first picture the five of them had taken in twenty-plus years. Following the pictures, Ed couldn't wait to get out of his uniform and began taking off his clothes in front of everyone. Ed's brother Andy jerked Ed's pants down while he took his shirt off.

Ed stood there in front of a crowd of over a hundred men, women, and children with his trousers around his ankles as if nothing were the matter. Jenny ran up and pulled his trousers up for him. He shrugged, pulled them back off, and put on some shorts. Embarrassed for him, Jenny shook her head and walked away. Ed laughed and headed for the cooler.

Ed overheard his dad tell his aunt, "Did you really think he was going to let his little brother get the best of him?"

The party was amazing. Pat introduced Ed to friends of his from Springfield, two Vietnam veterans, Kaiser and Rich. Kaiser served with the Rangers and 173rd, and Rich with the 101st Airborne. Ed thought they were both great men. Kaiser was more wild than Rich, but you could tell they had been friends for many years, and Ed knew the bond had been forged in their similar experiences. Ed stood there with the older men, forging his own bond with them, and decided he had two NARMY prospects. As they talked, Ed saw Pat on the phone, moving away from the gathering. Ed excused himself from their discussion and walked toward Pat.

As he approached, Ed could tell whatever Pat was hearing was not good news. He grabbed Pat's arm and led him farther from the party to a friend's camper. He opened the door and put him inside. Ed stood outside the hatch listening to the conversation. As he expected, their day just went to shit in a hurry. Pat got off the phone, frazzled.

"Are you OK?" Ed asked.

"I just lost two of my guys."

"I can get the truck, I can tell everyone to leave, or I will do whatever you want to do."

"I just want to drink."

"We can do that too." Ed grabbed his brother and said, "No need to tell anyone about this right now. They won't know how to react, and they will try to smother you. If it comes out, so be it. I will keep people off you, bro."

They returned to the party visibly shaken. Jenny and Pat's wife knew something was going on, but knew to stay out of whatever was going on with their husbands. Karen pushed the issue until Pat exploded and said, "If you need to know, two of my men were killed." She wished she hadn't asked.

"We are not going to discuss this today," Ed said. "Have I made myself clear? Bring it up again, and we are leaving."

The subject wasn't mentioned by any of the partygoers. People stayed and mingled for a while, but the tension made the party uncomfortable, and most decided to leave. By the end of the evening, only family and friends who were former military remained. Ed, his brothers, and friends walked over to a fire to toast Pat's fallen brothers. Pat reminisced about them and shared stories as the others listened. An awkward silence fell on the gathering.

"Pat, these dudes look like some good NARMY candidates to me," Ed said.

Pat smiled and said, "You are an idiot, but that's not a bad idea, considering what has gone on today. You have everything?"

"I'm sure I can find it. We just have to make a call and get approval from a third member."

Pat laughed loudly. "You took that shit way too seriously."

NARMY ceremonial wine in hand, a call and approval from Uncle Jerry complete, fire lit, and chairs in hand, Ed began the story of the NARMY. The recruits laughed at the fool's storytelling ability and gestures as he and Pat taught them the salute and greeting. With the command, "Burn in," the recruits threw their chairs on top of the fire. The NARMY grew in strength by seven members that evening, and the campground lost nine lawn chairs, because Pat burned two for his fallen brothers.

The devastation of losing a friend or loved one due to combat is something that is unexplainable. It can drive you to make rash decisions if you're not careful. Fortunately, Ed got a unique opportunity upon his third return from Iraq. Field Medical Service School (FMSS) had a position available as an instructor. With this type of duty comes great promotion opportunity, no deployments, and the ability to stay in the area.

This is a no-brainer, Ed thought. Jenny, on the other hand, was still reeling from the loss, dealing with her grief, and supporting her friend. With Ed's conversation and Pat's loss fresh on her mind, she wondered if moving on would be a better choice for the family. Every decision for a career military member is a family decision if you plan on staying married. Ed explained the benefits of instructor duty, and they decided to try it.

12

Moving Up

~

The offer was not as final as Ed thought. The following day, he received a call from a chief who used to work at the air station. He instructed Ed to pick up his service record from Camp Lejeune and report to Camp Johnson for an interview with FMSS's command master chief.

"The master chief has a lot of appointments today, so you need to be over here in fifteen minutes," he said, and hung up the phone. *Fifteen minutes?* Ed thought. *There is no way I can drive to Camp Lejeune, get to the personnel services detachment, get my record, and then drive to Camp Johnson in fifteen minutes. They are out of their minds.* Ed ran into admin at the clinic, told Chief Miller he was going to FMSS for an interview, and sprinted to his van. He may have set a land speed record in the old Rooster that morning. He didn't reach the master chief's office in fifteen minutes, but he managed to get there in under thirty and still waited an hour to see him.

Master Chief Munn was a tall, well-built older man with thin-rimmed glasses perched on his nose. Ed knew from the bubble and wings on his chest he was a force recon corpsman and guessed that he and his old nemesis Dark Helmet were comrades.

His suspicions were verified when the master chief said, "Blackhawk, Master Chief Johnson says you are a pain in the ass."

"I do not like being called Blackhawk, Master Chief," Ed said.

The master chief chuckled at Ed's response. "Come on in. No one likes the names that miserable old prick calls them."

That's a fact, Ed thought as he entered the office. The master chief told him to sit on the couch as he sat across from him in a chair. He asked him about his army experience, navy assignments, and combat assignments. Ed explained his career path.

The master chief then asked, "Why do you want to be a field med instructor?"

"I want to train corpsmen for combat service with the marines. I think I have the experience to do a good job."

"Any other reason?"

"No, Master Chief."

The master chief grinned and replied, "Good. Let's go meet the skipper."

Ed wasn't sure how the interview with the master chief went, but he assumed it went well if he was going to see the old man. He followed the master chief around the conference room of the command suite into the executive passageway and stood at the skipper's hatch as the master chief went in the commanding officer's office.

Ed heard a voice say, "HM2 Brannan, report."

Ed marched to the center of the commanding officer's desk, stopped three paces in front of the seated man, stood at attention, and said, "HM2 Brannan reporting as ordered, sir." The man before him was average height and build, with thin gray hair and glasses. He looked in his late fifties and spoke softly but directly.

He introduced himself. "HM2, I am Captain Alfred, the commanding officer of FMSS. I have been in the navy for thirty-five years, commissioned for the last twenty, and was a senior chief prior to that. It is nice to meet you. I have heard great things about you."

"Thank you, sir. It is nice to meet you too, sir."

The commanding officer stood and said, "At ease, Petty Officer," as he gestured for Ed and the master chief to join him at a small conference table at the side of the office. He took his seat, the master chief sat, and Ed took his chair. Ed sat straight at a modified position of attention, awkwardly nervous.

The commanding officer noticed his demeanor and said, "Please relax, HM2. I just want to know more about your career and family." Ed relaxed as they began to talk. The commanding officer discussed the training and daily schedule. He talked about the rigors his instructors had to deal with and the stress it put on their families.

"HM2, I understand you have recently returned from a third tour in three years. If you come here, you will spend a lot of time here. Are you sure this is what you and your family want to do?"

"Sir, my wife and I have already discussed the operational temperature of a training command, and we both agreed this is a good opportunity and the right thing for both of us," Ed said. The commanding officer seemed impressed by Ed's answers. He stood, and Ed rose to attention.

He reached his hand out, shook Ed's, and said, "Welcome aboard, HM2. We will have Personnel cut your orders ASAP. You are dismissed."

"Thank you, sir." Ed stepped to the side, did an about-face, and marched from the room. Ed waited outside in the executive passageway for the master chief.

The master chief came out and said, "Well, I guess you are hired. I will let Chief Day know and give your command a call to let them know to expect to see your orders in a few days."

"Thank you, Master Chief," Ed said and took the back hatch to the parking lot. As he left the building, he thought, *These people are crazy. I have never seen or heard of orders posting that fast. We will see.*

Ed headed to the van and went back to New River to brief Chief Miller.

As Ed entered the back entrance of the New River Clinic, he heard Chief Miller yell, "Damn, that was quick!"

Ed looked surprised and hollered back, "What do you mean?"

"You know what I mean. Chief Day already called and told me you nailed the interview and they are calling Personnel."

"I told them what they wanted to hear," Ed said.

Chief Miller laughed and said, "Brother, if you play your cards right, you will be a chief leaving that gig." Ed knew the potential for advancement with a successful tour as an instructor, but he also knew the potential for failure. Good sailors went and succeeded, but just as many went and screwed up. He only hoped he would be a success.

Ed finished the day and headed home to tell Jenny the news. They were contemplating buying a home in the area if he could get the orders, and he wanted to seriously discuss the opportunity with her. The deployments, Jenny's job, and her thrifty spending had brought them out of debt and set them up to start a new life. This would be an ideal time for them to continue to build their relationship and family. The kids were quickly outgrowing the small base accommodations, and their belongings were beginning to crowd the space. It was time to have their own home again.

When Ed arrived, he and Jenny sat and discussed the interview. Jenny asked him about the commanding officer, the master chief, and what he thought of the command. He told her what Chief Miller said about the career potential and asked, "Do you think we should look for a house?"

"I would love to, but we should probably wait till you get settled in over there."

"You're probably right. We need to wait and see if I get the orders. I am still skeptical if all of this is going to pan out the way everyone is saying it will."

Jenny laughed. "You are always expecting the worst, love."

Christopher and Clara came running in, and Ed asked them, "Do you two want a new house with your own yard?"

The kids jumped around, giggling and singing, "New house, new house, new house!" They all smiled and rejoiced at the thought of having their own home, praying never to be in a rundown old trailer again.

The following week, Ed received orders from navy personnel command to report to journeyman instructor training in Norfolk, Virginia, en route to Field Medical Service School for three-year orders in

September. Ed found receiving the orders was bittersweet for him. They marked the end of one chapter of his navy career and the beginning of the next.

The time frame left him little time to check out or prepare for training. In a sense, this was a relief for Ed. He focused solely on checking out and little on saying good-bye. The clinic and his comrades prepared a going-away ceremony on his last day. Keeping with tradition, they presented Ed with a paddle with the command logo, his name, warfare devices, the words "Fair winds and following seas," and his favorite saying, "Kick down the door and shoot 'em in the face." The commander and Chief Miller made brief remarks about Ed's time at New River and turned the floor over to him. Ed kept his statement short as well.

"Thank you. It has been an honor serving with all of you. I will always remember you, and I hope to serve with you again." They all shook hands and spoke briefly before he departed for the last time. As Ed got in his vehicle, leaving the clinic for the last time, he couldn't help but feel sad and wish he could stay on for a few more missions.

He returned home to Jenny and the kids that evening to pack and enjoy a couple of days before departing for two weeks of training in Virginia. There was no stress packing for this departure. Jenny and the kids found no reason to lock themselves in their room, and he had no gear to organize. They had grown over the last few years, and he was maturing, finally becoming the husband and father Jenny wanted. Prior to leaving home, Ed called an old friend who was now stationed in Virginia, Dr. Gallagher. He told him he would be in the area for a couple of weeks and would like to see him, Bug, and Reilly if their schedule permitted.

Ed arrived in Virginia for training, expecting a two-week formal instructor course. He realized immediately that he should have remembered navy training failed to meet his expectations. The course was designed for entry-level instructors and was easily completed in four days. The instructors were professional, and the material was good and formatted for sailors who had never spoken in public. Training consisted of an introduction, a five-minute class, a non-media class, a multimedia class, and three instructor peer reviews.

Ed completed his training in three days, but had to report to class for the entire two weeks. He spent most of his days at the navy lodge, reading and hanging out at restaurants. He did get to meet with Tom and Bug several times and enjoyed catching up and spending time with them.

When Ed returned to Camp Swampy, he checked into FMSS with Chief Day. Chief Day assigned him HM2 Tutko as a sponsor. HM2 Tutko had served with Second Marine Division in Kosovo and Iraq. HM2 Tutko was of Hispanic descent, around five foot nine and two hundred and ninety pounds of pure muscle, with no neck to speak of. He practiced mixed martial arts and had lifted weights since he was seven or eight, but had the demeanor of a huge cuddly teddy bear until he was provoked.

HM2 Tutko was a bit standoffish when he first met Ed. Chief Day had spoken highly of Ed, and HM2 Tutko didn't know what to expect. Ed won him over within a few hours, and they became instant friends. HM2 Tutko had pushed several classes as a lead instructor and was a wealth of knowledge concerning the workings of the schoolhouse. He took Ed around the command, introducing him to everyone and getting him checked into all the administrative shops. Field Med fell under Marine Corps Training Command. It was one of a few marine commands that had navy commanding officers.

The command master chief assigned Ed to the master-at-arms, Chief Day's section. The master-at-arms was in charge of security, legal, and students awaiting training/transfer (SAT/T). Daily duties included mustering and PTing the SAT/T platoon, handling legal issues, and conducting inspections, as well as instructing classes for platoons. The daily routine began at 0400 and did not end until 1700 to 1900. The work was grueling, exhausting, and rewarding.

Ed's collateral duties allowed him to teach with Fourth Platoon. The wife of Fourth Platoon's lead instructor, HM1 Kmetz, was a local Realtor. He and Ed became good friends, and Ed asked him if his wife would be interested in helping Jenny and him find a home.

HM1 Kmetz and his wife, Tina, were more than willing to help. Jenny and Ed discussed the price range they could afford, and Tina began searching for homes. The Veterans Administration home loan program was a wonderful program for service members. Ed and Jenny applied for certification through the VA and worked with an Internet mortgage lender to find a competitive lender within their budget. When they received a prequalification letter, they were ready to start looking. Tina found several homes within their price range and with the modest requirements they were looking for: three bedrooms, one bathroom, and a small yard in a decent neighborhood near a school.

Ed, Jenny, and the kids met with Tina at Exit Real Estate in downtown Jacksonville near city hall and Camp Johnson early Saturday morning. Tina had a list of three properties she wanted to show them that day. They decided to follow her to the properties, so they could discuss each property alone as they moved to the next.

The first house they visited was a petite three-bedroom bungalow with a converted front porch, three bedrooms, one bath, and a small yard. It was a nice home, but the property owners were looking for a quick sell and seemed more interested in selling to a property manager than a private owner. The home was five miles from Camp Johnson in a beautiful older neighborhood that they were interested in, but the house didn't meet their needs or draw their attraction. As they proceeded to the next location, they both agreed they wouldn't make an offer on the property.

The next home was two blocks away from the first, and as soon as they approached the home, it drew their attention. The house had a beautifully groomed, plush, green front yard with gorgeous shrubs, a partial brick front, a fireplace, and vinyl siding on a third-of-an-acre lot with a blacktop driveway. They pulled in the driveway, parked, and admired the house. Jenny gathered the kids as Ed got out and looked around the front of the home and scanned the roof, construction, foundation, and front porch. Tina joined them at the porch as an elderly woman opened the front door. Ms. Bourneman, an elderly woman and recent widow, had listed the house and was eager to talk about the home she and her husband had built and lived in for over forty years.

The showing turned into a trip down memory lane for Ms. Bourneman, but Ed, Jenny, and the kids enjoyed listening to the woman's stories. The home was meticulously maintained, but in desperate need of updating. The décor was from the early seventies, with multicolored plush and shag carpeting. The Bournemans were obviously John Wayne fans, because every room had a photo or movie relic of his on display. The home was a Sear's model home from the fifties: three bedrooms, one bathroom, kitchen, dinette, laundry room, central heat and air, with a large backyard and nice outside shed for lawn equipment and gardening supplies.

By the end of the history lesson, Ed and Jenny had made a decision. They all thanked Ms. Bourneman for the tour of her home and headed outside. Ed and Jenny told Tina they didn't need to see the other home, and they would meet her at the office to make an offer.

On the ride to Tina's office, the family all talked about the home as the kids laid claim to what rooms would be theirs. Ed and Jenny discussed the price, offer, and the VA process. Ed explained the VA required an appraisal by a VA-approved appraiser and that the loan approval would be based on that appraisal. He also told Jenny that based on his credit, the VA option would be the only way they could afford it, and if the house appraised lower than what Ms. Bourneman had it listed at, they may not get it. When they arrived at Tina's office, they went inside to begin the paperwork for the offer.

"Tina, my credit is not good," Ed said. "We have rebuilt it over the last few years and are prequalified for a VA loan, but if the house doesn't appraise for what she has it listed for, we can't buy it."

"We can make the offer for the list price with a clause contingent on the VA appraisal and give Ms. Bourneman the option to accept the VA appraisal or decline," Tina said. Ed and Jenny both agreed to the option and proceeded with the paperwork. With the arrangements made for the offer and appraisal, they awaited the results.

Ms. Bourneman and her Realtor accepted the offer, and Tina scheduled a VA appraiser to evaluate the home. Ed and Jenny anxiously awaited the results for two weeks. When they received the appraisal, they were heartbroken. The appraisal came in ten thousand dollars under the list price. They were both positive their offer would be declined, and they would have to begin searching for another home.

To their surprise, later that day, Tina called with the best news they had received in many years.

"Ms. Bourneman has accepted your offer, and we can set a final inspection and closing as soon as you can finalize the loan." Ed and Jenny were ecstatic with the joyous news. They had a home!

The loan process went smoothly. The final inspection came with a couple of hiccups. The home needed moderate electrical updates to meet VA standards, but Ed and Jenny had enough in savings to cover the cost and proceed with closing. Closing was scheduled, and the family received the keys to their new home on a beautiful Saturday morning in a local lawyer's office, with Tina, Ms. Bourneman, her Realtor, and a lawyer the loan company hired for closing. Ed, Jenny, and the kids left the office and headed directly to their new abode. The joyous feeling they all experienced as they turned the key and entered the home for the first time could never be expressed in words.

Ed and Jenny found that their humble belongings may have overrun their base home, but they barely filled a third of their new house. Fortunately, nothing could break their spirits. Ed stayed busy at work, and Jenny moved the household goods during the day. In the evening, they both moved the large items. They were quickly becoming a formidable team, and the kids were enjoying the new space and the adventure of their new area. The family made quick work of the move and checkout from housing. It was exhausting for all of them, but well worth their efforts, and they had an excuse to enjoy their favorite dinner—pizza—in the evening.

By the end of the first week, the move was complete, and they settled into their home. Now the process of making it their own could begin. The process would have to be slow. They had exhausted themselves and most of their savings during the move, but they made it happen together.

Things at work were going well for Ed as well. He quickly adapted to his roles at Field Med and was recognized as a good instructor and SAT/T platoon leader. His collateral duties within Fourth Platoon did not go unnoticed either. His rapport with the other instructors and students allowed him greater responsibility within the command, and he slowly got more opportunity as time drew on. In August, HM1 Kmetz was selected for chief petty officer, and his position in training as Fourth Platoon's medical adviser was available.

"Chief, I would like to request to go to training and assume the duties of Fourth Platoon's medical adviser," Ed told Chief Day.

"There are a lot of other instructors who want that position, but I will recommend you if that's what you want to do," Chief Day said.

"That is the reason I came here, and I would appreciate any assistance you can provide. I understand if I do not get the position based on seniority, but I want to put in the request."

"Route the request and see what happens, Shipmate."

"Thank you, Chief." Ed routed his request that day and went to discuss his request with the new Chief Select Kmetz.

Chief Select Kmetz was busy with chief transition training, but Ed found him in the training hooch.

"Chief Select, I know your position is open, and I was wondering if you think I am ready to come over to training."

"I can't think of anyone else I would rather have take over the platoon, and I will personally recommend you to the training officer."

"Awesome! I know that doesn't mean I will get it, but thank you. That means a lot to me!" The men shook hands, and Ed headed back to work.

That evening, Ed told Jenny he had requested to go to training and was waiting on a decision. He explained he wasn't sure he would get the position because he was not as senior as the other candidates were, but he wanted the opportunity.

"Honey bunny, you are great at what you do, and if you really want something, you always get it," she said.

Ed laughed and said, "I hope you are right, love."

The next morning, Ed was called over to the assistant training officer's office. The assistant training officer, training officer, and military adviser were waiting in the office when he arrived. Ed knocked and awaited orders to enter. He presented himself, and they told him to sit down. They explained to him that they had received his request, and Chief Select Kmetz had recommended him as his replacement. They also stated that he was not as senior as the other candidates were, but they wanted to interview him for the position, and they would make their decision that week. They proceeded with the interview and dismissed him. Ed left with little confidence he would receive the position, but knew the worst they would say was no.

At the end of the week, Ed received another call to report to the training officer's office. He was sure it was to receive news he wasn't selected for the position, and he prepared himself for the letdown as he walked to the meeting. When he arrived, the training officer was alone in his office, and the sight only confirmed his suspicion.

He knocked, and the training officer announced, "Enter." Ed entered the room and stood before the lieutenant.

"HM2 Brannan, I would like to congratulate you and welcome you to the training department. You will be the medical adviser for Fourth Platoon, and we expect great things from you."

Ed, flabbergasted by the news, stood with his mouth gaping wide open. He was speechless.

"HM2, did you hear me?"

Ed snapped out of his amazement. "Yes sir, I am just surprised. I thought I was called over for a different reason. Thank you, sir. I will not disappoint you."

The lieutenant laughed. "I do not expect you will, HM2. Please check out of the MAA shack and get with Senior Chief and the leading petty officer in training so you can begin immediate turnover with Chief Select Kmetz. Our next class will be on deck in two weeks."

"Yes, sir. Thank you, sir." Ed floated from the room as he headed back to the MAA shack to tell Chief Day and HM2 Tutko the news.

When he arrived at the shack, HM2 Tutko and Chief already knew of his selection and congratulated him. Ed told Chief Day thank you and asked HM2 Tutko to help him out with the classes due to his experience. He began the check-out process and proceeded back to the training department to see Senior and the leading petty officer to begin his new position.

Ed wondered if there would be any animosity among his peers because of the selection and didn't want it to disrupt their working relationship, but he was proud of the selection. Fortunately, since he was working with like-minded professionals, the only thing that mattered was training corpsmen to save marines, so there was no need to worry about pettiness. The following months, everyone bonded together and united to train the best in the business: the marine docs!

In September, another advancement exam came around. Like the ones prior, Jenny and the kids allowed Ed the time to study and prepare for the exam; and like the previous exams, when he left the room, he felt dumber. The bad thing about the navy exam was the wait for the results. The two- to three-month wait was grueling, and the best policy was to just begin studying for the next cycle.

Results came during field week as Ed's platoon was participating in the litter course. The litter course consisted of a quarter-mile mud-filled obstacle course in which four corpsmen maneuver a mannequin on a collapsible litter through simulated combat while being stressed and PT'd by the instructors. The instructors demonstrated the course prior to the students going through. This showed a couple of things. One, that the instructors could do and were willing to do everything they subjected the students to, and two, that the course was maneuverable. The assistant training officer arrived with the list of staff and students who had advanced. He announced the students first, and everyone congratulated the selected personnel.

When that evolution was complete, he called all the instructors to the side and said, "Two staff were selected as first classes." Everyone anxiously awaited the names. The assistant training officer continued. "Congratulations, HM1 Brannan and HM1 Pritchett." Ed looked at HM1 Pritchett and smiled. Everyone congratulated them, and they went back to work. Ed couldn't wait to get back to call Jenny.

By the end of the day, everyone was exhausted from the events and filthy from the exercises. Ed decided to shower, change, and head home to tell his family the outstanding news. When he arrived home, he pretended to be exhausted as usual and asked Jenny to draw him a bath.

"You look horrible, honey," Jenny said. "I will get you a bath and get you some supper."

Ed smiled. "I almost forgot. We made first class!"

Jenny jumped up and down. "I can't believe you pulled that crap. Congratulations! I love you!"

The following day, in a small ceremony in the command suite passageway, the commanding officer, executive officer, and command master chief had the families of Ed and Petty Officer Pritchett come up and pin them to HM1. The lives of Ed, Jenny, and the kids were steadily moving forward and finally on the right course. The commanding officer released him for the day to enjoy the time with his family.

13

Family Matters

As Ed's career blossomed, opportunity began to knock for Jenny. Chief Kmetz's wife, Tina, the family's Realtor, was also a postmaster. Tina recommended Jenny take the postal exam and apply for rural carrier positions in the area. Jenny requested the exam and awaited the test.

Meanwhile, Ed spent his days at work and evenings at home with Jenny and the kids. The command had an interesting group of instructors. They were all close friends and relied on one another at work and at home. They came from all walks of life, and the conversations in the instructor hooch were on a spectrum from very serious to outright insane.

Two months earlier, the training department had shifted from two primary instructors with training team members to a marine adviser, primary medical adviser, and two medical advisors with teaching team members. The changes allowed the instructors more face time with the students and more hands-on training. It also allowed more interaction with one another, which was dangerous, to say the least.

The training company consisted of four primary marine advisors, all marine infantry: Staff Sergeants Martinez, Gomes, Eichen, and Lipczak. The four primary medical advisors—Ed, HM2 Avila, HM1 Pritchett, and HM1 Sweeney—were all corpsmen with significant combat experience in ground, logistics, and air operations.

Each platoon had additional members that complemented the primaries' experience. Staff Sergeant Martinez and Ed's platoon had HM1 Schulter and HM2 Washburn, both with significant ground combat experience. The objective at Field Med was to train the students in all aspects of FMF medicine, so HM2 Washburn and HM1 Schulter's experience was invaluable to the platoon's training. All staff members outside of training were assigned as training team members to each of the platoons. They instructed classes and participated in major training evolutions. Ed was fortunate to have a robust team, with Chief Kmetz, HM1 Ayeni, and a female lance corporal who was the command's assistant armor, rounding out their training team.

The platoons constantly competed, but it was for the benefit of the students, not the instructors. Pennants were given for each platoon's guide-on for academic or physical triumph. The pennants pushed the students to form their own bond and team, and gave them bragging rights within the company. All of the instructors monitored one another and advised one another on ways to improve performance. The end goal was not to outperform one another, but to produce an outstanding FMF corpsman to send to the fleet.

Preparing a diverse group of eighteen- to twenty-four-year-old young adults in eight weeks to complete tasks expected of them was difficult. It took all of them working together many hours, developing and sharing skills they had all gained over numerous deployments. It also took a tremendous physical and mental toll on all of them. In order to pass on their skills, they each had to relive horrific moments they wanted to put behind them. They also had to prepare the students physically, which demanded they be in peak physical condition themselves. The students were not allowed to do anything the instructor was not doing with them.

At the end of the day, each instructor went home, ate, hydrated, medicated, rested, and began it all again before the students' alarms went off.

Although the schedule was demanding, the results were rewarding for the instructors. They all took great pride when a class graduated and moved on. When a class graduated, their ritual was simple: two weeks off, starting with a post party at Fast Freddie's for some adult beverages and laughs. The evening usually ended with the same core group of friends: Ed, HM2 Avila, Staff Sergeant Lipszak, Staff Sergeant Martinez, HM2 Book, HM1 Schulter, and Staff Sergeant Gomes. They were the partiers in the hooch. They were also the most experienced of the group and, no doubt, the ones who needed to blow off the most steam. After each class, they rallied at a local pub and blew off the froth of several beers, and then they partied until closing time, with a final call to Jenny around 0100.

Jenny received notice of an opening for a rural carrier in Burgaw, North Carolina. Burgaw was thirty miles south of Jacksonville, but the opportunity was too good to pass up. She interviewed, was offered the position, and accepted it. She trained in Wilmington, North Carolina, for two weeks before beginning her probationary period at the Burgaw Post Office. Ed and Jenny, forced to make a hasty decision on their old friend the Rooster, needed to buy another vehicle. Jenny couldn't deliver mail in the old girl, so they decided to trade her in on a used Toyota Matrix. Christopher didn't appreciate the decision.

The little boy cried his eyes out and screamed, "No, I want to keep the Rooster, Mommy!"

"Don't worry, buddy," Ed said. "We are getting something else too, and it is better than the Rooster. Daddy has been looking at the Silver Surfer!" While they were looking at cars for Jenny, Ed found a Silver Toyota Tundra they purchased as well. With Ed's promotion and Jenny's potential income, they were finally doing well financially and could afford to live like a middle-class family.

Christopher and Clara stayed active with youth activities. Christopher loved baseball, scouting, and anything outdoors. Clara enjoyed the outdoors and scouting but preferred to be a princess most of the time. Most of all, they loved having both their parents together. Although they were young, the endless deployments had taken their toll on the children as well. Spending quality time with their mommy and daddy camping and fishing was pure bliss for them.

Jenny's postal job required her to work Saturdays, so Ed had parenting duty one day a week. He enjoyed the time with them. It was his one chance a week to corrupt them. He loved taking them out to eat, mainly so he didn't have to cook, but he also liked to show them off.

Ed and a friend from work removed four cedar trees from the yard one weekend. He decided to utilize the tree trunks to make a tree house for the kids. He placed the four logs in a square eight feet apart, setting them in concrete in the ground. Then he built a treated lumber platform five feet off the ground, with steps, a slide, a climbing wall, and a rope railing. He constructed a four-foot-square clubhouse out of fencing material and a plastic roof set from Home Depot for the back corner. The kids played in, on, and below the tree house for hours every day. It was constructed well enough that Ed and his friends played on it too.

Traditions are a huge part of military life, and the annual navy ball was one tradition Jenny loved. It reminded her of the spring formals from high school and gave her an excuse to go buy a new dress and get her hair and nails done. The navy ball was a fabulous time. Members throughout the area gathered for a good meal, drink, and camaraderie. Ed loved the experience because it was the one night a year he could get away with telling people what he thought of them without serious repercussions.

As they grew as a family, they grew spiritually as well. They became regulars at Mass and enjoyed seeing the kids grow in their faith. They discovered that to have a true loving and lasting relationship, you needed more than just the husband, wife, and children. You had to have a spiritual connection. When they allowed that connection, their family grew as they had never believed possible. It was beautiful, and things continued to work out for them.

FMSS shared training with CREST, the training pipeline for religious program specialists (RPs) and chaplains being assigned to the marine corps. The cadre included a chaplain, chief, and lead instructor. The platoons integrated training with the RPs for marine-based training and separated for rate-specific training. Ed seemed to get the RPs the majority of the time, but he enjoyed having them. He had a great rapport with the chaplain, chief, and leading petty officer of CREST, and enjoyed their students.

During Ed's tenure at Field Med, he became a master training specialist and started to train other instructors. He had the opportunity to mentor the chaplain during his training to become a master training specialist as the chaplain mentored him on how to lead a more spiritual life. It was a fair trade, and both benefited from the venture, with the chaplain receiving his master training specialist and Ed learning to lead a better life.

That spring, Ed moved into the leading petty officer position of the training department. The position demanded more time, but gave him greater opportunity for future advancement, and he enjoyed the role. He worked closely with all the departments and enjoyed interacting with multiple people daily. He also enjoyed going to Camp Johnson Medical to mess with the clinic chief.

Chief Dittlinger, a navy independent duty corpsman, and Ed had met under not-so-pleasant terms, but had developed a kinship. They enjoyed giving each other crap and talking about the navy. Ed made an excuse to walk over weekly to give the chief crap, until ultimately the chief would tell him, "Get the hell out of my office!" They would both laugh and eagerly await the next duel.

Time was flying by, and life seemed to be on autopilot for Ed, Jenny, and the kids. Their careers, school, activities, home, and lives were smooth sailing. Friends were still coming and going, and life had its difficulties, but they were finally living a somewhat normal existence together. They were feeling blessed and truly believed nothing could derail them.

14

Not Again

~

The mission in Iraq had ended, and the administration began to refocus on Afghanistan. Operations intensified around Kabul, Kandahar, and the Afghan/Pakistan border regions. To date, the army had been engaged in the majority of the fighting. With operations in Helmand closing, the marine corps angled for a larger slice of the pie. The marines had sustained contingents of fighting elements within Afghanistan with Marine Expeditionary Units but were looking to reengage with a larger combat force.

Ed sat alone early Monday morning, preparing administrative and training data for the week prior to the arrival of the staff. Since becoming leading petty officer, he modified his routine to come in an hour earlier and stay later than the other staff members in order to prepare and finish his work without interruption. He was surprised to hear a door open so early in the morning, but continued with his work. When he heard the master chief's voice, he nearly jumped from his seat.

"Brannan, what the hell are you doing here so damn early?"

"I just have some things I need to get done before everyone gets in, and it's easier to do before everyone is in here running their mouths, Master Chief."

The master chief laughed and said, "Are you going to Afghanistan?"

"I'm going to Afghanistan?"

The master chief replied, "Great. Report to my office at oh-eight hundred, and I'll fill you in on all the specifics. Thanks for volunteering." The master chief then turned and exited the hooch.

Ed sat there stunned for several minutes, wondering if he was so exhausted, he had just dreamed or hallucinated that conversation. Then he realized he had drunk so much coffee that morning, there was no way he was asleep or had dreamed what had just happened, and he was sure he was not crazy. Somehow he had just volunteered to go to Afghanistan for a mission he knew nothing about. He then remembered messing around a few days prior in the hooch with his friends. He told them he could trick the master chief. They all laughed at him, and he swore to them he could do it and told them the next time he came over, he would show them.

The next time the master chief came barging in, he asked, "Brannan, where the hell is the training report?"

Ed had waved his hand and said, "You had it yesterday, Master Chief."

"I had it yesterday," the master chief had said and left the hooch. Everyone had laughed his butt off at the stunt and couldn't believe Ed had the stones to pull that on the old boy. Ed just realized the old man was the master. He didn't even have to use his hand to trick him.

The next few hours were grueling for Ed. He contemplated what the mission would be and how he would explain this predicament to Jenny. He also wondered why him and if he really wanted to deploy at a time when all was right in his life, but he knew this was his job, and it had to be done.

He reported to the master chief's office at 0800, knocked, and entered when beckoned. The master chief briefed Ed on the specifics of the mission. His assignment was as an embedded training team in a member marine adviser group to the Afghan National Army. Their role was to advise and train an Afghan infantry *kandak* (battalion) prior to and during deployment to the Nuristan District of Afghanistan.

Ed had no idea what all that meant, but it sounded familiar to the mission of a Special Forces Alpha team, so he was interested and wanted to go. Master Chief added the operation was time sensitive, and he would be leaving for training in two weeks. Ed's jaw hit the floor with the last information. He knew Jenny's head would literally spin off when she heard that news.

He was screwed, but he told the master chief, "Aye aye," and exited the office.

Ed headed over to the training department to inform the assistant training officer and training officer of the upcoming mission and to recommend a replacement leading petty officer. The two weren't happy with the blindside from the command suite, but understood the importance of the mission. Both asked Ed if this was what he wanted to do and not something he was being pushed into.

"I think you both understand I do not do anything I do not want to do, but thank you both for the consideration," he said. "I hate that I am leaving you with such short notice. I have everything pretty organized, and I can do a quick turnover with whomever you select to replace me." When he finished, he headed over to see his friends at the hooch. He knew this would be more difficult. As he expected, it was. All of them had spent multiple tours in Iraq and other not-so-nice places in the world and knew the dangers of deployment. The last thing they wanted to do was see a friend heading out again, but that was their job, and they accepted it with the typical half hug and three slaps on the back from each.

As Ed headed home, he pondered what he would say to Jenny. He finally thought he had the perfect solution. When he entered the house, she knew something was wrong. He never came home early from work on a Monday.

He asked her to sit down. "Jenny, sometimes life tends to throw you curve balls when you least expect, and we just got one. I was asked to go on an embedded training team mission to Afghanistan. The mission will be to train and advise the Afghan National Army in combat tactics and to work with them during operations. I broke the number one rule of family decision making and said yes without consulting you first. I'm sorry, honey, but this is a mission I have been waiting for my entire career. I hope you can understand."

"I can't believe you are doing this again," Jenny said as she began to cry. "Everything is going the way I have prayed for, and now here we go again. Why? What in the world are you thinking? Do you hate being around us that much? I'll never understand why you have to be the one to volunteer to go every time. Why can't someone else go? No, I don't understand, Ed!"

"This is not about me wanting to hurt or leave you and the kids, Jenny. It is something I started a long time ago, and I have an opportunity to put an end to this. I'm sorry, but I'm going to go."

The evening was tense, and the kids could tell their parents weren't being themselves. Clara sat with her daddy as Christopher snuggled in his mommy's legs. He affectionately called it his bunny hole. Jenny and Ed did not tell the kids he would be leaving them again very soon. They would know soon enough.

The following day, Ed reported to work and received his orders. He would report to Quantico for training in two weeks, and then move to Kabul, Afghanistan, with his assigned kandak. Upon arrival, his team would begin work-ups with the Afghan National Army for one month prior to deployment to a forward combat area. Ed was both excited and apprehensive about the assignment. He looked forward to the challenge, but had no desire to leave his family.

Ed and Jenny explained to Christopher and Clara that he would be leaving for training for two months and then deploying again. The kids were heartbroken. Christopher took it hard, but Clara was devastated. She was Daddy's girl, and she didn't want her daddy to leave.

She jumped in his arms and sang to him, "Never gonna let you, never gonna let you, never gonna let you go!"

Ed smiled and sang with her. Then he pointed to her heart and said, "I'm always right there with you, baby girl," and whispered in her ear, "I love you the most!" Then he winked at Christopher, and his son smiled and winked back, knowing his daddy was just comforting his little sister.

Ed reported to Quantico at the Marine Corps Liaison Office and was assigned to Embedded Training Team One-Two. The team consisted of a marine major officer in charge, a supply officer, three company commanders, a gunnery sergeant/senior enlisted leader, two additional gunnies, six staff sergeants, two sergeants, and one additional HM1 besides Ed. The team members were all from marine corps training and education commands: the Basic School, Tank School, Marine Combat Training, Mountain Warfare Training Center, Field Medical Service School, and the Staff Academy. It was truly a diverse group of the best, brightest, and most unique personalities each command could offer.

When they all completed their check-in procedures and were assigned billeting, they proceeded to an auditorium for their indoctrination training. Five groups of teams gathered in the auditorium for the briefing. Each team introduced itself and began to size each other up, which was typical of these situations. Ed sat at the rear of his group and watched the team interact. He remained quiet and politely answered the questions of his teammates. The liaison officer entered the auditorium and began the briefing. He introduced himself, passed out information about the training events, timeline, and departure schedule. When he completed the briefing, he released the teams to their respective officers in charge for team orientation.

Ed's officer in charge, Major Goodpasture, the executive officer of the Basic School, was a tanker. He introduced himself and Gunnery Sergeant Parsons, the senior enlisted leader and an instructor from the Staff Academy, and then had each team member introduce himself. The team included Captain O'Donnell from the Basic School; Captain Loignoin from Marine Corps Supply School; Captain Gafford from School of Infantry West; First Lieutenant Denman from School of Infantry West; Gunnery Sergeant Tirado from TBS; Gunnery Sergeant Wagner from SOI West; Staff Sergeant Lehrke from MWTC; Staff Sergeant Goulding from Communication School; Staff Sergeant Grandstaff from SOI East; Staff Sergeant Pugmire from Tank School;

Sergeant Hernandez from MWTC; Sergeant Lackey from MWTC; HM1 Melady From FMSS West; and Ed.

After introductions, Major Goodpasture released the team to the hotel and gave orders to be in the hotel lobby at 0500 for transportation to the backcountry driving course in the morning.

Ed went back to the hotel, stowed his gear, and prepared for the training in the morning. He ordered pizza and called Jenny and the kids. He talked to his family about the events of the day and meeting his new team. After supper, he watched TV and crashed out for the evening. The following morning, he woke early, did his morning routine, and headed to the lobby to meet the team for the convoy to the training site.

The backcountry driving course was in the Appalachian Mountains of West Virginia, about a three-hour drive from DC. The team took two vans to another hotel for the three-day course. After they checked in, they proceeded to the hotel conference room for classroom training. The instructors were some of the most country redneck folks Ed had ever encountered. The song "Dueling Banjos" echoed in his ears when they walked into the room. The men seemed to be nice, but they were country. They were also knowledgeable of all things four-wheel drive and mountain all-terrain driving.

The class lasted six hours, but it was a great time and informative. Ed had done a lot of four-wheeling as a kid, but these people taught him more in a few hours than he had learned in years of messing around. After class, the team decided to go out to dinner and start to bond.

Across the street from the hotel was a bowling alley with a lounge and grill. They decided that was a good enough place to hang out. After a few burgers and a few more beers, the beginning of a strong friendship began. They all understood they would be spending the next year with each other in some harsh conditions and would have to rely on one another, so it was best to get to know one another quickly. It was the first of many long bonding evenings.

The following day, the team moved to the training site with their redneck hosts. The good old boys had Toyota Land Cruisers for the team to beat up. Each vehicle had two team members and an instructor. They put the vehicle through the ringer, going up, down, around, and over anything and everything the instructor could think of to simulate what they may encounter in Afghanistan. It was a blast, and the company didn't mind if the vehicles got beat up a little. They encouraged it. They wanted the men to break something so they could show them how to fix it in the field with what they had in the vehicle or on them.

They learned an egg could fix a hole in a radiator. Chaining jumper cables to multiple batteries could make a welder. You could reinflate a tire with aerosol spray and a lighter. Ed's favorite was if you lost a rear tire, you could shove a strong tree branch in the rear axle, pull the rear drive shaft, lock in the front hubs, and ride it like a sled. The men even taught them how to manually winch overturned vehicles. It was all fun and beneficial training rare for the military.

The following day was mudding. That was just as much fun and gave Ed an opportunity to show off his skills. They were going through a deep trench that no one was able to get through when one of the instructors offered Ed an opportunity.

"Sir, I can make it through that hole, but I'm going to tear the front right quarter panel off that truck," Ed said.

The man laughed. "I have only seen one man make it through that hole, and if you can do it, go ahead and tear it up."

"You better back up then." Ed and Gunnery Sergeant Wagner got in the Land Cruiser and pulled around to the start. Ed looked at Gunnery Sergeant Wagner and said, "I'm going to hit that thing going about thirty and crank it to the right halfway through to climb up that right side and pop out of the hole. We might roll. You sure you want to go with me?"

Gunnery Sergeant Wagner looked pale and said, "You sure you can make it, Doc?"

"I can make it, Gunny."

"Go for it," Gunnery Sergeant Wagner said. Ed stomped it. He hit the hole going thirty miles an hour and dropped it into second gear. Halfway through the hole, he cranked the steering wheel to the right and mashed the accelerator. The front quarter panel smashed the right wall as the vehicle climbed up the wall and shot up the hole. The truck went vertical as marines and instructors went running. Ed was laughing as Gunnery Sergeant Wagner was screaming.

The Land Cruiser came down on the edge of the mudhole with the front axles all the way out and the rear tires barely resting on the edge of the drop-off. Ed eased off the gas and dropped the transmission into first gear. The vehicle lunged forward and came to a halt.

Ed shook his head in disgust and yelled, "Dammit!"

The instructors and marines came running back, yelling with joy. They couldn't believe he had made it out of the hole without a winch. Gunnery Sergeant Wagner sat in the passenger seat, shaking with fear and about to vomit. Ed was headbanging as if he were listening to Metallica. He told the marines to sit on the front of the vehicle to put some weight on the tires and pulled the truck forward. He gained some serious cool points with the team that day.

That evening, they had chow with the instructors at the bowling alley and talked about their crazy Doc. Ed enjoyed the compliments. The team enjoyed the evening, and the major briefed them on the following day's training package. They would be moving to another training site for a shooting package, so he advised them to make it a short night and be ready early.

The next morning, the team moved to the range. The range master did a safety brief and weapons familiarization, and went over the schedule for the day. They started with breaking down and putting together all the weapons the Afghan National Army worked with. Each member tested out on proficiency before moving on to the firing range. At the firing ranges, each member fired pistols first, then moved to the rifles, and finally the crew served weapons. Another great day of training complete, the team loaded up and headed back to DC.

Upon return, the team prepared to depart for the Mountain Warfare Training Center for a modified mountain training course. They packed, convoyed to Reagan International, and departed the following day to Reno. The team arrived a day early, so the major arranged for them to go to Lake Tahoe for a night of R and R. They all grouped up and got rooms together, and then headed to the casino. Ed walked in, dropped twenty dollars into a five-dollar poker machine, hit Spin, and won eight hundred dollars. He knew he was going to have a good night.

Ed headed over to the blackjack table and sat down. He had no idea how long he had been there when the major and Gunnery Sergeant Parsons sat down next to him. They asked how he was doing.

"I have eight hundred in my pocket, and it looks like I have a couple hundred on the table, so I think I am up a thousand." They both laughed and told him it was 0200 in the morning, and they were going to bed. "Holy shit," Ed said. "I didn't know it was that late, but I'm staying until I lose this money."

Ed kept playing, but didn't lose. He finally cashed out with another four hundred dollars in his pocket and found Sergeant Lackey at the bar. They sat BS'ing for a few hours until the breakfast bar opened, and they headed upstairs for chow. As they were eating, the team joined them, and after breakfast they all loaded up and headed to Bridgeport.

When the team arrived at Bridgeport, they checked in and stowed their gear in the barracks. Major Goodpasture scheduled PT for the following morning to acclimate to the altitude. It became clear to Ed immediately that the altitude was going to be a challenge. Just walking to the chow hall was difficult. In the morning, the team ran to the upper training area and back. The run, approximately three and a half miles, took over forty-five minutes. At sea level on a normal day, the run would have taken Ed around twenty-one minutes.

The team stretched, showered, and went to breakfast. After breakfast, they met the other teams in the classrooms for the briefing and received the training schedule. They would begin with a three-mile day-pack hike, followed by two days of classes, a five-mile full-pack hike, mule-pack training, and medical training, and then they would move out to the lower training area for the field operations.

They completed the scheduled training and staged at the barracks, ready to move out for the field operations. The other teams opted to take tents, heaters, and other comfort gear for the training exercise. Major Goodpasture and Gunnery Sergeant Parsons decided to make the training realistic. The motto in the mountains is, "Ounces are pounds, and pounds are pain," and the more gear, the more pain, so it was a logical assumption. However, the weather in the mountains could change dramatically, and it wasn't wise to underestimate the climate.

Ed packed a ranger roll consisting of a poncho, poncho liner, sleeping mat, and bungee cords, just in case. All the marines laughed at him because it was such a beautiful morning, and they thought the added weight was needless. Ed considered the extra pound a bonus if the weather went south, and he took the razzing.

The teams packed their mules, strapped on their packs, and moved out up the mountain toward the lower training area. The movement took quite a while due to the stubborn half-ass mules. When they reached the lower training area, the teams broke camp and began classes. The instructors taught knots, climbing, traversing, trapping, and cleaning small game. That evening was a beautiful starlit warm night, and everyone slept in his bevy sack.

The next morning, the team members individually plotted their own course to the upper training area and moved out in intervals. Sergeant Hernandez from Ed's team was a Mountain Warfare Training Center mountain instructor. He plotted and guided the team to the upper training area. The course he chose was directly up the mountain. It was not the easiest route, but the team was the first to arrive and enjoyed about three hours downtime before the last team made it in.

As they were waiting for the other teams, Ed took the time to make a lean-to shelter out of his poncho and bungee cords off a tree in the center of camp. He used his entrenching tool to dig around the sides of the poncho for a drainage ditch, in case it rained or snowed, and put his sleeping mat, sleeping bag, and gear under the makeshift tent.

After the teams gathered, the instructors passed out coordinates for a land navigation course and instructed each team to find five sets of coordinates and bring back the set of numbers at each box. The marines were eager to prove themselves and wanted to jump right in. Ed didn't care to do any more land navigation. He felt comfortable with his skill level, but he was interested in seeing if his comrades could navigate.

The first two coordinates went well. Unfortunately, Ed knew immediately the third would be an issue when he watched the person shoot his magnetic compass azimuth and saw he was several degrees south of his position.

Ed walked silently behind them until they reached their pace count. When there was no box, he said, "I think we are about five hundred meters down the ridge from where we are supposed to be."

The staff sergeant who had shot the azimuth was adamant he was correct, so Ed just walked up the ridge to look for the box. As he walked up, he saw the box was higher up the mountain. Gunnery Sergeant Parsons said he knew where the box was because he had it marked on GPS.

Ed laughed and said, "That's cheating, Gunny." They finally corralled the staff sergeant and found the box. Gunnery Sergeant Parsons grabbed Ed, gave him the map, compass, and protractor with coordinates, and told him to find the next box.

"OK, Gunny," Ed said. He plotted the coordinates, converted the azimuth, shot it, and moved out. When Ed reached a small stream, he pointed at a group of trees and told Gunnery Sergeant Parsons that was where the box would be.

"You are wrong," Gunnery Sergeant Parsons said. "The box is way up there."

"There is no way the box is way up there if these are the coordinates you gave me."

Gunnery Sergeant Parsons looked at his coordinates, smiled, and said, "Never mind, Doc. I was looking at the next box. You are right. Get us over this stream so we can get those numbers and get on to the next one." While they were looking for a crossing, the weather changed immediately. It began to snow horribly. Within an hour, more than four inches of snow covered the ground.

Ed smiled at the team and said, "I hope you waterproofed your gear. Ounces are pounds, and pounds are pain, and water is a lot of pain."

By the time they made it back to camp, there was about a foot of wet snow on the ground, and all the team's packs were soaked. Ed couldn't help but laugh. He crawled in his warm hooch, stripped down, and snuggled into his sleeping bag, peeking out at his team.

"Hey, if one of you wants to be little spoon, come on over, and Doc will keep you warm," he yelled. Then he closed the flap of the poncho and went to sleep.

The rest of the team didn't get much rest that evening. They did build a fire and stay warm, but there was no rest. The following morning, they all loaded up and hiked back to the barracks, cleaned up, and grabbed some hot chow.

Ed scheduled the next two days for medical training. The first day, he taught classroom PowerPoint Tactical Combat Casualty Care. The second day was all hands-on practical application and scenario-based drills. The team loved the training, and Ed loved teaching them. He explained to them why he knew this training was so important. If he were injured, he needed them to be able to perform as well as he would.

They must have learned something, because when they returned to Quantico for follow-on medical training, his team answered every question so accurately, the instructor dismissed them and allowed Ed to do their practical applications by himself. Ed was proud of the team and of his ability to instruct.

The time to leave drew closer, so Ed asked Jenny and the kids to join him at the hotel for the weekend. He wanted them to meet the team. Many of his other team members' families were in town as well, so they all decided to go eat at Carrabba's. They had a wonderful time, with great food, good wine, and outstanding people. Unfortunately, the night couldn't last forever, and they wouldn't see one another for a long time.

The next morning Ed, Jenny, and the kids said good-bye once again. He hugged, kissed, and wished them well as they drove off in the truck. Jenny didn't cry until he was out of sight. The kids didn't understand why their daddy had to leave again.

Ed stood in the parking lot wondering what he was doing and why he was leaving, praying he would see them all again.

15

Do Not Answer the Door

At 0300, the team gathered in the lobby of the hotel with all their gear, checked out of the hotel, had breakfast, and loaded the military vans. They proceeded to Quantico via the back gate and went directly to the armory to draw weapons, serialized gear, and night-vision equipment. The supply officer did his final inspection, locked each member's weapons cases, and then the team reloaded the vans and headed to Reagan International for the next leg of their trip.

Ed had never flown commercial on any of his previous deployments, so walking into a terminal in civvies, with a weapons case and duffel bags full of military gear, felt reminiscent of a spy novel. He thought it was cool until they hit customs and began the daunting task of checking the weapons and being searched. Then he thought, *Eff this, I'll take a military charter or C-130 any day!* Two hours later, on the other side of check-in and headed toward their terminal, the team stopped at a café for coffee and a short briefing.

Major Goodpasture and Gunnery Sergeant Parsons went over the flight schedule and estimated arrival times. They told everyone to get some rest, enjoy the flights, have drinks if they wanted them, but not to get stupid. Ed couldn't figure out why they looked directly at him and threw in "Doc" at the end of the sentence.

He laughed and said, "If I drink, it will be medicinal vodka, so it is perfectly legal, sir!" Major Goodpasture just shook his head as HM1 Melady slapped Ed upside his. Gunnery Sergeant Parsons explained when they reached Germany that Staff Sergeant Pugmire would lead the way, since he was fluent in German. *That's awesome,* Ed thought. *I didn't think Staff Sergeant Pugmire could read or write!* Ed loved messing with Staff Sergeant Pugmire, but thought the world of the man. When Ed taught the team tactical medicine at mountain warfare training, Staff Sergeant Pugmire was the most attentive and asked the most questions. He at least acted as if he wanted to learn, and during the practical application portion, he did better than many corpsman students Ed had taught.

After coffee, the team headed to its departure gate and grabbed some seats in the corner. They had several hours before their flight. As usual in the marine corps, it was an exercise in hurry up and wait. They all pulled out their books, audio devices, or pillows and did their own thing until the announcement came to board.

A commercial flight to Germany was not nearly as complementary as a military charter. Ed definitely didn't like his incognito status now. He did enjoy not being around a bunch of smelly jarheads talking about taking craps and asking him why it hurt when they pissed. As the flight landed and taxied, Gunnery Sergeant Parsons told the team to allow the other passengers to depart, and they would exit last and stay together on their way to the next terminal.

The team exited, gathered, and followed Staff Sergeant Pugmire through the terminal. Surprisingly, Staff Sergeant Pugmire did know German and took them directly to the next gate. They had another two-hour delay, so they each took buddy teams and went for chow and bathroom breaks. When everyone returned, it was back to books, sleep, and music until the next boarding call to Kuwait.

The mix of passengers flying to Kuwait from Germany was quite different from the previous flight. It was mostly Middle Eastern people, which made Ed uncomfortable. He knew stereotyping people was total BS, and he shouldn't think like that, but he couldn't shake the feeling.

He didn't sleep. He couldn't concentrate to read. All he could do was casually scan the aircraft until they landed at Kuwait International. Gunnery Sergeant Parsons announced again to remain on board until the other passengers deplaned. When the others departed, the team members got out of their seats and moved out. When they hit the terminal, they followed the signs to customs and proceeded through.

A marine liaison awaited them at baggage claim to assist with obtaining their weapons and bags and transporting them to Ali Al Salem for follow-on flights to their destination. The process was grueling, but they finally got in the vans and headed to the airfield to check in. When they arrived, Major Goodpasture and Gunnery Sergeant Parsons checked them in and got them billeting for the evening as the supply officer took care of their follow-on flights.

The team stowed weapons and gear, grabbed racks, posted a gear watch, and headed to chow. Everyone rotated through eating, calling home, and washing off the stink of travel before the major called a team meeting to discuss the follow-on travel plans. They were to depart in the morning to another air base in the old Soviet Union for a day. Depending on flights, they would travel within two to three days to Bagram, Afghanistan.

That morning, they all rose early, packed up, and headed to the terminal to depart on the next leg of their journey. They checked in for the flight, loaded their gear on pallets, and boarded a C-17 headed to Kyrgyzstan. The four-hour flight was not comfortable, and there were no snacks or drink carts.

The team sat together in uniform, lost in their thoughts, preparing themselves for the upcoming mission. The time was quickly approaching, and they were all putting their game faces on. The group that weeks ago had been partying and acting like frat boys was now looking like professionals. The transformation was amazing and strange—how easily all of them could switch it on and off without conscious thought. This was their career and their chosen path, something many could never understand. It was something their own families didn't understand, but they lived with it because they all loved the job.

As the flight touched down in the snowcapped mountains of the old Soviet Bloc, Ed thought, *This is a beautiful country. This is not how I imagined Russia would look.* Of course, he had no idea where he was geographically and had never heard of Kyrgyzstan before twenty-four hours ago.

They deplaned and were briefed and bused to a holding area for another briefing to be assigned billeting. The major and Gunnery Sergeant Parsons checked in with the marine liaison, and the supply officer went directly to work getting a flight to Bagram. The others grabbed the weapons and gear and made their way to the huge clamshells utilized for sleeping quarters. Each clamshell had approximately one hundred bunk beds and two hundred weapons racks in the center. The team claimed a corner next to a side entrance by the exterior heads, assigned a gear watch, and as usual, went to chow.

Following routine, they rotated through chow, head calls, phone calls, and ass washing until the major called his meeting. The major passed word the supply officer had arranged a flight the following afternoon. He also let the team know there was a bar on base. They could have two final beers before heading into country. He told them to enjoy their last night of freedom for the next several months, because after tonight it was time to go to work.

The team gathered that evening at the watering hole, minus the gear guard, and toasted to the upcoming mission, their training, and fallen comrades. They rotated the gear guard and did it again, and then headed back to the clamshell for a final night's rest. The next morning, they all prepped, had chow, made calls, gathered gear, and headed for staging. At staging, they palletized their gear, donned their personal protective equipment, grabbed their weapons, headed for the buses, and then boarded the C-17 for Bagram.

The flight to Bagram was similar to the previous flight into Kyrgyzstan. The team contemplated the mission and where they were headed. They were all in full-blown mission mode now, trained and ready for battle. They arrived at Bagram and met the marine ETT liaison. They grabbed gear, loaded vehicles, headed for billeting, checked in, and were briefed on the following day's convoy to the ANA camp in Kabul.

Bagram was not what Ed expected. It was a mini city. The base had a full-blown mall, dining facility, Burger King, KFC, Pizza Hut, and everything else a stateside base had. It was ridiculous. The whole team wanted to get off that base as fast as they could. The army ran the base, so it was a saluting area. You couldn't walk ten feet without popping a salute, and there were so many idiots, it was sickening.

Thankfully, the following day came quickly, and their convoy came in early. They were off in a flash, and the base was a distant memory. The desert landscape surrounding Bagram was not beautiful like Kyrgyzstan. The roads were pothole-filled nightmares. The beating the team took in the Hummers to Kabul made them all wish they were back in Bagram. The two-hour trip seemed like a lifetime, but they finally arrived at the gates of the ANA Kabul military training facility. They entered the base and proceeded to Camp Blackhorse, their home for the next month.

Jenny and the kids had returned to their normal routines: Christopher and Clara in school and Jenny back to the post office. Clara's first few weeks were trying on Jenny. She cried most evenings, and anytime Jenny refused to relent to her demands, she screamed for her daddy. But as time passed, the temper tantrums did as well. They all fell back easily into the beat of the old deployment rhythm. Family friends came around more. Neighbors would pick up the kids from school if Jenny ran late from work. The network was in full force to support her and the family.

As on base, Jenny had developed a strong friendship with her neighbors, many of whom were military spouses, one of them a marine's wife, born in Pakistan, named Charlotte. Charlotte was referred to as the Pakistani redneck due to her thick accent and common use of the word *y'all*. She was a kind and beautiful soul, raised Catholic in a region dominated by Islam. She was tough as nails, but gentle as the morning breeze. Charlotte lived next door to the Brannans with her husband, Johnny; son, Connor; and father-in-law, Pops.

※※

Ed's new friends were an interesting group as well. He felt they were some of the most interesting people he had ever met. In comparison to the Iraqis, the Afghan soldiers were professional and hardworking, the exact opposite of what Ed experienced in Iraq. Only a small number seemed to lack the motivation to stay in the military. Upon arrival, the team was assigned to First Kandak, Second Brigade of the 201st Corps. It was one of the original units formed after the dismantling of the Taliban. They were considered the commandos of the Afghan National Army, the elite. Some of these men were the original volunteers for the new army and had the most fighting experience.

The plan upon arrival was to complete turnover, introduce themselves to the Afghan National Army, and conduct training for one month prior to moving out to their forward operating area. That timeline shifted left or was reduced by one week instantaneously upon arrival. The team they were replacing did a simple "Here are the keys" turnover, loaded their gear, and departed on the same vehicles Ed's team arrived in. *God bless military efficiency*, Ed thought.

As with anything in the military, the team adjusted their schedule and proceeded with their plans. They proceeded on an expedited schedule and made it happen. All of them were careerists and instructors used to adjusting to meet deadlines, and that is what happened. They cut nonessential training from the schedule, reduced time off, and made a workable plan.

The team was working with soldiers who had been fighting a war for almost a decade, and some who had been fighting their entire lives, so all of this was nothing more than developing trust and getting to know one another. For Ed, it was more about teaching them combat medicine his way. He had no desire to go out in the middle of nowhere, be hit, and not have someone with the ability to treat him the way he would treat him.

The language barrier was difficult, but manageable. Fortunately for Ed, one of the interpreters happened to be a pathologist and could easily translate what Ed was saying. A prerequisite for the ANA medics was to be able to read and write. Ed was not sure of the proficiency level, but he knew they could, based on the pen each one carried in his pocket, a status symbol for the Afghan people, most of whom were not literate.

With the help of Ed's interpreter, Omar, the training went well, and Ed qualified the medics, who in turn qualified 25 percent of each platoon in combat lifesaving. Each graduate was given a certificate in a small graduation ceremony. The Afghan National Army loved certificates, pins, and photos. They were status symbols and items to show their families. Ed was amazed at the enthusiasm they showed and respected how much they desired to see their country free from the hostility. Training seemed to be over before it started, and they were loading trucks, preparing to depart for their forward operating bases.

The convoy through the mountain pass from Kabul to Jalalabad, then on to Camp Joyce along the Pech River road, took around fourteen hours. Thankfully, other than the frequent bathroom and chai breaks the ANA had to take, the journey was uneventful. As they traveled, Ed could not help but notice the extreme beauty of the land he was entering. Leaving Kabul and entering the steep mountain pass looking down from the perch of the turret, he imagined how many people had taken the same path over the centuries. This route dated back to the spice trade when Afghanistan was a thriving area. Sea trade, wars, other advances, and political maneuvering over the years had left Afghanistan in the past, but most of the people remained resilient despite the power-hungry oppressive forces driving their situation.

Coming down the pass into the river valley and entering Jalalabad were small fishing villages and lakes. The roads were lined with streetside vendors. Onlookers waved at the convoys from shacks selling fresh fish, fruit, nuts, spices, and modern items. Kids ran around playing as adults sat drinking chai, playing cards, and conversing, not bothered by the current situation of their country.

The convoy turned left onto the Pech River road, normally an improvised explosive device lane with ambushes. All the men were on alert, but the beauty was still present and the people still friendly. As they passed, onlookers waved the Hawaiian sign, with the thumb and smallest finger extended and the middle fingers curled. Some kids flew one-finger salutes, unknowingly insulting their guests. The salute no doubt came from the First Marine Division operating in the area and teaching them American traditions. Ed laughed to himself as he waved back at the kids yelling, "Candy, candy."

When the team entered Camp Joyce, they were greeted by the Afghan National Army and the team they were to relieve. The ANA split off to their compound as the Americans proceeded to their hilltop perch above the camp. Introductions complete and billeting assigned, they all sat down for a briefing of the situation and for chow. Once again, the planned turnover would be shifted left, and the team would take over operations immediately. *Why even have a plan?* Ed thought.

When the other team exited the chow hall, Major Goodpasture called a meeting and passed the plan. The supply officer was arranging transport for the different companies to immediately move out and turn over in place with the outlying assets of the current team. They would split into five separate entities to begin immediate counterinsurgent operations in the area of operation. Prior to leaving, they would have one final meal together with the Afghan leadership, and then go get it on.

The lead interpreter purchased goat, potatoes, rice, and all the trimmings for a traditional Afghan feast. The team and ANA leaders sat with the interpreters for a final meal, the last one together until they finished operations in the area and returned to Camp Joyce for departure back to Camp Blackhorse at an undisclosed time. Each team was given turnover, operation, communication instructions, and the plan of the day for the following morning before departing for the evening. That night, Ed called Jenny and the kids.

※※

Jenny didn't recognize the number and hoped it was Ed. When she answered the phone and heard the familiar dull noise and delay, she knew her honey bunny's voice would soon follow.

"Hi, love," Ed said.

"I love you," Jenny said. "I'm so glad to hear from you. Why haven't you called lately?"

"I told you we would be away for a while, baby. We're going to be out again. I wanted to talk to you and the kids before we head out. I'm not sure how long it will be before I speak to you again, and the mail will be slow, so don't worry. I'll be fine. I'm headed to a secure base, but the communication is shitty, though."

Jenny knew he was lying to ease her concern, but said, "OK, hon, please be safe. What are you going to be doing?"

"I'm just going to be helping out with some medical stuff. I will be fine. Let me talk to the kids, baby. I don't have a lot of time. I love you." He talked to Christopher and Clara, told each of them he loved them, and ended the conversation before he got homesick.

※※

The following day, all the men gathered their equipment, gear, and weapons. They mustered at the landing zone in their vehicles and readied for departure. Major Goodpasture and Gunnery Sergeant Parsons gave their final instructions, and like clockwork, each team rallied its ANA platoons and began the exodus to its respective area of responsibility. Ed and Staff Sergeant Grandstaff headed to Bella, a remote outpost in Nuristan next to the region's medical clinic. Flying into the base, Ed wondered who in the hell picked the location. The base was in the bottom of a fishbowl surrounded by steep mountains and streams on three sides. His first thought was, *If we get into a fight here, I may as well stick my head between my legs and kiss my ass good-bye!*

As they landed and off-loaded, a National Guardsman and ANA met them. The guardsman gave Ed an envelope and boarded the helicopter he had just departed. Ed wasn't sure what the hell had just happened until the helicopter was already in the air and gone. He ripped open the letter, began to read it, and gave it to Grandstaff. The letter was their turnover. Another fine example of military inefficiency!

The army's Tenth Mountain Division ran the outpost. Thankfully, Ed and Grandstaff would have someone to give them a briefing of the situation and guide them on their first patrols. The ANA had also operated in this area on previous deployments, so the situation was not as dire as Ed had initially thought, although it was far from ideal. Ed was skeptical about working with the Tenth due to his experience with them in Mogadishu, but that was many years ago, and the unit had a long, heroic battle history.

The following week, Ed and Grandstaff integrated with the army, and Ed made several visits to the local clinic to assess the supply needs and coordinate medical capabilities. He started to schedule regular visits and volunteered to treat local men in the region. The Afghan culture dictated he would not be allowed to treat any females of child-rearing age. The clinic was run by a nonprofit group based out of Sweden, and the manager, Niamtulah, who was a former Afghan refugee to Pakistan, spoke fluent English. He and Ed became fast friends.

Ed became familiar with the local doctor as well. He was actually a laboratory technician, but in Afghanistan, anyone with a medical background was considered a doctor. The actual doctor rotated throughout the region and was a physician assistant or the equivalent. The time Ed spent at the clinic mainly focused on readdressing what the lab tech misdiagnosed or mistreated and handling minor issues, such as colds and flus. He enjoyed the work and joked in letters home that it was the only time he would not be prosecuted for practicing medicine without a license.

The greater portion of his time was devoted to patrolling with Grandstaff and the ANA. They went out day and night on recon, raid, and ambush patrols, with Grandstaff as the infantry adviser and Ed as the medical adviser. Their roles intertwined many times, because they had to conduct patrols separately, and at times Grandstaff had to return to Camp Joyce and then proceed to Kabul for operating funds.

As time went on, they developed a strong relationship with the ANA. They lived, ate, and shared their free time with the men. They enjoyed watching movies, listening to them sing and dance, and sharing stories. They were an interesting group of men. Ed trusted most of them with his life, but there were a few he didn't want behind him on patrol. He could tell they weren't right and didn't want to be in the ANA.

The Afghan culture was amazing to Ed. The men were respectful, hardworking, and would rarely laugh at any of his and Grandstaff's missteps. On one patrol just outside camp, they were crossing a makeshift bridge. Grandstaff slipped and fell right into the freezing river, with his pack stuck between the rocks. Ed was laughing so hard, he fell to the ground, not realizing the danger his friend was in. Thankfully, the ANA sprang into action, freed Grandstaff, and retrieved him from the water before he drowned.

When Ed regained his composure and reached the other side, Grandstaff insisted he was OK and ready to proceed on patrol. Ed recognized immediately he was in the beginning stages of hypothermia and refused to allow him to continue. He ordered Faqula, the platoon sergeant, to have the ANA who assisted Grandstaff escort him back to camp and get him to shelter. He told Grandstaff to rewarm, and Ed would conduct the patrol. Grandstaff put up a typical marine fight until he realized Ed was right and headed back with his escorts.

Ed proceeded with the ANA to their first halt. When they halted, the ANA were laughing and making gestures, lying in the snow. Faqula slapped one in the head, and they all stopped immediately. Ed asked the interpreter Abdul Rahman what was said.

Abdul Rahman was reluctant to tell him, but relented and said, "They said Staff Sergeant Grandstaff looked like an upside-down turtle in the water." Ed laughed hysterically, flopped on his back, and kicked his arms and legs like a turtle on his back. This had all the ANA roaring with laughter once again, and Faqula even cracked a smile.

"Please tell Faqula I am not insulted," Ed told Abdul Rahman. "I am impressed his men had the sense to save my friend when I was being a fool, but it was funny. I won't tell Grandstaff we were making fun of him." Abdul passed the information along, and all were satisfied. They continued the patrol without further incident, occasionally laughing about the turtle as they returned to base.

Grandstaff and Ed's relationship with the ANA continued to grow throughout the deployment and their joint efforts dismantling enemy operations with the Tenth Mountain. Ed and Grandstaff relied heavily on one squad of the Tenth in particular. A young army staff sergeant, Jason Crawford, had one hell of a group they loved working with. Unfortunately, they rotated out frequently and were forced to work with other groups with whom they were not so comfortable. Ed remained vigilant around a few of the ANA due to their suspicious behavior, but saw most as his brothers-in-arms and trusted them implicitly.

Communication with Jenny and the kids sucked. Calls were intermittent, and when he was able to make them, they were often cut off due to signal loss. That made the situation difficult for Ed, Jenny, and the kids. Mail came in monthly. Ed and Grandstaff shared their packages with the ANA, which developed a stronger bond.

It was always funny to see their weapons decorated with stickers from care package items they had given them. It should not have been surprising, considering the age of some of the soldiers. Ed estimated one of the young men to be around fourteen. Ed requested he stay on base, but the teen still managed to sneak on patrol with them. The wry little shit even disappeared for a month once.

When he returned, Ed asked, "Where did you go?"

"I go home!" the young soldier replied with a smile. The interpreter explained the boy had walked to Jalalabad to take his check to his family and walked back. Ed could not believe the kid had the stones to leave his weapon and walk one hundred kilometers to Jalalabad in Indian country and back without fear.

Ed received word he was to be moved to another post for the remainder of the deployment. He was discouraged with the news because of the relationships he had groomed with these men and the clinic, but just as in the States, it was part of the job. He didn't tell the ANA and awaited his departure. On the day of his departure, he went to the clinic, said his good-byes, and headed through camp to do the same. As he stood on the landing zone with his gear, a soldier he had befriended approached and stood beside him. The interpreter Abdul walked up and had a heated discussion with the soldier.

Ed interrupted and asked, "What is going on?"

"He says he is going with you, Doctor," Abdul said.

"He can't go with me. He has to stay with his unit."

"I told him this, and he says he must go with you."

"Why must he go with me?"

"You are his friend, and you are here helping the Afghan people. If you die in Afghanistan, he loses his honor. He cannot allow you to die in Afghanistan."

Ed didn't know what to say. He stood silent for several moments, and then said, "Abdul Rahman, please tell him Doctor no die in Afghanistan. He is my friend, and he will always be. If anything happens to me, he will always have his honor, but he must stay and do his duty as I must go and do mine."

Abdul passed the information onto the warrior as his head slowly sank lower. Ed reached for his hand and said, "Salaam Alaikum, my friend."

The soldier raised his head, put his hand on his heart, and said, "Walaikum Salam, Doctor." He stood next to Ed until the helicopter retrieved him and transported him to Aranas.

As he landed in Aranas, it was clear the terrain was going to be much more challenging, but the base had been placed with more thought. It was put on the military crest, with better vantage points and more security. Ed was met by Sergeant Hernandez on the landing zone, and they transported his gear to their hooch, which was a beautiful little barn of mud and brick, with a tarp ceiling.

Sergeant Hernandez explained they had other houseguests—rats the size of raccoons—which amused the hell out of Ed, but scared the piss out of Sergeant Hernandez. Sergeant Hernandez introduced him to the ANA leadership, showed him the base, and took him to the Tenth's Tactical Operations Center.

They conducted a few joint patrols before learning they would be losing their kandak to the Special Forces and getting replacements. Neither Ed nor Sergeant Hernandez was overjoyed at this news. They both knew they were operating with the best in the Afghan National Army. They had no desire to train and to operate in the region with a group of untested soldiers, but they had no choice.

The turnover was conducted, and they met their new crew. As expected, the new group was not as seasoned as the commandos were, and many were quite sketchy. Ed hated patrolling with them. On more than one occasion, they lost contact with the front of the patrol, and Ed's rear element came into base thirty to forty minutes after Sergeant Hernandez.

Their concerns grew as they saw the new ANA interacting suspiciously with the locals. Even the interpreters were uneasy around this group. Tenth Mountain planned to place an Afghan National Police checkpoint on a finger/ridge overlooking a major intersection approximately three kilometers from Aranas. Sergeant Hernandez coordinated with Tenth to do security for the movement, and an operation order was issued.

They initiated movement to the designated checkpoints early in the morning. Ed felt uneasy from the start. Something felt off, and the ANA soldiers were acting strange. As they moved through the small town of Aranas, the rear element slowly began to fall back again. Ed radioed to Sergeant Hernandez and was requesting that he halt movement until they caught up, when all hell broke loose.

Ed heard a large explosion, then ringing in his ears, and felt warm liquid running down his face before his vision faded. His thoughts drifted to Jenny, Christopher, and Clara and how much he loved them and wished he were sitting with them at home.

❈❈❈

Jenny received a phone call, expecting it to be Ed. The voice on the other end was familiar, but it wasn't her honey. It was a voice she had not heard in quite some time, but one she loved dearly and missed. Jenny had comforted her during a time of deep sadness and enjoyed hearing from her. They enjoyed a brief conversation about their kids and careers. Andrea was just calling to see how Jenny and the kids were holding up with Ed deployed again.

When they finished speaking, Jenny lay awake hoping to hear from Ed until she drifted into a slumber. She awoke to the sounds of car doors shutting in front of the house. The one thing you never want to see pull up to your home when your husband is deployed is a government vehicle with people in dress uniform in it. She prayed she was still dreaming, but she heard a knock at the door.

16

Perimeter Is Formed

~

Jenny began to tremble as she moved to the door, tears already streaming from her eyes. She knew she was about to receive the worst news of her life. *If I don't open the door, maybe they'll go away, and this will all just be a dream.* She heard three more raps at the door. As she moved closer, her legs grew weak. She reached for the door handle, her hand shaking uncontrollably as she twisted the knob and opened the door.

Standing in front of her were four men in service dress blues. She recognized each of them from Ed's command, but HM2 Shannon Book was the most familiar; she had picked him and Ed up from the bar after classes, and he had been to the house for parties. As she pushed open the storm door, her head fell forward, and she went to her knees as the commanding officer reached for her. The men helped her to her feet and asked to come in.

Jenny, barely able to speak, muttered, "Yes."

They all entered the small living room and walked Jenny to the couch as they sat around her. What she heard next was exactly what she had imagined when she saw the vehicle.

"Mrs. Brannan, it is with my deepest regret that I inform you Ed was killed in action yesterday in Afghanistan," the commanding officer said. "He is currently being escorted back to the United States and will arrive in Dover, Maryland, on December fifth."

Jenny, unable to speak or contain her grief, rested her head on HM2 Book's shoulder and continued to cry aloud. The men sat in silence, allowing the young widow time to absorb the horror of her loss.

Jenny's thoughts raced as she sobbed. She had no idea what she would do without her love. And how could she ever tell her children their daddy would not be coming home? She knew Ed's family would be as devastated as she was, and she couldn't bear the fact she would have to face them. As full of sorrow as she was, she was just as angry he had left them.

She looked up at the commanding officer. "Why did you send my husband? Hadn't he done enough?" Jenny knew immediately from the man's look that was an unfair question, and it had hurt him deeply, but she could feel no compassion. She felt nothing but pain. She slowly gained her composure as the chaplain offered his condolences and the other men did the same. The commanding officer introduced the Casualty Assistance Calls Officer (CACO), Senior Chief Pittman.

Senior Chief Pittman offered his condolences and briefly explained his duties.

"Jenny, I will never know how difficult this is for you, and right now is not the time to go into detail about all the arrangements, but please know we are all here to assist you in any way we can," he said. "We all cared deeply for Ed. If you would let us, HM2 Book and I would like to stay with you until your family or friends can come be with you."

"I don't know what to do right now," Jenny said. "This is all so overwhelming. I can't believe he's gone. Please stay. I need to call Ed's parents and tell the kids. I don't want to be alone right now."

"We have made arrangements to notify Ed's parents, and Department of the Navy personnel are en route to their homes now," the commanding officer said. "They will notify me immediately when they have spoken to them, and you can call them directly."

Jenny was relieved and said, "Thank you."

The kids were still asleep, and Jenny had no desire to wake them. She offered to make coffee. HM2 Book stood and asked if she would like him to make some so she could sit and speak with the chaplain.

"That will be fine, Shannon. Do you know where everything is?"

Shannon smiled and said, "I think I remember. I'll take care of it, Jenny."

As he walked to the kitchen, Jenny thought of her friend Andrea, remembering how horrible Jenny had felt for her when they heard of Andrea's loss. The pain Jenny felt for her then was nothing compared to the pain she was experiencing at this moment.

"May I call one of my friends so she can come be with me?"

"Absolutely, Jenny," the commanding officer said. "We're just here to notify you and attempt to comfort you until you have some support. Please do whatever you wish to do." Jenny stood and retrieved her phone. She found the last number she received and hit Call.

The phone rang three times before Jenny heard Andrea's voice.

"I didn't expect to hear from you so soon!" Andrea said.

Jenny's voice cracked as she began to speak. She managed to say, "Ed was killed," but it was followed by crying and indecipherable speech. Andrea stood speechless and began to weep, remembering the day she had received the same news. She knew she had to get to her friend, the way Jenny had come to her.

"Jenny, I'll be there shortly. I'm so sorry for your loss, but hang on for a moment, and I'll be there."

As Jenny hung up the phone, the men in the room once again attempted to comfort her. The fog she was in seemed to be gradually lifting as the dread of waking her children and revealing to them this tragedy set in. She also felt a sense of horror at what she had just done to her friend. Although she needed her deeply, she knew she had just caused Andrea to relive her own nightmare and had asked her to be a part of her own.

She wished instantly she had waited. As Ed would have told her, "Stop, think, and suck it up, Jenny. These are our problems, no one else's." She knew Ed wouldn't want her to involve anyone in their business, but she also knew there was no way she could do this alone. The men around her were doing the best they could to comfort her, but they couldn't provide the same support as a fellow spouse.

Thankfully, true to her word, Andrea was at her door within minutes. The women embraced and held each other, now sharing an even deeper bond many would never know, one that neither woman would ever wish on anyone. The tension in the room lifted. Relieved, the men stood, knowing they could never provide the level of support that the young woman who had just arrived could.

"Jenny, we can stay as long as you would like, or we can leave you with your friend to handle your affairs," the commanding officer said.

"Thank you, sir. I think it would be easier for the kids if fewer people were here when they awake."

"We'll return to the command and attend to the arrangements. Jeremy and the CACO will return shortly to assist you with anything you need." With that cue, all the men offered Jenny their condolences one more time and headed to the door. Jenny thanked them all for coming and staying with her until Andrea arrived. She asked Shannon if he would bring his wife over when he returned. He agreed, and the men departed silently.

Jenny and Andrea stood silently in the doorway as the men filed into the van and departed. When they were gone, Andrea led Jenny to the couch and sat with her as she broke down once again.

"I'm so sorry to call and ask you to be with me," Jenny said. "I can't imagine the pain this must be causing you."

"Jenny, you were by my side when I needed you, and I will be here when you need me. That's what family is for. Please don't be concerned. I'm glad you called."

"I have no idea how to tell the kids. They're going to be devastated, and I'm afraid I don't have the strength for them."

Andrea reassured her. "Jenny, you're one of the strongest women I know, and you have always been the foundation of your family. You will be strong today, and I'll be right here with you. There's no need to wake them up to give them such horrible news. Let them sleep for now." Jenny agreed, and the women sat together, both lost in their own thoughts.

Christopher was the first to awaken and make his way to the living room. The little boy walked in, having no idea his world was about to be forever changed. He immediately recognized something was wrong. He could tell his mom was emotional and could feel the enormity of the situation. When his eyes met his mother's, she called him over and embraced him. As she wept, she explained to him that his father wasn't coming home, that he was now with God.

The little boy trembled and held his mother tightly while he cried loudly. Jenny summoned all her strength and gently rocked her oldest child in her arms, attempting to comfort him as she quaked inside from her own grief. She knew there were no words to comfort him, for there were no words that would comfort her. Time would be the only thing to heal this wound. The commotion woke Clara, and she soon made her way to the room. As Christopher had been alarmed, so was she. She ran directly to them and without knowing the enormity of the situation, began to cry with her family.

Jenny didn't know how hard Clara would take the news of her father's passing, but she knew how close she and Ed were. Jenny dreaded telling her, but she moved Christopher to one side of her lap and pulled Clara to the other as she stared deeply into the little girl's eyes. She explained what had happened. Clara's reaction was much worse than Christopher's. Jenny could barely hold her. She didn't speak, but she cried to the point of hyperventilation. Christopher attempted to console his little sister, but she was too deeply hurt to hear anyone. She held her mom and sobbed. Destroyed by the news, the small family sat together, speechless in mourning.

Andrea sat with them, comforting them the best she could. After several minutes, she made her way to the kitchen and began to prepare breakfast for the kids. She knew it was a futile effort, but she also needed to do something so she didn't add to the hysteria. Jenny sat rocking the kids, speaking gently to them both, reassuring them that they would all be OK.

After what seemed to be several hours, Jenny's phone rang. She looked at the caller ID and saw it was Ed's dad. Her heart sank once again. She didn't want to answer the phone, but knew her responsibilities didn't end with the children.

She answered and heard her father-in-law say, "Jenny, we were just informed. I can't imagine what you and the kids are going through. I just wanted to call and see if you all are doing all right and let you know we will be arranging to come to North Carolina." She could hear the devastation in Ed's voice. Jenny knew how close Ed and his dad were, and that this had to be killing him.

"I'm so sorry, Ed. I don't know what to say. The kids and I are overwhelmed. My friend is with us, and Eddie's command just left. They'll be back later. We're doing the best we can right now."

"We'll all get through this," Ed said. "Jenny, please call if you need anything. I know Karen will be calling soon, so I don't want to keep you. I just wanted to let you know how much we love you and that we will be out as soon as we can."

"Thank you. When the kids calm down, I'll call you back so they can talk to you. I know they will want to. I will talk to you soon."

Shortly after Jenny hung up the phone, she received a call from Ed's mom. Karen was as devastated as everyone else was, but she tried to remain calm and comfort Jenny, as Ed had. They spoke briefly, and Jenny told her she would call her back when things calmed down as well.

As the day proceeded, calls continued to come in from her family and from Ed's family, as well as their military family. Each call was much the same—awkward words of condolence followed by offers of prayers, and telling her to call if they could do anything. The calls were as comforting as they were difficult.

Shannon, his wife, and the CACO, Senior Chief Pittman, came back to the house as promised. Shannon's wife had prepared meals, and Senior Chief had all the paperwork needed to proceed with the arrangements. Senior Chief Pittman and Shannon were also prepared to stand watch. They both told Jenny they would answer any calls and direct any visitors to come back another time if she wished.

The seconds felt like hours, minutes like days, and hours like months as the calls and visitors continued to come in. Each person brought a different memory of her beloved husband and his crazy antics—some joyful, some frustrating, and all a reminder she would never have him in her arms again. Over the coming days, her family and Ed's family came in from across the country, and their military family was already there. The amount of love and support everyone provided them then and after was overwhelming.

She could never express in words the gratitude she felt for everyone's support, especially Andrea. She finally knew how Andrea felt and what she went through during her loss. Jenny couldn't overcome the hate she had festering inside her for the men her husband was sent to help. They had ripped her life and her children's lives from them, and she prayed she could forgive. Christopher was deeply wounded from the loss, but was strong and trying hard to maintain for his mom and sister. Clara had not stopped crying since hearing the news of her daddy's death and refused to speak. Thankfully, the most caring people in the universe surrounded them.

The morning of Ed's service, Jenny, the kids, and their families gathered for breakfast in her home. The mood remained somber, and everyone attempted to keep emotions in check. They all knew today would be a challenge, and Jenny understood Ed would want her to be strong. *He is not here, but I can still hear him telling me to suck it up and quit acting like a baby*, she thought. The memory of his strength gave her hope she could handle the day.

As she watched her children and family move through the house and prepare to leave, she stared at the door, wishing Ed would come through it and say this was all just a horrible mistake. Clara sat at the table, staring at her plate, with Christopher at her side, trying to get her to eat. Ed's dad was encouraging Pat to stay out of the beer until the services were over. Jenny could see the toll this tragedy had taken on all of them, but Pat was the only member of the family who had served, and he was lost without his brother.

When the time came to move toward Camp Lejeune for the service, they all proceeded to their vehicles. Senior Chief Pittman and Shannon arrived to drive Jenny and the kids and to escort the family to the chapel for the service. As the family drove, they all sat silently, remembering their loved one and praying for this day to be over.

As they entered the chapel, they were escorted to the front row. The chapel was filled to capacity. Jenny recognized many of the men and women as she walked to the front. Ed's commanding officer and command master chief sat across the aisle from her and the family with Senior Chief Pittman and several other staff members. The altar had a single photograph of Ed in his service dress blues. The chaplain stood at the lectern, and all in attendance received small programs with Ed's biographical data, family information, hometown, education, units, awards, decorations, and tours of duty. The program also had a summary of his service.

The service consisted of a prelude, posting of the colors, national anthem, and an invocation by the chaplain. HM2 Tutko reminisced about the time when he and Ed were instructors together. He talked about Ed's sense of humor and undying love for his family, friends, and country. After remarks by the commanding officer, followed by scripture readings, music, meditation, and a benediction by the chaplain, the master chief gave the last roll call. During the last roll call, the command prepared the battle cross for their fallen comrade. The cross consisted of the helmet and identification tags to signify the fallen member. The inverted rifle with bayonet signaled a time for prayer and a break in the action to pay tribute to their comrade. The combat boots represented the final march of the last battle. For Ed, they added his enlisted Fleet Marine Force warfare specialist badge, jump wings, and air crew and combat air crew wings. Each portion was slowly marched in and positioned by a member of the command, followed by a slow and solemn salute.

When the ceremony ended, everyone formed lines and walked past the photo and battle cross to pay respect to the fallen warrior. Some knelt and prayed. Others touched the helmet or tags, and some just paused briefly. Finally they proceeded to Jenny and the family to pay respects to the warrior's loved ones. Emotions filled the chapel, and tears filled everyone's eyes. Jenny stood strong as she knew her husband would want and was amazed at the outpouring of support and respect that people had for Ed.

Following the ceremony, Jenny invited Ed's closest friends and family to the house for what she knew he would want: an Irish wake. Ed had only discussed arrangements with her once, and his only requests had been, "Don't mourn my death; rejoice my life. Don't bury me in a national cemetery. I've spent enough of my life in rank and file. I want to spend eternity next to my Grandma Peg."

He was drunk when he told her what he wanted, but she knew he would haunt her if she didn't follow his wishes, so she did as he requested and threw a final party in his honor.

The booze and stories flowed. Ed's friends and family talked about all his antics as a child and as an adult. They laughed, cried, and enjoyed one another's company. Lifelong friendships were built throughout his life and remained after this tragedy. As the party dwindled down and people made their way home, Jenny and Pat found themselves alone outside. They talked about their loss and comforted each other until they had enough to drink to finally get some sleep.

The following day, the family headed to the airport for the flight back home. Jenny would ensure Ed's final request was met; he would be buried next to his grandma. After a grueling flight and drive, they all arrived at Ed's dad's house. Arrangements for the funeral were already made, and Ed's remains were at the funeral home. The family had to endure one more visitation and service.

The visitation, like his memorial service, was heart-wrenching, but the support from old friends and family was amazing. People traveled from far and wide to pay respects and to be with Jenny in her time of need. Ed's parents' friends also attended, remembering the wild young man they all enjoyed being around and wishing they were seeing their friends under different circumstances.

Military rites were conducted during the funeral, with an honor guard and flag detail. A solitary trumpet played "Taps" as Jenny was presented the US flag. Ed was laid to rest next to his grandmother, and his family was left to put together the pieces of their life that remained.

Jenny and the kids stayed home with family for a few days, attempting to relax and make sense of the tragedy. Jenny needed to return to work, and the kids needed to get back to school, so they made plans to return. They said their good-byes and headed home.

17

Strength

~

Arriving home to an empty house, knowing she would never share her bed with Ed again, caused Jenny to break down as she entered the doorway. Proceeding to the kitchen with tears in her eyes, she looked down at the table filled with hundreds of condolence letters and cards. Sitting on top, staring directly into her eyes, was one of Ed's favorite poems.

Footprints in the Sand

One night I dreamed I was walking along the beach with the Lord. Many scenes from my life flashed across the sky.

In each scene, I noticed footprints in the sand. Sometimes there were two sets of footprints, other times there was one only.

This bothered me because I noticed that during the low periods of my life, when I was suffering from anguish, sorrow or defeat, I could see only one set of footprints, so I said to the Lord, "You promised me, Lord, that if I followed you, you would walk with me always. However, I have noticed that during the most trying periods of my life, there has only been one set of footprints in the sand. Why, when I needed you most, have you not been there for me?"

The Lord replied, "The years when you have seen only one set of footprints, my child, is when I carried you."

(Mary Stevenson, 1936)

Jenny felt like Ed had just spoken to her. She felt the strength building within and knew she could carry on as she had always done for her and their children. She knew from that moment, she was not alone. Her faith, her family, and her friends would always be by her side.

Christopher and Clara's moods were much the same as their mom's. They moved through the house, slowly searching for their daddy, knowing he wasn't there. Proceeding to their rooms, they dropped their bags and headed back to the living room. Each of them wanted nothing more than to get back to a normal routine, but they knew nothing would be normal again.

Jenny hoped getting the kids home and back to school with their friends would help them move on faster, and she hoped getting back to work would help her cope as well. She understood only time would tell, but she prayed they would find some normalcy in the coming days. Christmas was coming soon, and she didn't want the kids to be miserable throughout their holiday break, though she knew it was going to be a difficult time.

They settled in that day, getting the house back in order from all the guests and preparing for work and school the following day. When the kids were in their rooms playing games and watching television, Jenny sat at the kitchen table to go through the letters and cards. She had a stack of thank-you letters to send out and wanted to personally send each of them.

Jenny and Ed had always sent thank-you cards together. *Sending personalized thank-you cards might have been the only thing Eddie and I totally agreed on!* The thought brought a smile to her face for the first time in days as she remembered the many times they sent cards to family and friends who sent them cards or gifts, or whom they had visited over the years.

As she read each card and letter, again she realized how much support and respect people had for the military, Ed, her, and her family. The outpouring of support touched her in a profound way and helped build her confidence and strengthen her resolve. Writing the thank-you cards allowed her to express her gratitude in a way she was unable to during the service and funeral.

Jenny always had Ed write the letters in the past, and she was dreading the task, but she found it therapeutic and enjoyed relaying her thoughts to each person who had supported her and the kids. She included cards to the commanding officer, master chief, chaplain, Senior Chief Pittman, the escort, Ed's team, Shannon, and her dear friend Andrea. She found some closure in the task.

As the family assumed its routine, it became apparent that not all was well. Christopher coped with the loss of his father and remained strong for his mom and sister, but Clara was devastated. The little girl could not understand or handle the tragedy. Jenny knew she needed to get Clara counseling and feared she had lost her too. Jenny had briefly discussed counseling for the entire family with the chaplain during the initial process, but through the turmoil of the events and the shock and speed of everything, she had lost focus.

Jenny arranged for her and the kids to meet with a grief counselor and got herself and the kids into treatment. She also contacted her chaplain for guidance. Her faith had always carried her through hard times, and she knew now was no time to turn away from her beliefs.

Jenny and the kids began therapy together and individual treatment. They also returned to the church and spent time with the chaplain. Jenny and Christopher benefited from the treatment, but Clara didn't seem to respond. Clara remained detached and silent, distant and broken. All she wanted was for her daddy to come home. She didn't act out or misbehave, but she cried often, and nights were brutal for her. Everyone reassured Jenny that with time, she would come around, but seeing her baby struggling was unbearable for a loving mother. All of this was bad enough so close to Christmas, but Jenny came home to another surprise.

18
Grief

~

The awful chain of events began three weeks before Christmas, when Jenny arrived home to three packages from her husband on her front porch. The items had been purchased and sent just days before his death. Jenny looked at the address labels and dates in shock. She couldn't believe what she was seeing and wondered if this was someone's idea of a sick joke. *We are all grieving, in counseling, and trying our best to cope and move on, and now this. How do I explain this to the kids, and how am I going to handle this?*

In tears, Jenny picked up the packages, moved them into the house, and placed them on the table. She sat down and stared at them in disbelief. She reached out, touching the one addressed to her to ensure it was real. As she touched the package, she knew it was no dream, and she remembered one of her last phone calls from Ed. He told her he was going to buy gifts for her and the kids, so he could have something for them under the Christmas tree even though he couldn't be with them. It was something he had always done in the past. He never missed a holiday, birthday, or occasion. He could be a real jerk, but he was a thoughtful man and always sent cards and gifts even if he couldn't be there.

With tears in her eyes and tremendous grief in her heart, she thought, *Even from the grave, he managed to make it to our last Christmas. I love and miss you so much, Eddie. Why did you leave us?*

Jenny sat silently, staring at the presents with tears running down her face, thinking of the Christmases they had spent together. She knew he never liked Christmas. Ed lost his grandma near Christmas, and his grandma had never enjoyed the holiday, because she never had the money to give her family as much as she wanted to. Ed had carried that with him through the years, but watching the kids grow and being able to give them more than he had lightened him up. Unfortunately, now none of that mattered.

Jenny rose, went to the attic, pulled down wrapping paper, and walked back to the table. She gathered tape and scissors, and began wrapping each box. Tears dripped from her eyes, staining the paper as she wrapped them.

"God, what is the plan?" Jenny asked as she wrapped. "I don't understand. I want to believe, but this is too much right now. Please give me the strength to carry on and bring my kids through this." She paused and said, "If Ed is with you, please tell him thank you, but as usual, his timing sucks!"

She finished wrapping the presents and hid them in her closet. Jenny still had no idea how she would explain this to her kids. They planned to decorate this weekend, and she had hoped it would brighten and lift their spirits for the holiday. She worried these gifts would restart the grief process, and she had no idea how the kids would react. The only thing she could do was pray for the best.

Jenny kept the information to herself and carried on throughout the week, dreading the day she had to unveil the gifts. She contemplated telling the kids they were from her, but knew that was wrong. The weekend came, and she mustered the courage to decorate with the kids. They all took the truck to get a tree, brought down all the decorations, and set up the house. As usual, the kids haphazardly decorated the tree with old ornaments, homemade ones, and unique trinkets acquired over the years. They hung their stockings on the mantel, four of them.

Clara hung her daddy's, staring silently at it after she placed it in its far left position. As Jenny watched her, she knew the gifts were going to be a bad idea, but she had no choice.

When they completed decorating, they all sat and admired their work. Christopher and Jenny chatted about how great it looked as Clara sat admiring the lights. This year they had added a decoration to the window that no family would want—a Gold Star flag recognizing their sacrifice. The light from the tree reflected off the window. The flag shone in the light, with its bright red border, white background, and centered, bright, gold star. As all their eyes were drawn to the emblem, Christopher asked what it meant.

Jenny choked up, not wanting to discuss it with the kids, but she swallowed the pain and said, "The flag represents that we have lost a family member in combat while he was serving in the military. It originated during World War II. It is for your daddy. Jeremy's dad gave it to us to display. He had it because he lost one of his sons."

Tears filled all of their eyes as the kids crawled into their mom's lap. They hugged and comforted one another as Jenny held them.

"We have all been through a lot the last few weeks," Jenny said. "You two have sacrificed more for your country in your young lives than most ever do, and I am very proud of you. Your daddy was very proud of both of you. Everything he did was to ensure you had a better life than he did. He loved you more than anything else in this world, and I have to show you something."

Jenny moved the kids to the side and asked them to stay on the couch as she went to the bedroom. Shaking, she retrieved the presents from the closet. She was filled with fear and doubt as she walked back into the living room with the presents in her hands. Christopher and Clara sat looking at her, puzzled.

"A few days ago, I came home and found these three presents on the porch. They are from your daddy." The kids' eyes widened, and they looked shocked. Jenny quickly added, "Your daddy bought and sent these to us before all of this happened, but the mail is slow, and we didn't get them until this week. He told me he would be sending presents for Christmas the last time we spoke, but I forgot about it. I didn't know how to tell you about this. I know this is hard for you, but I want you both to understand that your daddy wanted you to have a good Christmas."

Jenny put the presents under the tree. "We'll open them on Christmas Day with our other gifts, just like we would have if this hadn't happened." Christopher and Clara both sat staring at the presents as Jenny had, amazed they had received something from their lost father. They had no idea how to react. Each day for the next several days, they walked by the tree and presents, wondering what was inside.

19

Awakenings

~

Clara woke early on Christmas morning and found her way to the present from her daddy that had arrived days earlier. Rage took over as she began ripping the wrapping, and tears flowed from her eyes. A beautiful, warm light filled the room as the box opened. She didn't know if she was dreaming or not, but it seemed so real. As she opened the box further, the light increased and she saw an image move toward her. She couldn't believe her eyes. It was her daddy, smiling and holding a teddy bear. She ran as fast as she could to him. He swept her into his arms. She could smell, feel, and see him. She was in heaven. They moved to his chair, sat, and talked for hours. She woke feeling at peace in Ed's chair with the bear he had given her. Jenny was hovering over Clara, shocked and crying because she had opened the present.

Clara spoke for the first time since hearing the news of her father's death.

"Don't cry, Mommy. It's going to be OK. I'm OK now. Daddy is in heaven. I just forgot what Daddy always told me." She pointed to her heart. "He's always right here with me." Then she pointed to her mommy's heart. "He's right there with you too."

At that moment, a beautiful light shone directly through the Gold Star in the window, cascading a wonderful kaleidoscope of light over the Christmas tree.

※❈※

Afterword

Over the span of my adult life, I, like many others, have experienced loss. I pray to leave this world before my wife and children, but I have resigned myself to the fact I have little control over my ending. I wanted to create a happy ending to this book, but in keeping to the context of the book, I couldn't bring it together. I imagined a ending in which Jenny would awaken to a phone call from Eddie, and chapters 16–19 would have been just a horrible dream. I think that all Gold Star families hope the same thing when dealing with their tragedy. They desperately want to believe they are having an awful dream that they will awaken from and reunite with their loved ones.

I can only offer condolences and prayers to the mothers, fathers, spouses, and children of my brothers- and sisters-in-arms. Words and prayers seem so meaningless to me at a time of such great sorrow. I hope in some way this book brings awareness to the struggles of Gold Star families and support for charities that work with them. Thank you.

This book is not intended to push any religious or spiritual belief. Its sole intent is to spread awareness of military family issues and veterans' causes, and to show the potential growth through love, support, and dedication. My family, friends, and experiences were the research for this book, but it is a work of fiction, and none of the characters or events are real. Please move forward and do great things.

Fair winds and following seas.

Chief Brannan

63181612R00144

Made in the USA
Middletown, DE
30 January 2018